Civic
Duty

Other Bella Books by Laina Villeneuve

Birds of a Feather
Cowgirl 101
Cure for Insomnia
Falling All In
Kat's Nine Lives
Return to Paradise
The Right Thing Easy
Such Happiness as This
Take Only Pictures

About the Author

Laina Villeneuve has been called for jury service multiple times and served on one jury. While editing this book, her wife of twenty years served on her first jury. All three of their children are in high school, still too young to be called. The pups are too busy keeping peacocks out of the yard but have lots to say about justice.

Civic
Duty

Laina
Villeneuve

BELLA
BOOKS

Bella Books, Inc.
P.O. Box 10543
Tallahassee, FL 32302

First Edition - 2025

Editor: Heather Flournoy
Cover Designer: SJ Hardy

ISBN: 978-1-64247-654-5

PUBLISHER'S NOTE

Acknowledgments

My sister-in-law Katrina planted the seed for this story when she sent me her observations of the quirks she noted when she served on a grand jury for a year. We brainstormed quite a bit on a storyline with a grandmotherly character on trial for shuttling abortion pills across the border. In my research for that story, I remember reading about how traffickers hid the pills beneath jewelry or flower seeds, items that would bring light to the person at the end of the journey. While I loved that image, my story seed stubbornly refused to take root until Kay Acker suggested I watch *Jury Duty*, a show patterned off *The Truman Show*. That was the key to germination for the story you're holding now.

I would not have felt comfortable writing a story that takes place in court without the help of my book-signing-pal Alicia's friend Jennifer. So, thanks to Alicia for putting us in touch and to Jennifer for the hours of brainstorming the big-picture items like what case might work for the plot as well as the nitty-gritty of how the trial worked and what the characters would say to deliver the case. Thank you for helping to make it sound authentic but also understanding the fiction of it and where a bending of truth might make for better fiction. I apologize to anyone in the legal field who might find fault with my literary choices. Like *Jury Duty*, I took liberties with court proceedings.

Shawn Marie and Heather are the fairy godmothers of this project, having nurtured it through every step of the writing process. From Heather's excitement for the fake-jury storyline to Shawn Marie's invaluable encouragement as Spring Break pace pony and whole-story troubleshooter. Thank you, Jessica, for agreeing that Heather would be the perfect editor. You were right, as usual. How fortunate I've learned to listen!

Rae, thank you so much for the chapter-by-chapter cheerleading! I've said it before, but it bears repeating: your quick feedback keeps my cup full. It is such a joy to play with you in these imaginary worlds. Thanks also to Sarah, who gave me help with the ethical issues I ran into with this story. I was so happy she agreed that Sarah and her family fit into this story. Areej, thank you for help with the defense lawyer, Priscilla for fixing my fictional car, and Iris for help with astrological insights.

Many thanks to my wife for helping me brainstorm through the multiple layers of make-believe and then asking key questions of the first draft that made this a stronger story.

Most of all, I would like to thank my character Alex for challenging me. I dive into a story with the roughest of plans and was thrown for quite a loop when, early in the draft, they pointed out the binary language that opens a trial, thereby coming out and taking the story in a whole new direction. Thank you to the folks who created *Nonbinary Memoirs of Gender and Identity*, for the bloggers who share their stories, and for Jen for sharing experiences that helped me understand Alex's view of the world. Thanks to Ro for reading the parts I worried about and for saying that my character rings true.

Dedication

For all the beautiful nonbinary folks.

CHAPTER ONE

Alex

"My bailiff has advised me that the jury has reached a verdict. Who was elected foreman of the jury?" Judge Court asks with an air of indifference. She seems more concerned about how her black robes are arranged than the fact that we are about to close the case.

I raise my hand. "I was elected foreperson, Your Honor."

"Fore*person*." She assesses me over the rim of her dark-framed reading glasses. Despite the pounding of my heart, I stand a little taller, waiting for her to chastise me for correcting her. She doesn't. Instead, she seems to be holding back a smile. "My apologies. Have you reached a verdict?"

"Yes we have, Your Honor," I say, trying to project confidence that does not come naturally to me.

"Please hand the verdict form to the bailiff."

I'm happy with the verdict I hand to the bailiff. I am savoring the feeling that justice is about to be served. I am satisfied that the jury has served its purpose but avoid looking at either the plaintiff or the defendant. I can't figure out where to focus my attention as I wait for the bailiff to return our verdict. I glance at Vicki, and she gives me a reassuring smile. So do Sarah and the other members of the jury. Are they avoiding looking at the plaintiff and defendant as well? It sure feels like all the attention is on me. It's everything I can do to keep myself still.

Finally, the bailiff returns the paper, and the judge asks me to read the verdict.

"We the jury, in the case of Aschbran versus Menjivar, render the following verdict. To the question of a legal contract with a noncompetition clause existing between the parties, we find that there was no legal contract. Therefore, there can be no breach of contract and no damages, financial or emotional."

From the corner of my eye, I see the defendant grab her lawyer's hand. I can sense her relief from where I stand in the jury box. She looks stunned. Her lawyer leans forward to whisper in her ear and the defendant throws her arms around her, tears streaming down her face. The plaintiff is arguing with his lawyer, but the judge is smiling hugely. She regards me as though we've done the right thing with our verdict.

Are judges allowed to show such emotion?

I'm about to sit to wait for our next instruction when Judge Court motions for me to keep standing. "Just a moment, Juror Eleven." She shuffles through the papers in front of her. "Alexandria Verita."

"Yes," I say. Am I in trouble here? The air in the courtroom crackles with tension. She's no longer smiling, and the delay is as painful as the dramatic pause reality TV shows use before they eliminate a contestant.

"You said this was your first experience serving on a jury."

"I did."

She removes her glasses, carefully folds them, and sets them on the bench. "I didn't mention it as the trial started, but this is my first experience as a judge."

I cock my head in confusion. Why is she telling me this?

"You see, while you believed you were being filmed for a documentary about what it is like to serve on a jury, the subject of this show is really you."

I don't understand and glance from defendant to plaintiff to bailiff to my fellow jurors.

"Every person in this room is an actor. None of what we have done this week was real. The case was fictitious. The lawyers? Actors. The courthouse? Well, it was a courthouse once, but it has not seen a real case in years."

I'm starting to feel lightheaded, but I'm acutely aware of the cameras that are filming. I know they are trained on me. I hiccup from the shock of what I am trying to ignore. I turn to the jury, these people I've grown so close to over the course of the week, in hopes they will help me grasp what the judge means.

"Actors," Judge Court says as my eyes land on Vicki.

"Actor?" I whisper, barely able to vocalize the word. I'm having trouble breathing, and my vision is starting to narrow. Sarah is suddenly next to me and encouraging me to sit. Vicki tries to take my hand, and I snatch it away. I can't speak, but I want more answers. How is this show about me?

"And though none of this proceeding was real, humanity was on trial this week. We live in a time of apathy. People draw conclusions of innocence and guilt largely based on appearance, yet you rejected that. Your keen attention to detail kept our writers on their toes as they scripted the court case."

The lawyers are smiling at me now, but I have no control over the muscles in my face to smile in return. My instinct is to run from the building, away from everyone watching me, but I am stuck in the jury box. I've seen reality TV. They're waiting for me to laugh and join in this revelation. The judge keeps talking about my amazing leadership of the jury, but I'm stuck on how none of it was real. Sarah Cooper is real. I've listened to her podcast. Read her book. But Vicki… She's an actress?

You lied, I mouth at Vicki.

"Alex," she says so quietly.

My name on her lips is a punch in my gut, and I push myself to my feet, the echo of her whispered *Alex* ringing in my ears.

"She hasn't gotten to the best part," Vicki says, trying to take my hand again, trying to hold me in place. I step out of her reach. If she touches me, I will lose it. My heart is hammering so hard it's difficult to catch my breath.

I try to focus on what Judge Court is saying, but it's like her words scramble and float around the room instead of traveling to my ears and brain. Everyone is applauding and cheering, and I can't. I scan the room, desperate to ground myself. Sarah appears next to me and asks if I'm okay.

"I need to get out of here."

Without another word, she has her hands on my shoulders, guiding me past the other jurors and out of the courtroom. I worry I'm letting everyone down, but I can't stay in the room a second longer.

CHAPTER TWO

Alex

One Week Earlier

Sit down! Everyone is staring at you. Sweat beads along my spine, and my inner voice is only making it worse.

I can't sit. There are very few open seats in the room, and the only ones that don't require sandwiching myself in between two people are right next to the most gorgeous human I have ever seen. I'll stand. How long does it take for the court to call in the jury for the selection process? I try to ignore the feeling of being watched. I've agreed to participate in a documentary about the judicial process, so I'm going to have to get comfortable with cameras filming if I make it onto this jury.

There are no cameras yet, which is good because I don't know what to do with myself when the woman smiles at something on her phone, which sends my stomach flying like a dog released to chase a flock of birds off the sand. She's got serious dimple action and perfect teeth, and I swear she senses that I'm watching her out of the corner of my eye when she glances up and rearranges her bountiful hair. Her golden highlights perfectly complement her light-brown skin.

A woman shuffles into the juror holding room—at least, I think she's a woman. It's difficult to make out the shape of her in the baggy black pants and shapeless button-down shirt she's got on. She looks as though she cobbled together an outfit from a donation bin. Her grayed hair is braided, and a cloud of patchouli follows her from the window where prospective jurors check in. She eyes the available seats by the beautiful woman. It's now or never.

I rush forward and sit with one seat in between me and the woman I won't allow myself to look at, because at close range, if I do, I am positive I won't be able to tear my eyes away from her. I keep myself focused, picking at the corner of my name tag with the number fifty on it trying to free the sticky side. My hands are shaking. Why are my hands shaking this badly?

The gorgeous woman crosses and recrosses her legs. She's wearing black leather pants with heels the exact shade of green as her formfitting green shirt. She makes my khaki shorts and rust button-down feel inappropriately casual.

The crone narrows her eyes, and I'm praying that she picks the seat across the room.

She doesn't. She sits right smack between us.

I open my phone to keep her from talking to me, but she leans over and croaks, "What's your sign?"

Her voice is Disney-villain gravel, and I'm surprised she doesn't end her thought with "dearie."

"Excuse me?"

"Your astrological sign."

Is she serious? Another prospective juror approaches the window. Her outfit suggests she's a run-of-the-mill career woman. I wish she'd been the one to take the seat next to me. I jump when the crone sticks a bony finger in my arm.

"Your sign?"

"Virgo," I say.

"Oh, dear." She turns to the beautiful woman and asks for her sign.

I hear her voice for the first time and feel myself pulled toward her even though she's just said one word. And that one word makes my jaw drop. "Virgo."

The crone stands up as the new woman approaches.

"Holy shit. You're Sarah Cooper!" The beautiful woman stands as well and extends her hand. "I'm Vicki. I'm *such* a fan!"

Sarah slips sunglasses on and raises a finger to her lips before she clasps Vicki's hand. "Thanks, but I'd rather not make a big fuss about it." She turns in my direction. "And you are?"

"Alex," I say. "I'm sorry I don't recognize you."

"Neither do I," the crone booms. "Are you sure she's famous?"

People glance up from their books and phones. I cringe on Sarah's behalf.

"Please, I'd prefer to keep a low profile here." She moves to claim the seat between me and the beautiful woman.

Unbelievably, the crone stays her with a hand to her shoulder and asks for her sign.

Sarah shifts her gaze from me to Vicki. We shrug in unison. Cautiously, she says, "Pisces?"

The crone crosses her arms, hips tipped out in her ridiculous old-man pants. "You don't know your sign?"

"I don't know why you're asking."

"It should be obvious! I'm an Aries. I can't sit next to these Virgos. Especially that one." She points right to me. "She's vibrating at such a high frequency, it would be better if I sat in a completely different row, but do you see anyone moving their things to offer me a seat?"

All four of us scan the room. Absolutely everyone buries their head in their laps. Probably because the crone stinks to high heaven.

Like a conductor, she directs Vicki to collect her bag and scoot to the right and points Sarah to take the vacated seat. She sits on the far side, leaving the one by Vicki for me. Grateful to be a few people away from the patchouli cloud, I sit. Without looking directly at Vicki, because I'm sure that if I did, I would lose myself forever, I whisper, "Who is Sarah Cooper?"

"Do you not watch TV? Her book has been on the *New York Times* bestseller list for weeks. She was on *Ellen*!" She pats Sarah's shoulder as she says this, pulling her into the conversation. "I wish I had a copy of *The Family Sarapist* for you to sign."

That rings a bell. "Wait. You do that podcast *The Sarapist is In*?"

"I do," she says modestly.

"Didn't you...Not to be rude, but didn't you, um, piss off a bunch of people when you hooked up with someone after saying single parents shouldn't date?" I ask.

The smile disappears, and I feel rotten. Vicki pats her shoulder again. "She owned up to it, so it's all in the past."

"I'm sorry," I offer.

"You're fine. It wasn't pretty. I'm the first to admit that." She perches the sunglasses she's been hiding behind on top of her blond hair. "Are you okay? You look pale."

I do feel sick, partly from embarrassment but also because patchouli literally turns my stomach, and I'm too close to the scent-soaked crone. I rush to explain, leaning close to Vicki so the crone doesn't overhear. "I'm feeling ill. Patchouli gives me migraines."

"I love patchouli," Sarah says.

Vicki studies me and leans over to stage-whisper, "I'd count that as a strike against her. Patchouli is definitely not my favorite."

She's close enough that I'm more aware of her scent. I try to keep how nice it would be to bury my face in the space behind her ear off my too-expressive face. I lean closer and breathe her in. My eyes close. She smells so good. I want to stay exactly where I am until I can identify all the layers. The notes of cinnamon are obvious, but there's something else, too. Pepper? Eucalyptus? I open my eyes, and both Vicki and Sarah are staring at me. I've lost myself for a moment and have to remind myself of the conversational thread. "Oh, no. I didn't mean for you to think I was being critical. Of your podcast or if you like patchouli."

"Don't hold back!" Vicki laughs. The dimple she flashes takes away the sting of her words. "What did you say your name was?"

"Alex."

She's taking in my short hair, and my neck and ears grow warm. "You look like a young Alison Bechdel. People must tell you that all the time."

"You're the first," I say, surprised she knows Alison Bechdel. Or is she offering me a clue that she's queer? I'm spinning, not sure if I'm supposed to follow up with a comment about *Fun Home*. Now doesn't really feel appropriate, so I switch topics. "Have you done this before? Been on a jury?"

She nods and holds up one finger before turning to Sarah, who agrees. "I've been on several, always civil." The crone hears and chimes in with a story of how she was close to serving on a criminal jury once, but it was for a drug case. When they asked if there was a reason that would prevent them from being fair and impartial, she had to disclose that she'd lived in Humboldt County for twenty years.

Sarah wears a puzzled expression, but Vicki laughs again. "Pot capitol of the US, isn't it?"

"You know more than that prosecutor did! It would have been fun to see seen how it all played out. A court this size, I'm sure this will be a civil trial, nothing juicy or controversial, but whatever the case, this is my civic duty. I personally think it's an honor to serve."

"Sure, but it's like your cycle," Vicki says. "Always coming at the most inconvenient time."

"I second that," Sarah says.

I shrug. "This popped up at the perfect time for me. I'm between jobs right now, so I'm excited to pick up a little extra cash and see how this all this works."

A stern bailiff enters the room, commanding in his crisp uniform, to escort the prospective jurors to the courtroom.

"Here we go," Vicki whispers, and I'm praying that we both get selected for this jury because I have to see this woman again.

CHAPTER THREE

Vicki

"What the hell are you doing?" Sarah whispers as we follow the herd to the courtroom.

"Shh! What if she hears you?" I hiss.

She stalls me with a hand on my elbow. "Tell me you were not flirting with Star?"

So much for hoping no one would notice. "I couldn't help myself. She's freaking adorable."

"Something the lesbian podcaster can point out, but not you! Aren't you supposed to be dating Mr. Right?"

"I know, I know."

"The number one priority is to make sure that Star isn't damaged at all in this whole process."

"I've got this. I'm a professional." I roll my eyes because I'm the actor here, not her. I'm aware that production brought her on board because she is a marriage and family therapist. She's basically the grown-up who will make sure that nothing goes too far while we're shooting *Civic Duty*. Literally everyone in the building is part of this reality TV show, but Alex—or "Star," as she is referred to in the scripts we've been working with—believes she's participating in a documentary focusing on the inner workings of jury service. I'm pretty sure that Sarah's worried about her plotline since Star barely recognized her. "Are your feelings hurt that all she knows about your show is the bad press you got?" I ask.

Sarah waves her hand. "Not at all. I think it'll work in our favor. She's perfect, isn't she?"

"She really is." I follow the bailiff's direction into the row where he's sent Star. He directs Sarah to the other side of the aisle. That means the producer must like the spark I felt with Alex. I relax a bit and prepare myself for voir dire. This is the first time I've ever done improv, and I'm hopeful that the footage the camera crew was capturing in the holding room has promise. We've rehearsed the jury selection process, though, and I can't wait to see how Alex reacts to the content the scriptwriters have created. Everything about this experience is wildly different than my day-to-day routine in my home studio recording audiobooks. I love the energy on set, even if I can't compare notes with the other actors as we are to behave like we are in a real courtroom, never as if we are on set.

"All rise," the bailiff calls, and we follow his direction and wait for Judge Court to enter. She sweeps in, a huge presence in her formidable black robes. I love how diverse our cast is. The bailiff is Filipino; Judge Court, Black. One lawyer is Japanese, the other Indian. Like any court, they've called more prospective jurors than will serve, but only a few are white, so the jury box is going to be majority BIPOC no matter who they decide will work best with Alex. She is the palest in the room. Does she register the diversity, or does this feel like the status quo for her living in Southern California?

Judge Court taps her gavel and invites us to sit. She says, "This is a civil dispute involving a suit for monetary damages. In a moment, I'll have the plaintiff and defense attorneys introduce themselves and their clients and the witnesses they plan on calling. Before we get started, the clerk will swear you in."

The clerk, an androgynous young person wearing a tidy gray suit, stands and has us all raise our right hand. We're asked if we understand the importance of being accurate and truthful when we answer questions about our ability to serve on the jury. When we collectively agree, the judge asks if there is any reason anyone in the room feels they will not be able to serve on a trial that will run up to a week.

As discreetly as possible, I watch Alex as the judge excuses one prospective juror for a root canal, another for being a primary caregiver of his sick grandfather, and one for severe anxiety. Alex looks attentive but bored. The cast has been prepared ahead of time that much of the filming will be long and dull to build the believability of the trial. Waverly, on cue, raises her hand to explain how she lived behind the Redwood Curtain for twenty years.

"Why would that be relevant?" Judge Court asks.

"I wondered, given that the defendant seems to fall on the more granola end of the social spectrum, if I might be perceived as having a bias."

The defendant is beaming at Waverly, but the judge shakes her head. "That will be determined in voir dire. I'm asking if there is something that will keep you from performing your service."

"Oh, no. I can devote my full attention to this case," Waverly says.

Next to me, Alex tries to muffle a laugh. I lean over and whisper, "She says she wants to serve, but it sure sounds like she was hoping that would get her excused again."

"Right?" Alex replies, and her eyes meet mine. She's so adorable, I want to throw my arms around her. She doesn't wear any makeup, but her complexion is flawless, and it's clear that her appearance is important to her. She's had a recent haircut, so her fade is perfect. She has a severe part that sets off the longer part of her hair that she's styled up from her forehead. And her eyebrows are carefully shaped into delicate arcs that give her a curious and engaged appearance. I break eye contact and try not to think about how her breath felt when she leaned in to whisper in my ear. With the energy between us, I am reluctant to deliver my lines, but when a tall white dude with spiky dark hair raises his hand, I know I'm up next.

He stands and pushes heavy tortoiseshell glasses up his nose. He glances nervously toward the prosecution's table and clears his throat. "I'm a bartender, Judge, and I've seen the plaintiff's lawyer drunk off his ass."

Again, Alex meets my eyes, and hers widen as if to say *Can you believe this?*

I know! I mouth.

Judge Court shoots daggers at the prosecution's table, and Mr. Patel hangs his head. "Counsel, will you both stipulate that Prospective Juror Number Twenty will be excused?"

They both nod, and the man leaves.

Adrenaline spikes in me. It's my turn. What I'm about to say will shift everything. Before I met Alex, I was excited about my reveal, but now I'd give anything to fade into the woodwork. I can't avoid it, though, so I raise my hand and stand.

"Yes." Judge Court's tone is clipped.

"I already have plans in the next week to attend my boyfriend's high school reunion."

"You're saying it's not *your* reunion," Judge Court tips her chin down, peering over the rim of her glasses. While I should feel pierced by her stare, it's Alex's gaze I feel. I don't have to look at her to feel her surprise and disappointment.

"No. But. We've been going out for a while, and his ex-girlfriend is going to be at the reunion, so I have to be there, you know, to keep an eye on my man."

Judge Court waves her hand as if she's trying to erase what I've said. I wish I could, too.

"You're trying to use a social engagement to evade your civic duty."

"No! I know jury duty is important, but I want to make sure nothing, you know…happens during this reunion. You hear stories about high school sweethearts…reconnecting."

"One would hope that a relationship between adults would be stronger than teenage lust. Sit down. Is there anything else?"

The entire courtroom is silent as I take my seat, which serves to amplify the questions in Alex's eyes. When I accepted the role of Vicki, I never once considered that there would be any ramification for pretending to be in a relationship. How could I have known that I would feel this energy between me and the person chosen as Star? I can't explain to Alex that this attraction is real, and that rattles me.

I blindly fill out the questionnaire the lawyers will use to begin voir dire and am barely present for the round of questioning. I try to maintain the same air of disengagement when Alex is speaking, but I can't help taking in details that, were we not meeting on this show, would pique my interest. She's from Kentucky and has been living in Southern California for a year. She's twenty-eight, the same age as my faux boyfriend, two years younger than me. She shares a house with four other people because the rent is cheap, not because they are friends.

I hear in her voice that she craves connection, that she wants more than the camaraderie she feels for her roommates. I would like to build that with her. The producers want for us to forge an honest connection with Star, and based on her personality, that will be very easy. My problem is going to be ignoring the obvious chemistry we have and keeping firm emotional boundaries in place.

CHAPTER FOUR

Alex

I'm trying to pay attention to the questions the lawyers are asking when they move to voir dire. The plaintiff's lawyer, the perfect example of professionalism in his tailored suit and shiny black shoes, explains that voir dire literally means *to speak the truth*, so I recognize how important it is to listen, but I can't stop thinking about how Vicki wanted to get out of jury duty to attend her boyfriend's high school reunion. Now her comment about trials coming at an inconvenient time makes sense, but what am I supposed to do with her comment about Alison Bechdel? I was sure she'd been flirting with me. Why would she do that if she has a boyfriend? It doesn't make any sense at all. Thinking that if I keep my attention directed toward the person speaking, I'll be able to direct my thoughts, I turn my head only to find Vicki watching me.

Electricity zings through my body, and I shut my eyes. This is not the time or place to be distracted by chemistry. And I definitely feel chemistry. If I weren't in public, I'd literally smack myself in the head. The word *boyfriend* paired with Vicki's feminine appearance short-circuited my brain, temporarily depositing me back in the world of binaries where feminine women are into men. With a smirk, my queer brain challenges my assumption that a woman who looks like Vicki wouldn't be into women or men. Or both.

"Prospective Juror Number Fifty," the man says, snapping me back to attention. "You looked down when the judge was talking about the business in question stemming from a friendship the plaintiff and the defendant have that spans back to their college days. Would you speak to why that affected you?"

Am I allowed to say no? The judge must see the question in my eyes because she asks if I would rather step into her chambers with her and the two lawyers to give my answer. My reason is personal, but does it matter? I don't know anyone here, so why am I worried about their judgment?

"No, Your Honor. I can answer here." I bite my lip. "It hit a sore spot because I'm no longer in touch with a close friend."

"Did the two of you have a business plan that dissolved?"

"No. We had a relationship that failed."

"I see. Would that interfere with your ability to fairly hear and decide on this case?"

"I don't think so." I can't help glancing at Vicki from the corner of my eye. As I suspected, she's looking at me again. Now her eyes are full of sympathy, like she's gazing at an abandoned puppy.

I'm thankful the focus is taken off me when a short man with chiseled cheeks and tidy, short hair who looks as though he was pulled into the courtroom from a basketball or tennis court raises his hand. "I'm currently in college and have a lot of friends."

"Having friends in college is not relevant," the lawyer says. "Unless there has been a conflict with your friends that might cloud your judgment."

"No, sir."

The lawyer consults his notes and says, "Number Eight, you stated that your spouse is a pool technician."

"No." Sarah's tone snaps the man's attention away from the papers on the podium. She says very clearly, "I said my wife is a pool technician."

"Ah, yes. You're rather public about your relationship with her."

"Many podcasters use material from their relationship on their show," Sarah says. "Would you question a male podcaster's use of anecdotal material that includes his wife?"

I want to give Sarah a fist bump or high five for pushing back when the lawyer changed wife to spouse. As someone who uses they/them pronouns, I understand how important words are and how they can either inflate or pop your emotional balloon.

The lawyer is asking a question about what kind of contract Sarah had with her pool technician before they became a couple when the judge holds up her hand.

"Excuse me," she says. "I'm sorry to interrupt. Is someone wearing patchouli in my courtroom."

My eyes go wide. I can't help it.

"Prospective Juror Number Fifty, are you wearing patchouli?"

"No, Judge."

"Can you tell me who is wearing patchouli?"

I gulp. Even though the smell makes me sick, I don't want to get the crone in trouble. "No, Judge." I will not look at the crone. I will not look anywhere but at the judge's gavel. I can't bring myself to meet her stern gaze.

"Let's be clear, people. Strong perfume or cologne will not be permitted in this courtroom. I encourage you to wear deodorant, but no additional scents."

Is she directing this at the crone? I can't tell, but I'm having my own personal panic about deodorant. I don't wear deodorant or use antiperspirant. My mom says that the absence of body odor is our shared superpower, so I've never bothered with the stuff. Am I going to need to buy some if I end up on this jury?

Sports Guy raises his hand again. "I mix two deodorants for maximum control of sweat and odor."

"I'm sure we all appreciate your attention to personal hygiene," the judge says.

As voir dire continues, the lawyer reminds us that the businesses in question were equine-based and offered both physical and behavioral therapy, and asks more specific follow-up questions. He excuses someone after he shares that a horse threw him and stepped on his testicles when he was on vacation.

Sports Guy interjects that he has never been on a horse before.

Another juror is excused after she discloses that her son receives Applied Behavior Analysis therapy.

Sports Guy raises his hand. "My neighbor has a cousin who might be autistic."

I try my best not to roll my eyes. How can the lawyers and judge keep their patience the way this juror keeps interrupting? I'm learning that what I've seen of courtrooms on TV is not a good gauge for real life, but I am still annoyed by this guy and wish he would keep his mouth shut so we can get our jury set and get to the rest of the trial. As if he senses what I'm thinking, he says, "I just thought it might be important."

It takes another hour for the lawyers to complete jury selection and for the clerk to swear us in again, this time agreeing that we will render a verdict from the evidence that we are presented with during the trial and that we will follow the instructions of the court, which specify that we are not to talk about the case outside of the courtroom, jury deliberation room and, in the case of this trial, with the documentarians. We are told not even to discuss the case with each other until we are released to deliberate.

I'm numb in both body and mind and past ready to call it a day when the jury is excused, but Nick, who introduced himself as the documentarian as we entered the courtroom, raises his hand. "Folks who are first-timers, we need you to stick around a few more minutes to talk about the jury selection process." Three of us stay behind and follow Nick to the break room for what he calls the "talking-head interviews." In here, there's one camera on a tripod.

I smile at the other two as we settle into the hard plastic chairs they've set in a line opposite the tripod.

The Latina woman to my right extends her hand. "My name is Ripley," she says.

"As in Believe it or Not?"

"Same spelling, but it's actually for Ellen Ripley. My mom is a huge *Aliens* fan."

Like me and Ripley, the man appears to be under thirty, and I wonder where they work that they opted to do their jury duty for this documentary. He shakes my hand as well. "Joseph," he says with a nod. His skin tone is closer to Ripley's than mine, though I've noticed that nobody is as pale as I am. Even Sarah's skin holds the sun opposite to how mine rejects it. I stand out in Southern California in a way I don't back in Kentucky.

I shouldn't be disappointed that Vicki didn't stay for this after hearing that she's practically engaged, but that fact doesn't dampen the spark that flares whenever our eyes meet. I'm thinking about the podcast I listened to where Sarah described meeting Jass, the pull she felt to be closer. That's what I have been feeling all day. It isn't fair for my body to react like that with someone who is unavailable.

Nick gives each of us a microphone to clip to our shirt and asks us for our impression of jury selection, directing my thoughts away from the unproductive musings about my attraction to Vicki.

CHAPTER FIVE

Vicki

"Yesterday went really well, everyone," our producer, Brittany, says. "Remember that we're filming for content that is going to make good television. We're riding a fine line between believable and entertaining. I hope you brought your bored poker faces for the presentation of witnesses. Everyone have the rough sketch of today's schedule?"

The cast has gathered in the courtroom four hours before Alex is due to arrive, going over the rough scripts the writers have prepared for us, especially for the actors who will be presenting the case. Those of us who are interacting more directly with Star have more room for improv. The writers have given us what they hope to get filmed as the trial proceeds, but the footage will depend on how Alex reacts to today's plot points.

Brittany releases the folks on the jury, so we can exit the building without being seen in order to arrive with Alex.

My stomach flutters. Part of it is this role and all the unknowns of the day. The pressure of maintaining the ruse is palpable. The way she was checking me out, I couldn't help but flirt with Alex, and it was easy to read the interest in her eyes.

Before I met Star, I had no reservations playing the part of Vicki, who has a boyfriend. Now it feels wrong to make Alex believe I'm invested in hanging on to him.

I'm waiting in the parking lot when she pulls in, driving an orange Honda Civic that has seen many miles. I admire her fluidity as she unfolds from the driver's seat and the purpose in her stride. She is definitely invested in this trial. I watch her hesitate and glance over each shoulder when several reporters run up in front of her. Relief and confusion flash across her face when she sees Sarah crossing the parking lot and the reporters descend on her.

"Why are you here?"

"Is it true you're being sued for the impact your show has had on listeners?"

"Are you on trial yourself, or are you serving on a jury?"

"Are you testifying in support of LGBTQIA-plus families?"

Sarah slips on sunglasses and tries to walk by them, but they form a wall. I'm about to jog across the parking lot to offer support, but Alex is already stepping forward.

The reporters turn their attention to her. "Are you a friend of Ms. Cooper?"

"What can you tell us about this case?"

She whispers something to Sarah and wraps one arm around Sarah's shoulders and extends the other to push through the reporters.

I scoot around the cluster to hold open the door for them, and we all breathe a sigh of relief to be in the quiet of the foyer with folks waiting to go through security.

"Should we send security out there? That's insane," Alex says.

I shrug. "Comes with the territory, doesn't it?"

Alex stares at me, wide-eyed, and again, I think about how innocent she comes across.

"Not at that level," Sarah says. "Unfortunately, not everyone is a fan of how I defend the queer parenting community. Or, like you pointed out yesterday, how I changed my stance on single parents dating."

"I wanted to apologize for judging you about that. I listened to the episode where you explained how you fell for Jasmine. It was genuine and heartfelt, and I feel really bad for regurgitating what I'd heard other people say about you."

"Thank you, Alex. I'm so touched you listened to it."

"You've got a ton of podcasts! I downloaded a bunch to listen to during our downtime. It seems like all of this takes forever, doesn't it?"

"It does," I agree. The line for us to pass through security would test my patience if I didn't know that the security guard has been told to move the line slowly if Alex is talking to us.

"You excited to hear what the case is?" I ask Alex.

"Yeah." She doesn't look at me, and I want to blame it on the distraction from the reporters, but I sense that it's my storyline that is making her more distant than she was yesterday.

"When does your boyfriend leave for the reunion?" she asks, confirming my guess.

"Tomorrow."

She nods. "How long have you been together?"

"Going on a year."

"So, pretty serious."

I want to answer her question as myself, Emelynn Rivas, unquestionably single actress, but that's not who I am right now. I have to answer as Vicki, and Vicki is really serious about Malcolm. "I think so. He's met my parents, and this is when I was supposed to meet his. But now I'm stuck here."

"Is he still hung up on his ex? Is that why you're worried?"

"He says he's not, but he has a picture of her on his bedside table. He says he's only keeping it because he looks good in it, but it doesn't sit well with me. Would it bother you?"

"A hundred percent. I'd be worried."

"What about you? You seeing anyone?" The writers haven't said anything about gathering information about Star's dating status, but I'm curious and can't help myself. I hope she notices that I didn't ask if she has a boyfriend.

She looks away. "Nope. Nobody in the picture."

It is not relevant to the case in any way, but I want to know more about why she's single. If I weren't playing a part right now, I would ask her out. But I am playing a part, and once we're through security, I join the collective energy of the cast and keep myself focused on Vicki and her role.

"All rise," the bailiff calls after he has filed us into the jury box. "Trial court of the State of California Seventeenth District is now in session, The Honorable Judge Court is presiding."

"Sit down, sit down." She motions with her hand as if she's doing Whac-A-Mole until she gets to Sarah. "Except you. Can you please explain to me why the entrance to my courtroom suggests that an important criminal case is being heard here?"

Sarah wrings her hands. "No, I cannot."

"Did you talk to any of the reporters? Are they under the impression that you are going to offer any information about the proceedings of this court?"

"I did not, Your Honor."

The judge scowls collectively at the jury. "Let me be clear as patchouli about this. Nobody on the jury talks to the press. You don't talk to each other about the case unless you are in the deliberation room or meeting with the documentary staff. Understood?"

I nod along with the rest of the jury.

"Then let's get this trial started." She settles her glasses close to the end of her nose. "Mr. Patel, are you ready to offer your opening remarks?"

CHAPTER SIX

Vicki

Though the jurists are largely unscripted, working more with ideas than scripts, the lawyers have been able to run rehearsal of things like opening statements for the case. We have not been told about the case, only the general idea of how they intend to test how assumptions impact judgment and thereby verdicts, so we are all coming in at the same place as Alex is. As the plaintiff's attorney begins with his opening argument, I'm attuned to her reaction as much as I am to the lawyer's words.

"Ladies and gentlemen of the jury…"

A frustrated huff escapes from Alex, and she shakes her head. I'm confused. He hasn't even said anything, and she's upset. I nudge her and raise my eyebrows in question.

She scribbles something on her notepad and tips it for me to read.

Stupid gendered language.

I turn my gaze to the lawyer, who is painting his picture of how his client has been wronged. At the same time, I draw a question mark on my notepad.

Gender isn't binary. One. Or the other.

Realization smacks me. *He could say...* I try to think of gender-neutral salutations I've heard. *Beardos and weirdos isn't right.*

She can't hold in a small snort, and that tiny sound makes me beam inside.

I jot down another suggestion. I can't help myself. I want her full attention. *Ladies, gentlemen and gentle... Them? Person?*

She rolls her eyes and quickly jots down *Members of the jury.*

Oh. The solution is so simple. Is it that easy to remove gender? I wish I could express support for the observation about our rigidly gendered society, but she's turned her attention back to the lawyer. Glad she's distracted, I hurriedly tap out a text to a crew member and hope they can communicate with the defense lawyer. The lawyer is explaining how we will determine the intentional infliction of emotional distress the plaintiff suffered when Judge Court interrupts him.

"Excuse me, Counselor. I hate to interrupt you, but it appears that Juror Six has something more pressing at the moment."

All eyes turn to me, and even though I can't get in real trouble here, I break into a sweat.

"Pray tell, Juror Six. What is more important than Mr. Patel's opening statement for the plaintiff?" I peek at Alex's notepad to see if she's caught more than I have of the opening statement.

She's crossed out the gender observation and jotted down *Business dispute. Lost Revenue. Reputation. Emotional distress.*

Okay. So I have no idea what's going on. I hold up my phone and hope I'm making the right choice here. "I'm sorry, Your Honor." I glance at my phone as if it is taking all my willpower to leave it off. "It's my fiancé. Boyfriend. Soon to be fiancé. My little sister just texted me that she saw a picture of him..." I make my voice crack and press my fist to my solar plexus. "I need a moment, ma'am. Can I step out to the restroom?"

"No, you may not. If it's so important, you can share with your peers what has the attention that should be focused on this trial at hand."

I auditioned for this show largely because I've always wanted to try the challenge of improv like this, and the casting call said that the shooting would frequently include working without a net, so I have to come up with an idea on the spot and hope that it creates good content for the show. "There's a picture of him with his high school sweetheart at a pancake house sharing a waffle with strawberries and whipped cream."

"You are holding up my trial for this? Do you have any idea how valuable my time is? The lawyers? How do you think their clients feel knowing your mind is elsewhere?"

"Not good."

"Not good, indeed." Judge Court studies me over the top of her dark-framed glasses. "Do we have your attention now?"

Her tone invites me to press into this thread. "I'd feel better, Your Honor, if I could show you the picture, so you can see for yourself why it's important for me to get to his reunion. It's not fair that I'm stuck here, leaving him wide open for the high school sweetheart to make her move."

"Bailiff!" Judge shouts, and he shuttles my phone to the judge. She studies my phone's screen, which I hope is still open to the text exchange letting the crew know about how Alex reacted to the phrasing of the first lawyer's opening remarks, and then levels me with a sardonic smirk. "His arm isn't even touching her. It's resting on the booth." She sets the phone down on her bench. "Let me remind all of you that the use of cell phones is prohibited in my courtroom. Thus, I am confiscating this for the remainder of the day. Now, do we have your permission to proceed?"

Sheepishly, I nod, and the plaintiff's lawyer clears his throat and begins again. "Ladies and gentlemen of the jury…"

Alex bristles next to me again but doesn't jot anything on her pad. However, she takes careful notes as Mr. Patel delivers his opening argument outlining how his client, Mr. Aschbran, is suing for damages, including financial compensation for lost revenue, damage to his reputation and future revenue, and for intentional infliction of emotional distress, which "…we believe the evidence will show was caused by the defendant's calculated and deliberate breach of the noncompetition clause of the binding contract they created when they were in college."

Vicki is supposed to be bored by the whole court process, so I doodle on my notepad as I wait for the defense attorney. When the lawyers have traded positions, I tune back in for a moment before returning to my drawing.

The defense attorney, Ms. Saqsaq, stands and smiles at the jury. She is wearing a maroon hijab that accents the wide stripes of her tunic. "Esteemed members of the jury," she says.

I turn to observe how Alex will react to this just as Saqsaq starts to hum part of a tune. At first, I think I'm imagining it, but the expression on Alex's face offers confirmation. There is something familiar in the rhythm of what she's humming, but before I can identify it, the lawyer continues. "My apologies. Excuse me. Where was I?" She squints at the jury as if she is trying to place how she knows us. "Members of the jury!" She sounds surprised, as if we have appeared out of thin air, and I have to bite my tongue to avoid laughing. She turns to retrieve a pad of paper from the table. She hums a few more bars of the tune as she turns a page of her thick, yellow notepad, then snaps to attention, smiling brightly. "It is true that my client agreed to go into business with Mr. Aschbran. However, this agreement was little more than a memorandum of understanding. It was…"

After such a strong beginning, her extended pause creates an air of suspense throughout the room. Ms. Saqsaq is studying the corner of the ceiling as if trying to decipher words from a teleprompter. Alex shoots me a quizzical look. I lift a shoulder, and I'm not acting. This content has not been rehearsed, so the entire jury is experiencing this together.

When Ms. Saqsaq finds her voice again, she enunciates with such force that we collectively jump in our seats. "…never reviewed by an attorney, never legally formalized in any way."

Again, she pauses, pulling us collectively forward before she blasts her next sentence. "It was just a dream, members of the jury, a dream that came to a close." She pauses long enough I begin to wonder if she's finished, but as before, she launches into the next idea. "Thus, you will see that there is no breach of contract. How could there be when there was no contract, in fact, to breach? As far as damages are concerned, my client should not be held financially responsible because Mr. Aschbran is not able to maintain a successful business."

She surveys the ceiling again, and her internal teleprompter must be blank because she squints our way again, nods once, and returns to sit next to her client, Ms. Menjivar.

CHAPTER SEVEN

Alex

"I know I'm supposed to have an open mind and all," a tatted-out guy says, "but I can't say that…What was the second lawyer's name? Suck Suck? I don't trust her."

The jury has been excused for the day, which surprises me. Most of the day we're waiting, and by the time we get into court, we've barely done anything, so it makes no sense that they are already excusing us. It works for the documentary crew, who have pulled us back into the break room to interview us as a group about our impression of the opening statements.

One of the other men nods in agreement. "No offense to the ladies, but she doesn't seem very professional showing up to court with that scarf thingy on her head. I honestly spent more time wondering whether that's appropriate court attire than I did listening to her opening argument." This guy has an air of authority. The way he squares his shoulders in his neatly pressed shirt suggests that he expects us to listen to him. He's over six feet, always in a suit, and wearing shined leather shoes. He has a baby-round face and short blond hair swept off his forehead.

He resembles Fred from *Scooby Doo*. Fred always acted like the leader of the gang, and this guy will no doubt try to take charge of the jury.

He's got the floor and continues, "She obviously doesn't know what she's doing. It's like she was waiting for someone to feed her the stuff she's saying through an earpiece."

"I'm not sure she knows what the case is about. Have you noticed how she and her client just sit and stare toward the front of the courtroom?" This observation comes from a Latina woman who wears her hair in a severe ponytail. She shakes her head. "The way she doesn't look at the jury?" She hums her disapproval and shakes her head again. "Makes her look guilty."

I can't believe what I'm hearing from the jurors around me. We haven't heard anything except for the opening statements, and they sound like they've already decided the outcome of the case. I want to stop the conversation, but it's hard when nobody else seems to have a problem with their comments, the crew included. Their impression is so different from mine. I'm already aware of the bias I have for the plaintiff, a tall, muscular man with a buzz cut. Even before the opening statements, he came across as an entitled cis-het white guy. I get the impression he's suing his friend because he didn't get exactly what he wanted.

I have a lot of sympathy for the defendant. I agree that she hasn't presented as well as the plaintiff has. She's overweight and clearly wore a borrowed skirt suit to court. A size too small, the buttons pulled at her chest, accentuating both her gender and her weight. She'd look better in a man's suit, but I bet her attorney told her that dressing feminine would garner more sympathy from the jury. Her thick hair is cut in a helmet shape that screams "lesbian" to me, reinforcing my conclusion that she's trying to present as more "normal." It's certainly backfiring with the selected jury.

Juror Two, a Latino man with a heavy mustache says, "*Ella me parece tortiella*" to the woman, and they both laugh.

One of the crew asks them to translate.

The woman purses her lips defiantly. "She looks like a lesbian."

She did not just say that out loud! I whip my head around to catch Sarah's eye. I obviously don't know her well, but her lips are pursed like she's upset. She doesn't say anything. Unbelievable. Not even the out-and-proud podcaster can find a voice to counter what is being said in the room.

"Juror Eleven?" I don't figure out that Nick is talking to me until he follows up with, "Alex?"

I meet his gaze but cannot form a response.

"What is your experience so far?"

"This isn't what I expected at all," I'm able to say.

"Can you say more? What part isn't what you expected?"

I wish I could hide my ears. I can feel they've turned bright red under the scrutiny of the film crew and the jury. "I don't know. It feels more like reality TV than court. The plaintiff and his attorney come off as flawless, and the women are being scrutinized for their appearance or whether they're qualified. The defense's attorney might not have the polished delivery of the plaintiff's, but she stated her side. We're supposed to listen to the evidence. So shouldn't we be waiting to hear the evidence?"

If only I had a turtle shell I could pull into… Feeling everyone's eyes on me makes me extremely uncomfortable. I knew that we would have these follow-up interviews, but I was not prepared for this shallow commentary.

"That's a fair point. What's your impression of the process so far?"

I glance at the other jurists, hoping someone else will take a turn talking. Everything suddenly feels focused entirely on me.

"I found the voir dire fascinating," Sarah says. My shoulders ease as the spotlight shifts. She talks about the strategy involved and how she enjoyed guessing who the attorneys would want to dismiss. "I feel humbled to be a part of this jury. This might not be a big murder case, but it obviously impacts these individuals, and it will be up to us as a group to, like Alex said, listen to the evidence closely and deliver a verdict. That is a lot of responsibility."

I nod my agreement. This is what I anticipated the process would be like. The rest of this documentary interview covers the range of boredom jurors are experiencing and whether they are inconvenienced or excited about the possibility of the trial lasting up to seven days. I'm past ready to be gone by the time the crew says they have enough footage for the day. As quickly as I can, I scoot out the door and head toward the parking lot, grateful to be out of the stale confines of the courthouse.

They've released us early enough that I should be able to get in a good workout. I'll have to go to the gym. I don't want to risk the trails of the San Gabriels as dusk comes on. I am not a fan of sharing the trail with coyotes.

I pull the choke lever and crank the key to the old Honda Civic wagon I bought from a friend of Tom's when we got to California. It doesn't have a whole lot of miles on it, but it's a cranky old thing that often refuses to start. Of course, today is one of the days the engine revs without turning over. I rest my head on the hard plastic steering wheel. I do not need this today. I'm startled by a tap on my window. It's Vicki. My insides go *zing!* in a totally inappropriate way. I remind myself: A) She's got a boyfriend, and B) She's got a BOYfriend. There is no reason for my body to respond to her.

I motion for her to step back, so I can get out of the car. I'd roll down the window, but sometimes it falls off the track. I don't need that on top of it not starting.

"You okay?" she asks.

"I'm fine. The car is a different story."

"You need a ride?"

I hate how I must come across to her right now. Everything about her screams put together: her clothes, her posture, her perfectly sculptured eyebrows, highlighted hair, and flawless lipstick.

"Let me give you a ride," she says into the silence that has stretched out while I've been comparing myself to her and coming up short.

Of course she has a car built this century. It suits her, black, sleek, and sporty.

"Where to?" she says, as though it's her job to chauffer me around.

I open my mouth to give my address but then remember how I had planned to stop by the store on my way home today. I have zero options for dinner.

"I promise I am not a stalker." She laughs.

"No. It's not that. I need to stop by the grocery store is all. You can drop me there, and I'll catch an Uber when I'm finished." I don't have the money for an Uber or to get my car fixed, but she doesn't need to hear all that.

"I got zero else on my schedule today. Let me help, okay?" She rests her hand on my thigh for the briefest moment before snatching it back.

It's not just me, I think before immediately reminding myself that she has a boyfriend and I cannot be having any reaction at all to this woman.

Once I've told her I shop at the Stater Bros on Route 66 and we're on the street, she says, "I'm sorry about your car but also a little thankful because I wanted to thank you."

"Thank me?" I'm surprised. "For what?"

"For what you said during the follow-up interview."

I know I haven't hidden my reactions when she continues, "Those guys were pissing me off, too."

"But you didn't say anything." I didn't expect her to be mad about the lesbian comment, but she didn't say anything about how the men discredited the defense lawyer, either.

"And give them the perfect clip of the 'fiery Latina' for their documentary? No thank you."

I sit with that a moment and wonder if it was Sarah's whiteness or status as a podcaster that made me hope she would speak up. I've been living in Southern California for just over a year and am very aware of how often I'm the minority living in Azusa, a predominately Hispanic community. I wish I could talk to her about how I worry that guy in the suit is going to take point on the jury since he is white like the plaintiff. I contemplate the observations Sarah made about the jury selection process. Does the plaintiff fear that the jury is stacked against him with only four of us being white? I remember his lawyer saying that the plaintiff and defendant came up with their business plan back in college. What must have happened for these once-close friends to end up in court, one suing the other?

It's not a question I can float to Vicki. The judge made it clear that we can't talk about the case outside of court, the jury room, and the documentary interviews. It's all a nice distraction from the mess of my car and lack of direction I have right now. I lean my head back and fantasize about what Vicki's life must be like, on the cusp of engagement.

CHAPTER EIGHT

Vicki

I have put myself in a real pickle here, offering Alex a ride home, but how could I help myself when she was sitting there so utterly deflated? We're not allowed to talk about the trial at all, but to talk about our personal lives will force me to stay in character. *You've got a boyfriend that you'd never cheat on*, I tell myself. I picture the handsome man in the photograph the tech team texted me. He deserves my faithfulness.

I sense Alex's eyes on me, so I keep my gaze fixed to the road. "What are your plans for the car?" I ask. "Are you bringing tools to fix it during our breaks?"

"I am not that handy. You think I can work on cars?"

I can't help but peek at her now. She's got a slight build, but I can tell she's fit. She comes across as a take-charge soft butch who could fix a leaky faucet and make dinner. I wouldn't mind her taking charge of me. I boot that thought out of my head as quick as I can. I shrug. "Old car like that...It's possible. It's not like these new ones with service policies and a bunch of electronics to worry about."

"How do you know so much about cars?" she asks. Her eyebrows are raised again and, good lord, those eyebrows might undo me.

"My brothers are always under one hood or another." Did that sound suggestive? I didn't mean it to be, but the air between us feels alive with energy. I pull into the parking lot and ease into a space. "I could ask if one of 'em has time to take a look at it?"

She has her hand on the door, but she hasn't opened it yet. "Why would you do that? You don't even know me."

It's a good question, one my brothers are going to ask me as well. Why should they drop whatever they are doing and drive to the courthouse to take a look at some stranger's car. I can't tell her it's because she looks like an abandoned kitten. Or that the filming team has drilled into us how important it is to take care of our star. This, of course, falls outside of filming, and I am also caught wondering whether anyone associated with the show would question my offer. "I heard you talking about your family and friends. It doesn't sound like you have anyone you could call for help. I know how that feels. So I'm offering."

She eyes my phone. "I guess. Yeah. That would be...really nice."

The way she says it confirms my impression that she is all alone here in Southern California. "Good. What's the make and model?"

"Honda Civic. A seventy-six."

"Got it. You do your shopping. I'll stay here. I've got a few calls to make."

"Gotta keep an eye on your man," she says as she slips out of the car.

"That's right!" I say, trying to keep my tone playful.

There's too much to convey for a text, so I pull up my contacts and dial Cesar first. He's an electrician and has a more flexible schedule than our brother Mateo. Plus, Cesar is way more likely to go along with me when I have to stay in character.

"Whattayawant and whyareyoucallingme?" he barks into the phone.

"You on a job?"

"Finishing up now, why?" he asks skeptically.

"There's an old Honda Civic that could use some help. I'd owe you," I acknowledge, drawing out *owe* several beats.

"More than dinner," he says.

"But dinner is a good start, isn't it? And listen, my name is Vicki and I'm dating a guy, okay?"

"The fuck?" He cackles. "Who is this person you told you're dating a guy?"

"Shut up. I can't explain right now. It has to do with an acting gig, okay? Promise me you'll roll with it."

"I promise."

"And the house is mine, okay? No talking about how we're flipping it."

"What? Why?"

"I'll explain later," I promise. "I'll text you the address and meet you there." I'm just hanging up with him when Alex emerges with a bag of groceries in each hand.

"Good news! My brother can take a look at the car. He's meeting us there. Do you need to swing by your place first to put anything in the fridge?"

"I don't want to take up more of your time."

"Stop. We're taking Cesar out to dinner after he fixes the car, so it's best if we unload the groceries." When she doesn't rattle off her address, I fail to rein in an eye roll. "Not a stalker, remember? I will not sell your address."

"I don't understand why you're doing all this," she mumbles, but she accepts my phone and adds her address, which I immediately map.

We're quiet for a few blocks, and then she asks if I got ahold of my boyfriend. "I did. I could barely hear him over the music. He hardly ever goes home, so his parents are having a big party before the reunion."

"Why doesn't he like to go home?"

"He complains that it boxes him in. He got out, you know, escaped to the big city, so it's hard to go back. His family doesn't grasp why he didn't stay. Small town, girlfriend who adored him and the family expected him to marry. You can see why I worry."

"Where's he from?"

"Small town in Virginia." I have got to redirect the conversation, partly because the more I share with her, the more I have to keep track of, but also because I want to learn more about her. "Is your story the same? Are you here in California alone because you're escaping a small town in Kentucky?"

"My family lives in a small town, yeah. They run this museum that has old ore wagons, the ones that used to be pulled by a twenty-mule team. There's a guy out here in California who has the mules and gear to pull them. He comes out for the Fourth of July parade every year. He kinda dared me to come back to California with him, so I did. Turns out the boots are the only part of the cowboy experience that worked for me."

"Why would he dare you to come out to California?"

My map signals a turn, and Alex holds up a finger to pause the question. "Mine's the yellow two-story on the right." I've barely stopped the car when she hops out with a "Stay here!"

She runs in and in less than a minute is back on the porch and running down the stairs. "Okay! Ready."

"I feel like I'm driving a getaway car. Is that how you left Kentucky?"

"Pretty much." She laughs but then turns somber. "It wasn't easy leaving. My family's been there forever. I believed I'd stay in that town till the day I died. But they all betrayed me. Every last one of them. You think you know someone, you know?" She turns her head to look out the window. She doesn't expect an answer from me, and what can I say when I can't tell her who I really am? I'm battling between wanting to help this stranded soul and maintaining the promise we've all made to do no harm to Alex in the making of this documentary.

I'm relieved that Cesar is already parked next to Alex's funky orange station wagon when we pull up at the courthouse.

"Alex, this is my brother Cesar. Cesar, Alex."

"Thank you for your help. I owe you. Vicki and I didn't talk about money, and I want to be up front. I don't have a whole lot of cash right now, but if you need something painted..."

Cesar holds up his hand. "Whoa! Slow down! It's my sister who owes me. You can talk to her about payment. But are you seriously a painter? Like a good one?"

"Cesar!" I say, punching his arm.

He jumps, pretending I've hurt him, little weasel. He and Mateo deliver a lot worse than that when they are messing around.

"I think I'm good," Alex says.

"Interior? Exterior?"

"Both," she says.

Cesar rubs his hands together. "This is perfect! I hope your engine needs a lot of work because I have a lot of painting that needs to be done."

"Shut it!" I jab him again. "She doesn't owe you, remember?"

He leans close to Alex and puts a hand up like it will give him privacy. "Her place needs your help."

"Enough!" I shout. "Pop the hood, will you, before we run out of light."

CHAPTER NINE

Alex

"Okay, so, Alex. You'll bring the Orange Beast by the house soon, and Mateo and I will fix it up good. Sis, you said you'd start with dinner. In-N-Out? The one up by the 210?"

"Alex? You game for a burger?" Vicki asks me.

"I'm good now that I can drive home. I picked up stuff for dinner, remember?"

"Oh, no," Cesar breaks in. He's every bit as intense as his sister is, but had they not told me they are related, I would not have guessed. His hair is way too short to show the kink Vicki's does, but their build is completely different. He is wiry where she is all curves. "We're still going to talk about your skills, but I'm starved and it's disrespectful to turn down a free dinner, isn't it, sis?"

"Very." Vicki's eyes search mine, and that damned spark flares again. I should go home. "You know the In-N-Out he's talking about?"

"I've never been," I say.

Cesar drops his jaw, dumbstruck. "How?"

"She's from Kentucky," Vicki explains.

"How long you been here?" he asks.

"A little more than a year," I say. My stomach is in knots, wishing I had a go-to strategy for how to talk to people I've just met about pronouns. Vicki seemed open-minded when I criticized the lawyer's gendered language, but she hasn't asked me about my pronouns.

He tsks as he shakes his head.

He's about to reply, but I interrupt. "Wait. Can I say something?"

Vicki and Cesar wear matching expressions of confusion. I hate the feeling of the spotlight. Best not to draw it out. "I use they/them pronouns."

Vicki smacks her head. "Of course! I should have asked after the opening statements. I'm sorry."

I shrug. I don't want her to be sorry. I just want them to have a more accurate picture of me if we're going to spend time together.

"Got it," Cesar says. "Hate to say it, but you got a crappy welcome crew if you've never had In-N-Out. We're gonna fix that now. Sandwich caravan. Me, you, Vicki, so you don't bail on us. Let's go!"

"Sorry about him," Vicki says as she heads to her car. "He has ADHD. You get used to it."

His energy doesn't bother me at all, especially since he was so quick to take in the pronoun change.

"You're good?" Vicki asks. "See you at In-N-Out?" Cesar has already started his car and is tapping the horn, so what can I say but yes? I jump in line and follow them to the burger place, my head spinning. I'm having a difficult time reading Vicki's brother. He's made quick work of something to do with the choke cable to get the car to turn over, which feels like a miracle. I pat the cracked dashboard to let the car know I'm grateful for this small grace. But Cesar warned me that it is due for some serious time with a mechanic, and soon. He said a lot more words than that, but what it boils down to is the car needing a cash infusion and me needing to be cautious about how far I drive it if I don't move repairs up on my list of priorities. None of this is news to me, and I've been more interested in studying Vicki and Cesar.

Their easy banter achingly reminds me of home, back when my brothers ribbed me the way Cesar ribs Vicki. Why the comment about Vicki's place needing painting? It feels like the jokes Billy used to make about me and Lilian when he was trying to figure out what we were to each other. Only Cesar's ribbing doesn't have an edge to it like Billy's always did. I set that on the shelf in my memory next to Vicki's comment about looking like a young Alison Bechdel. If it weren't for the boyfriend, I would have such a different read on Vicki. I tell myself I need to be cautious, but it is difficult not to get swept along by Vicki and her brother.

At the restaurant, a chain I've passed many times before—I mean, what's the big deal about one more burger joint?—Cesar tells me about the secret menu. I'll leave the Animal Style 3x3 to him and stick with a standard cheeseburger, but he does talk me into a Lemon Up, lemonade mixed with 7-Up.

We're sitting at round cement tables with plastic red-and-white umbrellas, waiting for the food when Cesar asks me why I am painting here instead of in Kentucky.

"Here is not where my family is," shoots out of my mouth before I can curb myself. The siblings exchange a look. Being around them has scrambled my emotions. "I came out here with a wrangler who worked for my parents. When he figured out how bad I am with horses, he helped me get on my feet. He had a friend who was fixing up a house. He let me live there rent free and taught me how to prep and paint. We finished his place, and since then, he's tried to funnel a steady stream of business my way. I work job to job and wasn't doing anything when I saw the docu—"

Vicki interrupts me. "We're on the same job this week."

I'm taken aback by the way Vicki jumped in, and it sounds weird for her to call jury duty a job, but I guess technically it is our job this week, and her brother doesn't seem to question it.

"You look legit with all the equipment in your wagon there."

He nods in my car's direction and leans to pull his wallet from his pocket. He pulls out a card and tosses it across the table to me. "Shoot me a text, and I can pass your number to a few contractors."

"Seriously?" I quickly scan the card. He's a licensed electrician. I'm so overwhelmed by his kindness that words escape me for a minute. "That would be amazing. Thank you."

"First you gotta help my sis out with her crappy-ass place. I've been telling her it needs work."

"I'd be happy to take a look at it," I say. "But probably after your boyfriend is back from his trip." The siblings make eye contact, more evidence to support the hunch I have that the chemistry I feel for her is not one-sided. "Sorry. I assumed you lived together. My bad."

"No. Yeah," Vicki stammers. "I should talk with him about it before I make any decisions." I don't understand the daggers she's glaring at her brother. What's the backstory there?

"Boyfriend," Cesar says dismissively. "You know I think you could do better."

"We are so not talking about this right now." Vicki's tone shuts him up completely.

We're sitting in awkward silence, weird energy between the siblings that I can't translate at all, when mercifully, our number blares from the speakers. Cesar is immediately on his feet, waving off our offer to help retrieve the food.

"Sorry." Vicki won't meet my eye.

"Don't worry," I say, wishing I had time to ask what it is he doesn't like about the boyfriend and even more so find out how he would feel about her dating a woman before he comes back with the food. "I could never talk to my family about who I was with."

I'm pretty sure from the sympathy in her eyes that she intuits my ex is a woman, but she doesn't have time to comment before her brother returns with our burgers and fries. I can't imagine how this guy can possibly eat a burger with three patties, but he has no trouble chomping it down with a waggle of his eyebrows. I've only eaten a few bites when he crinkles the paper wrapper and unfolds himself from the bench. "Can't wait for you slowpokes. Text me about the car, okay?" He points at me. "And don't wait too long."

"I won't."

He and Vicki fist-bump, and then he's gone, jogging across the parking lot.

"Don't take it personal. He never stops," Vicki says, popping a ketchup-dipped fry in her mouth. She licks the salt from her fingers, and my belly tightens. *Stop!* I tell myself, quickly turning away.

"He's amazing. You're amazing."

"Stop. I'm happy to help." She points at my burger. "Have we made a convert out of you?"

"The burger is okay. The fries are amazing. I've never seen a potato get smashed through that thing that turns it into fries."

"That's why they are so good."

I glance back, and she's licking her fingers again. Why am I doing this to myself? Because this could lead to more work. If only I didn't want more with Vicki. "So, Cesar's an electrician. What do you do when you're not on a jury?"

"Boring office work," she says.

"Kind of a nice break, then?"

"Yeah. Nice change of pace."

We eat in silence with the drone of the freeway filling in the background. I want to ask why her brother figures she can do better than reunion boyfriend. Whatever it is, I'd second it. It doesn't seem fair to meet someone who makes my heart race like this when she's already taken. My helpful brain supplies me a song lyric I've heard on the radio about meeting the man of your dreams and then his beautiful wife. Good thing for me my life can't be reduced to a song lyric. I'm not interested in finding the perfect man, and considering how Cesar dismissed the boyfriend, maybe the spark I feel with Vicki could actually do more than just flare. Maybe it could catch and grow.

CHAPTER TEN

Vicki

I am in such hot water. I barely slept last night because I couldn't stop musing about Alex and wanting to see her again. Not on the show but on a date, and I can't date Alex. Not right now. But could we after? I should not have given her a ride. I swear my car still holds the faintest hint of her perfume. Wait...I shake my head, reviewing all the things I just thought and revise. I want to see them again. My car holds their scent, and would they wear perfume or cologne?

We're gathered in the jury room. I haven't seen Alex yet, and just as my mind flip-flopped all night long, it continues, going from wanting them to arrive with time to chat before the day begins to hoping they squeak in on the dot so I can reestablish a professional distance today.

"Good morning," Sarah says, sitting next to me. At my mumbled "Good morning," she assesses me and furrows her brow. "Everything okay?"

"No! Nothing is okay!" I blurt. I grab her by the sleeve of her denim jacket and haul her to the small kitchen space off the holding room. I cross my fingers nobody will need the fridge or microwave this early. "I fucked up," I say.

"Say more," she says, and it's like I'm a guest on her podcast. She would probably invite me onto her show to talk about questionable morals and choices. I push aside the thought. It only makes me feel worse.

"I hung out with Alex after the show yesterday."

"In what capacity?"

"They needed help with their car. I gave them a ride."

"They?" Sarah asks, cocking her head. "That means pronouns came up?"

"They did."

I can see Sarah weighing this. "Which means she trusts you. *They* trust you. So you were genuine with them. You created a space that made them comfortable."

"Yes."

"And you stayed in character?"

"Obviously," I huff.

"And you didn't talk about the case? If this were a real trial, that would be problematic, so it would throw a wrinkle in filming if you had to divulge that."

"No, we didn't talk about the case. But we talked. A lot. And my brother helped fix up her car. Their car. And then we had dinner. I told my brother I'd be in character and he had to play along, but he said he thinks I can do better than my made-up boyfriend, which is so bad because I feel this amazing chemistry with Alex."

"Oh, no."

"That's bad, right? I fucked up."

Sarah's face doesn't hide her disapproval. It's as bad as I feared, maybe worse. "You need to tell the team, so they can assess what to do. Maybe they'll give your boyfriend a medical emergency and rotate in an alternate."

"I want to be on the show!"

"But you and Alex clearly have chemistry. If the two of you start to have feelings for each other, that could seriously mess with Alex's head. They cannot think they've been messed with emotionally. That's why I'm here, to make sure that Alex isn't harmed in this process."

"I know. But I'm not lying about being attracted to them."

"I know that, but they think you're Vicki. You're not, and you're blurring dangerous lines by inserting them into your real life. That's why you wanted to talk to me. You already know you can't do that."

I nod. That is exactly why I pulled Sarah aside to talk to her. Damnit if my eyes aren't pricking with emotion. I don't want to be Vicki. I want to be myself so badly right now. Even though I barely know Alex, there's this sense of possibility that I can't bear to let go.

"I'm sorry," Sarah says, wrapping her arms around me. "I can tell that this is all really hard."

"Oh!"

Both Sarah and I start at the sound and step out of the hug to witness a very surprised Alex standing awkwardly by the door with a lunch bag in their hand. Those eyebrows… It's like they are attached to all my nerve endings. When they go up like they are now, I feel the pull everywhere.

"Sorry." They turn as if to go, and I have to stop them.

"Alex!"

I glance at Sarah, and something passes between us. I hear her warning about not harming Alex in any way. If we are spending time together, even if it is only in this fictional world the writers have created, I cannot have her thinking that I'm seriously dating a guy. "Malcolm broke up with me."

This brings Alex to my side. Today they're wearing cowboy boots and jeans with a formfitting green T-shirt tucked in. Have they decided to present more masc of center since sharing their pronouns with me? The pressed shorts and button-down shirts they've worn on previous days present significantly more androgynous. Today they carry themself with more certainty. They rest a hand on my shoulder. "Oh, I'm so sorry. When did that happen?"

"He literally just texted me. He knows we'll be going into court, so I can't call."

Sarah's eyes bore into me, but I will not meet her eyes. I'll get a sense for what kind of wrench I've crammed into the gears when we meet with the producers and scriptwriters.

"Can I get you anything?" Alex asks. "I could go check out the vending machine. Chocolate always helps, right?"

"Always," I say with a twinge of guilt.

"Okay. I got you. Are you an M&M's kind of person? Snickers? Twix?"

"Plain M&M's, if they have them?"

They squeeze my hand. "Peanut are better, but I'll get you plain if they have 'em," they say and rush from the room.

Now I can't avoid Sarah's gaze. "You're playing with fire here, *Vicki*."

"I know. Oh, I know."

"And they're right. Peanut are way better than plain."

"You can lecture me on both after trial today."

Outside, the doors to the court are now open, and Alex is waiting there with a bag of M&M's they hand to me as we enter the courtroom and take our seats.

Once the judge has called the court to order, she invites counsel to call his first witness.

"Your Honor, for my first witness, I call Geoff Aschbran to the stand."

The plaintiff stands, adjusts his tie, and buttons his coat purely to cross the courtroom and sit down to be sworn in by the clerk.

"Do you solemnly swear or affirm that the testimony you are about to give in this issue of matters shall be the truth, the whole truth, and nothing but the truth?"

Geoff sits straight-backed, very solemn and, I'd add, entitled as he holds up his hand and says, "I do."

We've been warned that real court can be boring, but watching paint dry must be more exciting than listening to this guy spell his name and confirm that he's the plaintiff. Why does he have to confirm that he's the plaintiff and that he knows the woman sitting at the defense table? He's suing her! Of course he knows who she is. I can't understand why it takes so long to get to the point. Is it important for us to know that he was studying psychology or that she was studying animal husbandry?

Alex is writing furiously on their notepad, so I at least jot down what they were studying in college even though I seriously want to ask Alex if this is more boring than watching paint dry.

"How did the two of you meet?" The lawyer has his hand in his pocket, his posture relaxed. He consults a notepad from time to time, moving his pen as he progresses through his prepared questions, and from what it seems, this is a game of a lot more than twenty questions.

Geoff nods. He has clearly rehearsed this.

"I was dating her roommate. She was never ready on time, and we'd get to talking."

"Did the two of you talk about going into business?"

"We talked about it, yes."

"And how did that come about?"

"We quickly saw the overlap between horseback riding and therapy. My brother has cerebral palsy, and we talked about the benefits of horseback riding. There are stables that offer therapeutic riding, but we got the idea for a mobile unit because we were always waiting on Janet…"

"Janet was your girlfriend?"

"Yes, and Ms. Menjivar's roommate," Geoff says.

Alex underlines something forcefully, so I steal a peek at her notes. She's written *Roommate?* and underlined it twice.

They catch me peeking and make a face as if they're thinking, *Roommates. Yeah, right.*

Roommates? This sparks an idea I can take to the writers, one that might make the water I'm sitting in less hot.

CHAPTER ELEVEN

Alex

There is something about the way Mr. Aschbran says *roommate* that moves my attention back to the defendant. She's not showing any emotion at all as he describes how they fell into a friendship that outlasted both the dorm roommate assignment and the relationship. She never looks his way, yet he keeps a steady eye on her as he explains how they brainstormed ways to make therapeutic riding more accessible.

I'm writing notes as the alleged contract that the friends wrote together is entered into evidence and given to the jury to examine. I take note of how few of the other jurors even give the contract a once-over as it is passed from person to person. Most of the other folks don't even have their notepads out. Sports Guy holds the contract in his left hand and after a moment swings an imaginary racket as if he is volleying the contract to Waverly, the old crone. She takes forever to find a stopping place in her knitting or crocheting—I don't know the difference—before she can take the contract. At least she studies it briefly before passing it down the line.

This is only the first witness, and nobody appears to be listening. Even Vicki is distracted, thumbing candy into her mouth and chewing with exaggerated slowness that, in my opinion, amplifies the crunch. I want to tell her we're in court, not at the movies, but I can't. I'm the one who got her the chocolate in the first place.

Our fingers brush when she passes the contract to me, and though it feels utterly inappropriate, my insides whisper *She's single!* But that doesn't make her available. Maybe there are rules against jurors seeing each other. Beyond that, I am not gaming to be Vicki's rebound.

Am I?

The document that has been entered into evidence as the contract doesn't resemble any legally binding document I've ever seen. It's scribbled on the back of a handout from one of their classes and is stained with grease and rings from cups or bottles. It reads more like a grocery list than a business. *Ponies! Wheels! Accessible! City parks? More than rich suburbs.* The most important thing is scrawled in all block letters: *IN IT TOGETHER OR NOT AT ALL!*

I make a note of that and pass it to my left, but Scooby Doo Fred is snoozing. I poke him with the cap side of my pen, and he startles awake. Dude. We're on the first witness, and he is already nodding off? I try for a *What the hell!* look but can hear my brother teasing me about how ineffective my face is at conveying disappointment.

"You gotta get rid of the permanent smile," he'd said. "Or nobody's ever going to take you seriously. You ever seen a smiling cowboy? No. The Marlboro Man is stern. Tough. Not all sunshine."

Hanging out with Vicki's brother yesterday has opened a floodgate of memories about my family. I'm literally thousands of miles away from them, but they're still in my head.

The defense lawyer stands up and smooths her hijab. Today it is saffron, which matches something close to a paisley pattern in her shirt. I'm pretty sure she's humming the way she does as she gathers her thoughts. It's too quiet to identify what the tune is, but her lips are in an "O" shape, and her head is bobbing.

She approaches the stand and smiles at Mr. Aschbran. Then she tips her chin up, again as though there are teleprompters in the corners of the court ceiling. "Isn't it true, Mr. Aschbran, that you and Ms. Menjivar did, in fact open a business together, thereby satisfying your agreement?"

"Yes, that is correct."

The lawyer takes a deep breath and hums another refrain before asking, "And isn't it also true that you asked your cousin, who is a lawyer, if this is a binding document?"

"I did."

"At that time, had your cousin passed the bar in California?"

"No. He had not."

"And did it take twenty-five attempts for your cousin to pass the bar?"

"Yes."

"No further questions, Your Honor."

"Counsel, call your next witness," Judge Court says.

The handsome lawyer stands. Today's suit is just as pressed as yesterday's. Every hair is swept into place, and he smiles at all of us like we are the best of friends. "As my second witness, I call the CPA for TheraPony, Lance Wood."

I glance at Scooby Doo Fred as the CPA takes the oath, spells his name, and confirms his schooling and how long he has been an accountant. Scooby Doo Fred is leaning forward and blinking like a long-haul driver trying his best to stay awake at the wheel. Am I the only one paying attention? I surreptitiously glance around at the other jurors. Two have the notebooks we've been given open on their laps, and I'm pretty sure that Ripley, the woman who did the first talking-head interview with me, is doodling from the way she keeps tipping her head to examine the page. Even Vicki's notepad is on the floor. She discreetly tips the bag of M&M's I bought her in my direction. I shake my head, again thinking we aren't at the movies, and it's like she can hear what I'm thinking because she folds the edge of the wrapper and tucks it into her bag.

Still, she doesn't pick up the notepad. Why would they provide us with one unless we are supposed to be taking notes? I have no desire to be foreperson once we get to deliberations, but if nobody else is keeping track of the evidence, then how are we ever supposed to assess it critically? We are supposed to be a jury of the defendant's peers. Maybe I am more invested because she so obviously falls outside of social norms, but I know that even if it were Mr. Clean Cut in the defendant's seat, I'd be keeping track like I am now.

The accountant is finally past all the stuff that they must have to go through for the court reporter and gets to information that seems relevant to the charges we will be deciding.

"During the years employed by the business, do you have a record of how much money they made?"

"Yes. At its peak, TheraPony was bringing in two hundred thousand dollars a year."

"Did you continue to be the accountant after Ms. Menjivar breached the agreement?"

"Objection!" the defense lawyer says, standing.

We are all waiting for her to state what she objects to. Even the judge holds out her hands as if to prompt the lawyer to continue.

She's humming again, louder, like she's agitated or nervous. I think I recognize the tune now and turn to see whether anyone else is reacting to what I'm pretty sure is "Baby Shark."

"There is no evidence that there was a noncompetition agreement..." She searches the ceiling for more words. "Without an agreement, there can be no breach."

"Sustained," the judge says, making a note. "Counsel, proceed."

"What was the annual income after Ms. Menjivar opened No More Stubborn Mules?" the plaintiff's attorney rephrases.

"Seventy-five thousand, the base operating cost of TheraPony."

I'm relieved that the judge calls for lunch after the cross-examination. We're instructed to leave our notebooks and return in an hour and a half. All morning I have been wanting to talk to Vicki. Her offer to share candy makes me wonder if she would go to the movies with me. Not like a date or anything, but as something to do to take her mind off the breakup.

Before I get out into the hallway, she and Sarah are already walking side by side down the hall. Disappointed, I settle for finding a quiet place to eat my lunch.

I am conditioned to search outside since I'm usually trying to escape paint fumes during a break in my workday. At this time of day, there is no line to enter the building through security. Several of the jurors from my trial have the same idea I do and push through the exit doors.

Eyeing my bag, Waverly gestures and says, "I think there is a picnic bench around this side of the building. Since you brought a lunch, too?"

"I did," I acknowledge reluctantly. Once I admit that, I can't say I'd rather sit by myself.

I needn't have worried, because shortly after Waverly and I settle on the concrete picnic table under a canopy of shade trees, a bunch of the other jurors who bought lunch from the food truck join us. Sports Guy is inhaling a chicken wrap and talking to Waverly about how it's too hard to get the calories he needs without eating meat.

They look expectantly at me and the sandwich I'm eating. "Cheese and pickle," I say, relieved I didn't make myself a turkey sandwich this morning.

"I could feel that," Waverly says.

"Feel what?"

"Your sandwich doesn't give off the same air of suffering," she explains.

Sports Guy studies his wrap. "My wrap has an air of suffering?"

She nods. "I wouldn't be able to stomach it." She points to the other meals that include meat. The nachos with ground beef that Scooby Doo Fred is eating exudes "suffering," as does the hot dog a goateed Latino guy is eating. "I didn't think that anything could feel worse than the courtroom, but this is about to make me start crying."

"What's wrong with the courtroom?" Scooby Doo Fred asks.

"You don't feel all the residual conflict from prior cases?" She scrutinizes everyone at the table.

Nobody responds. I make the mistake of looking her way and meet her eyes. "There have been terrible, horrible cases those walls have heard, and from the feel of it, it's never once been cleansed. It has to impact the new cases, and I have a bad feeling about this one. The walls tell me that many women have cried in that space. Do you think the judge would be open to a smudging?"

Scooby Doo Fred chokes on the soda he is sipping through a straw. "You can't be serious," he says when he recovers from the drink he aspirated.

"I am quite serious," Waverly says. She lays eyes on each of us at the table in turn. "This court has upheld sexist expectations of women and punished them when they have dared to walk their own path. I tried to balance the energy after sensing the grave suffering trapped in this space. I put smoky quartz under each of the jury seats to promote healing and balance our masculine and feminine energy, but it's not working."

"Are you crazy?" Scooby Doo Fred exclaims.

"Can that hurt us?" Sports Guy asks. "I'm in training for a pickleball tournament. I don't want you messing with my energy."

"It should improve your game. These stones help you with balance. When you are at harmony with yourself, you'll notice how in tune you are with the world around you."

Scooby Doo Fred angrily crumples his trash. "The judge is going to hear about this. You're not allowed to bias the trial."

"But it is already biased!" Waverly cries. "That you don't feel it is more evidence that the room favors men."

"This is a load of crap," Scooby Doo Fred grumbles.

My palms are starting to sweat from their conflict. My heart is racing. It gets worse as others join Scooby Doo Fred's side and demand that she collect her stones. I want to ask how they could possibly hurt anything. None of us even knew she put them under our chairs. I don't care that there is one under mine. I can't imagine that a bunch of rocks can undo bad energy, and contemplating how messed up and imbalanced our society is, it kind of makes sense to me that a space could be biased. Isn't that what I felt strictly by looking at Mr. Clean Cut plaintiff and the defendant that Waverly said was on the granola end of the spectrum? The guys at the table seem threatened by Waverly. It's all about power, I think. It always is.

"I'm with a lot of you here," I'm surprised to hear myself say.

The whole table goes quiet, which is a relief and terrifying at the same time.

I gulp. "I don't get the whole energy thing, but it's clearly important to Waverly. We have to work together on this case, so it's important for us to listen and respect each other, even if we don't understand. I've never once thought about what a room might hold." I shrug, not really knowing where I'm going with this.

"That's true," Goatee Guy says. "When my uncle bought his house, they had to…I forget what the word for it is, but they had to tell him someone had died there."

"Disclose," Waverly says.

"Yeah, disclose," Goatee Guy says.

"Guy in my neighborhood shot himself, and the house is still on the market. Nobody wants to buy it," Sports Guy says.

Waverly excitedly points at him. "Exactly! Because a lot of people can feel the negative energy that stayed in the house. Negative energy stays in all sorts of spaces, and it would be better if we cleansed the courtroom."

For some reason everyone stares straight at me like it's my decision. "We can't stop you from asking the judge if it's possible," I say. "Right?"

I'm surprised when even Scooby Doo Fred begrudgingly says, "Whatever. Let the judge decide."

I'm not going to lie. It feels like a small victory, and I'm glad I spoke up.

CHAPTER TWELVE

Vicki

"We should run with this," Hiroki, one of my favorite writers, says. "I knew the two of you had chemistry. *This* is what makes great TV! Why wouldn't we let this play out and see where it goes?"

"I wonder how often people hook up when they serve on a jury," Ryan says.

"What you're suggesting is highly inadvisable and exactly why the producers asked me to take part in this," Sarah says. "My job is to preserve Alex's emotional well-being, and allowing Alex to form an emotional connection to a fictional character is anything but."

"Ignoring the chemistry between us will hurt them," I say. "I can tell that my dating a guy threw them off. We don't want them doubting themself and their read on people, do we?"

"What if you come out as bi?" Ryan suggests.

"And your boyfriend comes around? That would make you safer to hang out with but also help ease Alex's confusion?" Hiroki looks at Sarah as he says this.

She's weighing this against my impetuous decision to say my fake boyfriend dumped me.

"That won't work," I say. "Vicki's whole fear of sending her boyfriend off to the reunion alone is rooted in the old girlfriend snagging him back. It isn't believable for him to come running back so soon."

"Unless he dumped Vicki to hook up with the girlfriend and immediately learns he has misjudged her interest," Hiroki muses.

"What was your long game when you ended the relationship?" one of the producers asks.

I can't tell him that my long game is for Alex to still like me after the reveal, to more than like me. I can't tell him that I want for Vicki to be more like me, so I can assure Alex that who I have been with them is not a lie. "They're not seeing anyone, and I get the sense that they were dumped."

"Wait," the producer says. "Are we talking about Alex here?"

"Yeah. Alex uses they/them pronouns." I can feel Sarah's eyes on me, but I can't look at her because I'm unsure about how much to divulge about my interaction with them yesterday. "I drove them home yesterday, and we ended up having dinner."

Hiroki's eyes light up "Are you driving her—"

"Them," Sarah and I say in unison.

"Them," Hiroki repeats. "Are you driving them home again today? Can we set up a camera on them? All the jurors are reminded not to talk about the case. So we could follow them and record what the jurors do end up talking about?"

"I didn't drive them today," I say.

"Totally inappropriate," Sarah says.

The producer says, "Is it though? She's agreed..."

"They," I say in time with Sarah and Hiroki.

The producer bows his head. "They signed a contract agreeing to be filmed. The mobile camera is on everyone having lunch out at the picnic table. What's the difference if the camera covers Vicki and Alex if they get together outside of court? As long as Vicki is in character, we're getting more backstory on Alex, seeing how they think, right? We might score some material that will tie in with deliberation and verdict."

Sarah voices her doubt. "That's quite an extension from jury service."

"Is it, though?" Ryan asks. "Remember we brainstormed about sequestering them to get more material? This would be similar, only without the expense of putting everyone up at a hotel. This is perfect!"

"And you're comfortable spending more time on the clock?" the producer asks.

"Absolutely," I say, ignoring the cautionary look Sarah directs at me. "They wrote something down during court today that I need to follow up on. When Geoff was talking about Marlene being roommates with his girlfriend in college, they underlined 'roommate' a bunch of times. I think they're hypothesizing that Marlene and the girlfriend were more than roommates. Could we work that into the case?"

"How so?"

I'm jazzed that Hiroki wants to run with the idea and do my best to create a legitimate suggestion. "I haven't had very much time to consider, but Waverly has already pointed out that Marlene is granola. That would track with her being lesbian."

"Being granola does not make her a lesbian," Sarah interrupts. "Plenty of straight folks are granola, and plenty of the lesbian population is far from granola." She points to herself as an example.

"I know it plays to the stereotype, but this is TV. Isn't Geoff as much a caricature of the entitled straight white guy as Marlene is a granola queer? Isn't our whole purpose here to challenge how quickly people assume innocence or guilt-based on how 'presentable' a person is?"

"Does using they/them pronouns make Alex queer?" the producer asks. "Because I like the idea of pulling an important part of their identity into the deciding of the case. That aligns with our wanting viewers to reflect on the potential consequence of snap judgments people make largely based on appearance."

"Exactly," I say, excited. "What if the business split because Geoff's wife left him for Marlene?"

"So it's not about the money as much as it's about hurt feelings," Hiroki says.

"Bingo. Jealousy makes good TV," I say.

"We could brainstorm how to bring in an ex," Hiroki offers. "It would help if we had the rest of the day to work out a new scenario."

"We'll create a diversion," the producer says, and we're released back to court for whatever will transpire for the rest of the day if we aren't returning for more testimony.

The collaborative brainstorming as the team considers the angles of an idea and develops it further is so exciting. I love being part of this energy and creativity and knowing that the next time we meet, I'll be able to see where the writers take this small idea I've given them.

"That wasn't exactly coming clean," Sarah says as we leave to grab lunch before we're due back in the courtroom.

"You steered them away from the love interest idea. Isn't that the important part?" I ask.

"It would be better if they knew how accurate they are about you being attracted to each other."

"You think they're attracted to me?" I whisper.

Sarah playfully shoves me. "'Duh,' as my daughter would say."

"So all I have to do is be as authentic as I can be during the rest of the trial. Then when it's all over, I can ask them out."

We've walked out to the food truck to collect our lunches, and Sarah's silence unnerves me. I want so badly for her to agree with me. "They're going to feel betrayed, Vicki. They trust you. I worry that it would have been better for you to stay with the boyfriend. Then when it's all over, you could say that everything was made up."

"Except for how much I really like them."

"That cannot be your focus right now. Use the time together to help establish that their insights as a nonbinary and queer person are important. Bolster their confidence, but do not play with their emotions."

The lunch group that includes Alex is headed back to the entrance, and my insides flutter as Alex slows and separates from them.

"Are you doing okay?" They look like they want to hug me, and I would love a hug. Emelynn would love a hug. Vicki has a reason to be hugged. I cannot hug them. I put my hands in my pockets and curl my shoulders protectively. Sarah reaches over and gently wraps her arm around me.

"I hope you know you can talk to me about it anytime. I am happy to help," Sarah says.

"I feel bad making you work when you're on jury duty," I say.

"Nonsense. I went into marriage and family therapy precisely because I enjoy helping people. Alex? Anything troubling you? My calendar is free when they dismiss us for the day."

"No, thank you," they say so formally I expect them to tack a *ma'am* on for good measure.

Sarah squeezes my shoulder, and I see it from Alex's eyes as the supportive action for someone still stinging from being dumped, but I feel in it the cautionary reminder that I must stay in character.

The tenderness of the gesture makes tears spring to my eyes, which I brush away with the swipe of my wrist.

Alex pulls a pressed handkerchief from their back pocket. Who carries a handkerchief anymore?

They shrug apologetically. "It's old, but it's clean. I promise."

I take it, and the cloth is soft with age. I gently press it to the corners of my eyes. My voice cracks when I thank them. "You carry a handkerchief that you don't use? Are you on a quest to find a damsel in distress?"

"You're no damsel in distress," they say. "You're a real person having a shitty day. I know how it feels."

Their voice quavers, and they swallow hard as they try to push away the emotion. They look so vulnerable that tears spring to my eyes again, and now I'm genuinely crying for how tangled this all is.

"Can I hug you?" they ask quietly.

I should say no. To accept is to step onto a slippery slope, but I can't help myself. I nod once, and then their arms are around me, and my face is resting against their shoulder. I am absolutely me when I press into them and breathe them in. They smell like the mountains, like a field of wild grass and clear blue skies.

"Alex!"

We step apart much too soon and well after the damage is done. Hiroki and a camera operator have approached to ask about filming home segments for the jurors, but Alex isn't listening. The way their eyes stay on me, I know they are as lost in the hug we shared as I am, as if the body contact has plucked a chord that continues to resonate. I am meant to be in their arms. I felt it. They felt it.

I press the soft handkerchief to my face again. I am in such hot water.

CHAPTER THIRTEEN

Alex

I was nervous enough about going over to Vicki's house after court without the added weirdness of a camera coming home to shoot a segment completely focused on me. When we're in the courtroom, I'm so focused on the details of the trial that I don't even notice the camera. I was aware of the portable camera following us to lunch but similarly tuned it out once Waverly got to talking about crystals. That whole conversation was so freaking weird it felt like we were shooting some kind of reality TV show.

I pull out my phone to tap out a note to bring up the crystals tomorrow when we return to court. As soon as we got through security, we were shuttled right back outside. Something about the building losing water and not being able to resume court if the bathrooms are not in working order. There are sure a lot of delays. I would have a hard time if my workday was as consistently cut short as our time in court has been.

It crosses my mind that reality TV often is built around interviews like the one I'm about to do, but I dismiss the idea.

Documentaries must do individual interviews as well. I hastily tidy my room before Nick, the documentarian, arrives to film my home segment. Apparently, they've already been shooting the other members of the jury, which seems a little weird. Nobody has talked about it, and they didn't tell us at the beginning that they would be following us once we left court. Now, they're interested in filming us outside of court as the trial progresses to see how who we are as individuals ties into how the trial is decided. It's similar to the voir dire process the lawyers did at the beginning of the trial, but visual for television.

I keep my room tidy, but there's not a whole lot I can do about the spaces I share with my roommates. All I can do is hope that Nick will want to use my room to do the interview. I'm wiping crumbs from the counter when the doorbell rings. Nick is there with a familiar camera operator behind him. I lift my hand in greeting, and he simply nods.

"Do you mind if we film from the beginning? Part of filming a documentary is that you never know what tape is going to be useful."

"That's fine," I say. "Come on in." What was the living room at one time is walled off to make another private room. I lead them through the kitchen with its small circular table. "I mostly spend my time in my room if I'm here," I explain as the camera operator does a sweep of the kitchen. It's super old with tuna-colored tile and terrible lighting, but I'm not home that much, which I explain to them.

"How many people do you share the house with?" Nick asks.

"There's five of us. Two downstairs and three upstairs. We each have a section of the fridge." I open the door to show them the shelves that have tape with our names to identify where we can store food. On the outside of the fridge is a list of common chores—taking out the garbage, sweeping the kitchen, and such—on a wheel that rotates, giving each of us a different job each week. "My room's this way."

I lead them by the tiny downstairs bathroom. It's convenient that my room is closer to the bathroom, but the downside is all the noise from the kitchen that filters through at all hours of the day. I've decorated my room with castoffs from jobs—a dresser I patched up, a desk with a missing drawer. "I didn't have any savings when I left Kentucky. I didn't even have a car, just hitched a ride with a family friend who also helped me find this place when it didn't end up working for me to stay out at his barn."

"Are you a cowgirl?" He motions at my boots and then to a rope I have hanging on the wall.

"I can barely catch a kitchen chair."

He smiles. "Show us?"

"It won't make any good video. I tried to learn from Tom. He's the one who brings a twenty-mule team to pull a bunch of ore wagons in the Fourth of July parade." I pick up a picture and hand it to him, pausing for the camera operator to capture the image. "My parents run the museum that owns the wagons. That's them." I point. "And Tom."

"Do you have other photos of your family?"

I kind of laugh at that, at the assumption I have that picture out because my mom and dad are in it. I keep it despite the fact that they're in it. I keep it because when my parents tried to tell Tom what an embarrassment I'd turned out to be, he said he'd never had any luck asking a mule to be a horse or a horse to be a mule. After driving across the country with him, I got to understanding what he meant by that. We had stops along the way where I earned my keep by helping unload and care for the animals. As hard as I tried to follow Tom's instructions, I never got the hang of working with those enormous animals. I did admire his ability to read all the differing personalities of the mules, especially since that skill contributed to my parents recognizing that he got me better than they ever did. Tom agreed and said California would be a better place for me to live and invited me to come out here with him. My parents kept praying for my salvation, and those twenty mules turned out to be the answer.

"Are you still in touch with your family?"

"No need," I say. "They're only interested in my coming home if I'll be the girl they raised me to be." I run my hand through my buzzed hair and smile. "It would take a long-ass time to grow my hair out long enough to even think about going back."

"Does that make this Tom fellow your family now?"

Tom's a businessman. He doesn't keep stock in his barn that don't work for him. I wonder for a moment if he's ever sold any of his stock to one of the businesses we're hearing about in this trial. Too bad I can't ask him with the judge's orders not to discuss the case outside of her courtroom. "I guess he's kind of like the uncle you see every other Christmas. But most of the time you don't think about them."

"What about your roommates here, or a coworker? Anyone we could get on camera to round out the picture of who Alex is?"

I shake my head. All I hear are the voices I left back in Kentucky telling me I was the girl in their photo album pictures. I was only lovable if I stayed the girl in those pictures. My family I could comprehend. Lilian I couldn't. For a second, I imagine what the Lilian I'd been so happy with might have said about me to this camera. Risk-taker. She'd told me that once, that she admired the risks I took. She said they made her feel brave, too.

Wasn't that partly why I'd believed I could be even more of myself with her? But when I cut my hair and bound my chest, I'd lost her, too.

"I'm not attracted to boys." Her words are seared into my brain.

"But I'm not a boy," I'd insisted.

"But now you look like one. That's how everyone sees you," she had complained. I couldn't be who she wanted me to be. I'd never be a good Christian, either, in anyone's eyes. And I know there's no way I'd change any minds staying there.

"Sorry," I say. "It's just me."

"No, no apology," Nick says. "This is good stuff. Tell us about your business."

It's awkward, at first, talking about myself so much, but the longer I talk, the more relaxed I am. I explain how I started with Tom's place as a way to compensate for my keep and then branched out to people he knew until I'd gotten enough word-of-mouth praise that contractors started hiring out their paint jobs to me. "I'm proud to do a good job. A job well done makes me feel good. A nice, evenly coated wall or clean lines on my trim...It's satisfying, you know?' I'm a little self-conscious saying that. It seems like such a small thing to take pride in your work, but I guess that's not everyone's priority.

"I get the sense that there's a lot of folks out there who focus on speed and don't care at all if their work is sloppy. Everything I paint, I do it like it was my home, like I am going to be the person staring at that wall every day. I want it to be perfect."

"I'd say it's a rare thing for someone today to be driven by that kind of inner code."

I blush at the compliment, but I hold on to it like a treasure I can take out of my pocket later to enjoy again.

"Are you on a job now?"

"I actually might be. I kinda owe Vicki for some help she gave me with my car. She said I could repay her by doing a paint job. I haven't seen what she needs yet."

"Fantastic! I'd love to get footage of you doing your painting thing, and we could grab Vicki's interview at the same time. What do you think?"

Butterflies rise in my stomach at the thought of seeing Vicki outside of court again. "You don't think it would be a problem to do that when we're still on the jury?"

He waves away my concern. "As long as you don't discuss the case, I don't see why it would be a problem at all."

"It's not really part of being on a jury, though," I say, finding it weird that they would want to bother following up on my painting. Watching someone paint is about as exciting as waiting for paint to dry.

"Like you said, you and Vicki can't talk about the case. It would be great for the documentary to explore how difficult that might be."

I shrug. "Guess I'm game if she is. Since she'll be doing one of these, too."

"We'll set it up." He motions to the camera operator to cut the recording and pack up.

They're gone within minutes, and I'm left in the quiet speculating about what it will be like to see Vicki at her house but with cameras. It's about repaying my debt, not about testing the waters of whether she might like me or not. As if that's a fair thing to presume when she just got dumped. I run my hands through my hair. The trial has thrown us together at such a bad time. I cross my fingers that the painting thing will help me sustain a connection to Vicki beyond the trial.

CHAPTER FOURTEEN

Vicki

When we reenter the courtroom the next day, assured that water has been restored, several of the jurors crouch in front of their chairs before taking a seat. I don't understand and look to Alex.

"Waverly told us at lunch yesterday that she put rocks under our chairs."

"Not rocks," Waverly corrects. "Smoky quartz. I brought them to counter all the negative energy in the room."

Alex kneels and extracts a rock—no, a piece of smoky quartz—from under their chair and hands it to Waverly. Is there one under my chair as well? I investigate and find what appears to be a chunk of brown glass. With a quizzical look, I hand it to Waverly. She's collecting them from all of us, stowing them in a reusable cloth bag. "There's negative energy in the room?"

Waverly places her finger over her lips and subtly shakes her head, her gaze on the plaintiff and the defendant. "We shouldn't discuss it in front of them."

Happy for the excuse, I lean close to Alex and whisper, "What's she talking about?"

"She says that all the past cases are going to prejudice the court in favor of the plaintiff since he's a guy. The quartz was supposed to neutralize the energy."

"Do you buy it?"

Alex shrugs. "I mean, it's probably true. Historically, I would guess things have gone better in court for men than women."

"Can I keep mine?" I hear the athlete from the jury ask. "I think you were right about balance. If I keep it in my pickleball bag, will it help me improve my game?"

"Give me the smoky crystal." Waverly holds out one hand while putting her other into her coat pocket. She places the chunk in the bag, freeing up her left hand. From her pocket, she has extracted a fistful of smaller stones that are all smooth and shiny, which she pours into her open palm. She pushes through them with a finger, and I want to do the same. They look so soothing. "What is it you seek? Balance? Confidence? Strength?"

"Training for this tournament has knocked my confidence." He reaches for a green stone.

"That's peridot. It's good for a detox. Could reduce your stress, but it's more for reducing anxiety or anger in relationships. I don't think that's what you're going for."

"But it's green. That feels appropriate for pickleball."

"How about amazonite?" Waverly says, plucking another green one from her palm. "It'll soothe your nerves."

How does she know all this? She must be making it up as she goes along. I peek at Alex to see how this is landing, and they look as transfixed as I feel.

"All rise," the bailiff says as he does each morning. "Trial court of the State of California Seventeenth District is now in session. The Honorable Judge Court is presiding."

"How about a tiger's eye?" Waverly whispers. "It's great for power and motivation. It'll neutralize self-doubt."

"Oh, that sounds good!" he says. He plucks it from her fingers.

"How does it feel?"

Judge Court bustles into the room, but they don't acknowledge her at all.

"Heavier than I thought," the athlete says. He closes his eyes and curls his fingers around it and appears to be centering himself for meditation. "But it feels warm, too, maybe...encouraging?"

"Good, that means..."

Judge Court clears her throat loudly. She's leaning on her bench, fingers splayed, eyebrows high. "I'm sorry, am I interrupting something important?"

"Clearly," Waverly says. I have to bite my lip to keep from laughing out loud, and Court struggles to suppress a smile.

Waverly pockets the little stones again. Then she raises up her cloth bag. "You see, Judge, I have healing stones. I carry many in my pocket to help balance various energies. You never know what kind of support you might require, especially when you have to spend long periods of time in an enclosed space with a lot of history. I brought pieces of smoky quartz to help with this space, but my fellow jurors asked me to remove them from under their chairs. With your permission, may I leave the others?"

"There are more crystals?"

"Yes, Your Honor."

"In my courtroom."

"Well, not all of them are crystals. I put a blue lace agate under your bench to amplify the voice of justice."

They've locked eyes, and the energy suspended between them is like a rubber band stretched to its limit. Judge Court has to be wondering whether she should check under her bench. This isn't rehearsed—at least, not to my knowledge. Is this something the writers worked on with Waverly?

As if accepting a dare, the judge ducks beneath the bench and reemerges holding something between her thumb and forefinger. "Bailiff!" she cries.

The bailiff bustles to the front of the courtroom. She's about to hand him the rock, and Waverly is gesticulating wildly. "Please don't hand it to him. You might perceive it as simply a rock, but it is not. It has important energy and should only be handled by someone who presides over legal order. Otherwise..."

The entire court is waiting.

"Otherwise?" Judge Court says.

I figure Waverly must be waiting for one of the writers to feed her script to her through her earpiece, but she turns to me, and I can see that she is searching for words. She's hit a wall. Watching the scene has been like watching someone running at breakneck speed down a hill. She's faltered, and she's terrified she's going down. I search for ideas to help her but come up blank. Suddenly, I flush hot. Is this where it ends? I'm not just picturing Waverly biting it at the bottom of the steep hill. Now I'm imagining the entire crew on the hill. If she goes down, we will all be a tangled mess, bouncing and rolling toward the bottom of the ravine.

"Excuse me? Judge?"

Alex? I spin to look at them, replaying the way they said *judge*. Was it how any regular person would say judge? Or is this the tipping point, and they are calling out our "judge"?

"Yes?" the judge says.

"The way Juror Seven was talking about the crystals yesterday...She's an expert about this stuff. I don't...I don't feel the energy she's talking about, but this is a scary place."

With all the attention on them, they are exposed and vulnerable. I'm standing close enough to watch the blush creep up their neck and turn their ears bright red. But their posture doesn't falter.

"She was really brave to tell us what she experiences in this room, and she knows what she's talking about. Sports Guy said the stone Juror Seven gave him feels significant. Maybe the one you are holding does, too. Maybe you don't feel it, but she does. We might not understand..."

They swallow hard, and I wish I could take their hand. I can imagine the amount of courage they have had to muster to say as much as they have. I am curious about what else they want to say.

"When I don't understand someone," they amend, "I try to be aware when people are confused by my asking them to use more inclusive language and try real hard to respect where they're coming from. Give respect to gain respect, you know?"

The judge has been standing there with the stone pinched between her fingers the whole time Alex was talking. She rolls her wrist and lets the stone drop to her palm. As she regards it, she strokes it with her thumb. "For the time being, I will hold on to the rock."

"It's an agate, Your Honor," Waverly says.

Judge Court lifts her gavel and raps it loudly against the bench. "Enough. Court is in session. All right, we are back on the record in the case of Aschbran versus Menjivar. Counsel and the parties are present. I believe that the plaintiffs had concluded their examination and the defense was going to proceed with cross-examination. Mr. Tally, you can retake your seat in the witness chair, and I want to remind you that you are still under oath."

What follows is testimony after testimony about the emotional distress Mr. Aschbran suffered when his business started losing money. Today's plan is to immerse everyone in the minutia of procedure to strengthen the argument that what we are doing is legitimate court. It would be difficult to believe that any TV show would film this many hours with absolutely nothing happening. The prosecution spends the entire morning calling every damn person Mr. Aschbran has ever known, from his therapist all the way to his second cousin's third wife. *We get it!* I want to shout. He fell apart. Can we please move on? The prosecution never calls a spouse, though, which piques my interest because it must mean that they have scripted something with the *roommate* idea we discussed yesterday.

In real court, would the prosecution call so many character witnesses to establish how well he had treated his business partner and how her betrayal completely wrecked him? In my eyes, they have gone above and beyond to give us an experience that must go beyond the tedium of real court. After three or four witnesses essentially saying the same thing, I can tell that even Alex is finding it difficult to pay attention, which means their plan to bore us to tears is working. What they've created today brings to mind nature documentaries and how many hours of mind-numbing footage they must film when they are waiting for something interesting to happen. I'm clearly not cut out for that career path.

Several hours in, even Judge Court's energy seems to be flagging. "Does the plaintiff wish to call additional witnesses?" she asks, chin resting in her palm.

"No, Your Honor." Mr. Patel rises about three-quarters of the way from his chair. Today he's wearing a beautiful tan suit. They went all out with the wardrobe for Patel and Aschbran to paint them in the most favorable light. Mr. Patel places a hand on his navy-blue tie and bows slightly, all grace and deference to the judge. "The plaintiff rests."

"Very well. Will the defense call its first witness?"

The defense attorney leans over to talk to Marlene. She's in a turquoise hijab today that accentuates her beautiful blue eyes. When she stands, she directs her words to the left-hand corner of the courtroom. Her face is turned away from the jury, so we can barely hear her when she says, "Your Honor, the defense requests a cleansing of the space before we call our first witness."

Judge Court closes her eyes. "Counsel, please approach the bench."

Alex leans over, their shoulder brushing against mine. "I hope the cleansing doesn't involve us. I need a break."

I should not be focused on how good their breath feels on my neck.

"You and me both. I don't even care if it works or not if it gets me out of that seat for a minute."

They beam at me and bump my shoulder. "Hey, no disrespect for what you don't understand. Selfishly, I'm kind of hoping the judge says yes to the defense doing whatever they want to do. The longer this trial takes, the more days I get to sit next to you. Am I allowed to say that?"

"Absolutely." I return the bump, wishing I knew whether more days together playing this farce is going make things better or worse.

CHAPTER FIFTEEN

Alex

She bumped back! I want to put my hand on my shoulder as if I can hold in place the way it makes me feel inside. I'm proud of myself for finding the courage to say something to the judge about Waverly's crystals. It was much more difficult to defend Waverly today because I wasn't sure if I could be held in contempt of court. Now the judge has taken the two lawyers to her chambers and sent us back to the jury room with the admonishment to not talk about the facts of the case or form any opinions about the facts until all the evidence has been presented.

Waverly is immediately surrounded by folks asking about the stones she has in her pocket, but the bailiff quickly returns to ask Waverly to join the judge in her chambers. Sports Guy becomes the new center of attention, holding his tiger's eye out for display and speculating about how he hopes it will improve his game.

Vicki sees me watching them and leans close to me, but not so close our shoulders bump again, sadly. "He's not letting anyone hold the stone she gave him."

"Nope. I appreciate that. He's one of the ones who was kind of being a dick about things yesterday when Waverly told us about the smoky crystals."

"And now he's a believer, probably thanks to you."

My ears start to heat up again. I can't look directly at her or they will burn like lanterns. "You ever play this game he's going on about?"

"No. You?"

"Nah." I'd play in a heartbeat if she was interested, but I already said that thing about wanting to sit next to her, and I don't want to seem like some sort of stalker, especially since she got dumped.

"I'd try it out, though. If you were interested, I mean." She shrugs. "It sounds kind of fun."

I'm so surprised I can't stop myself from laughing out loud.

"What?" she asks. Her dimple is showing, and her hand is on my shoulder again.

"I literally just thought that, but I didn't want to say it."

"Why?" She crosses her arms. Is it because she realizes how frequently she touches me?

I search for Sarah, remembering how she got to hold Vicki yesterday when she was so upset about her boyfriend. She got dumped yesterday, I reprimand myself. How can I be standing here today thinking about how much I'd like to wrap my arm around her?

"This is the second time today that I've wished you had a thought bubble above your head so I can see what all you're thinking about and not saying."

"Oh, no!" I chuckle and hide my face. "You do not want to know what's going through my head right now."

"I'm sure I do."

She steps closer to me, and I smell her sweet perfume, like a breeze fluttering clean sheets on a clothesline. She tucks her curls behind her ear, exposing her neck. I can picture her doing the same motion to dab on her perfume in the morning. I cannot be imagining what this woman would look like in the morning, and yet I can so easily picture myself lounging in bed, watching her get ready for work. Her in front of the mirror in nothing but a white button-down shirt, pushing her hair back to put in earrings, catching me watching in the mirror...

"Hey." Sarah's voice jolts me out of my fantasy.

"Sarah! How are you?" Vicki asks.

"Funny, that's what I came to ask you. You doing okay today?"

"Yeah, I'm good, I guess. Still doesn't feel real, probably because he's out of town."

"Ugh. Do you have to wait for him to come home to get all your stuff sorted out? Disentangling is so difficult."

"Yeah, no. He's never lived with me, so it's not the stuff. It's more that I haven't told my family yet."

"Are they super attached to him?" Sarah asks.

"My parents are. They worry about me less when I 'have a partner to take care of me.'" She says the last part in what I presume is the accented English of her parents and rolls her eyes.

"I'm sorry." She wraps an arm around Vicki's shoulder exactly how I'd wanted to.

"No. It's fine. It is what it is."

"True," Sarah acknowledges. "But that doesn't make it suck any less. Tell me if there's anything I can do?"

"I appreciate that. I'll be fine if I can keep myself distracted. Maybe I can finally get some work on my place done."

"Are you ready for paint?" I ask. "Because I was serious about repaying you for your help with my car the other day."

Something passes between Vicki and Sarah that I can't decode. It's like Sarah is cautioning Vicki. Has she observed how much I like Vicki? For the third time this morning, I feel my ears burning. *It really is about repaying her brother for the time he spent on my car*, I want to say. Except in my heart, it is more than that. It's how important seeing her at the courthouse each day has become and how I don't want that to end when this trial is over.

"Well, if you need to get out of the house, one of the guys is teaching a bunch of us how to play pickleball tomorrow morning. He says to get there early to secure a court. My daughter is still up at the crack of dawn on weekend mornings, so I'm planning to go see what all the fuss is about."

"I've been curious," Vicki says. Her eyes are back on me the way they were when I said I had been thinking I'd play pickleball if she was interested, so I'm sure she hasn't forgotten that I never answered why I hadn't said what was in my head.

I want to spend time with her and for her to know that. I would love to be able to casually say that I didn't want her to think I was rushing her when she so recently got out of a relationship, but it all feels like too much. I'm too much.

"What about you?" Now Sarah's hand is on my shoulder.

"I'm in," I say without pause because I already have too many thoughts clogging my thinker.

"Great!" She and Vicki laugh in a way that back in Kentucky would have made me feel like an outsider but here makes me feel like the accepted sidekick.

"So after court today, maybe we can talk painting, and then tomorrow…" Vicki breaks off.

Sarah immediately fills in the rest. "We meet up at the park. He said he has plenty of gear, so all you need to bring is yourself. And your self is really okay? You're sure you don't need anything?"

I'm watching Vicki for signs of grief. Either she's not very broken up about this breakup—which would be strange seeing as how at the beginning of the week she was practically engaged to the guy—or she's better at masking it than I ever was. After Lilian left me, all I had to do was think about her, and my nose would be red as a flying reindeer.

"I'm sure," Vicki says. When Sarah is gone, it only takes a second for Vicki to ask why I hadn't said I'd give pickleball a try if she was interested.

"Because…" I stall, hoping we'll get called back into court. No such luck. *What the hell*, I think and say, "I was worried that saying I'd play if you were interested would sound like I was maybe interested in you, in spending time with you because I'm into you. Which is stupid. You're obviously not looking to hook up with anyone right now. It's stupid. Forget I said anything, okay? Please?"

Before she can reply, the bailiff pokes his head into the jury room. "Recess is over, folks. Back to court."

Vicki looks like she's about to respond, but I am first to the door, hustling back to my seat. I fist-bump the bailiff as I pass to thank him for using *folks* and wish I could keep walking straight out of the courtroom. What was I thinking telling Vicki I'm into her? I keep my attention focused on the courtroom, the lawyers, and the people they're representing and remind myself that I'm here for a serious court case, not to be crushing on a probably straight woman.

"Ladies and gent..." Judge Court begins once we're all settled into the jury box again. Then she locks eyes with me. "Members of the jury, I have talked to both counsels and it is agreed that we will cleanse the courtroom."

We must have the most woke judge in the history of judges. I glance at Waverly. Her posture is nothing short of regal. I can't look at Waverly without turning my head toward Vicki. Her eyes are on me, and I'm caught.

"Juror Seven will lead the cleansing. You need an hour to set up?"

"An hour is plenty of time, yes," Waverly says.

"So if I combine this with lunch, we could resume in two hours?"

"Yes, Your Honor."

She bangs the gavel and swoops out of the courtroom. Nick jumps up. "I have a camera set up outside and ask that some of you to stop and record your reaction to the cleansing that will take place after lunch."

We are all standing, collecting our things, and I sense that Vicki is waiting for me. "I'm going to do the talking head." I shrug. She hasn't challenged me, but I feel compelled to explain. "Since I said we should let Waverly perform the cleansing."

"Yeah. I get it. Talk later." She squeezes my elbow and is gone. I'm disappointed. I'd hoped she would go with me to give her own statement about the cleansing. I'd hoped she'd want to talk to me about the chemistry I thought we were both feeling.

CHAPTER SIXTEEN

Vicki

I stop so abruptly when I step back into the courtroom that Alex smacks into me. Their hands are on my shoulders for an instant as they regain their balance, and I have to tell myself not to place my hands over theirs to keep them there. Now they are standing next to me, awed to a standstill as well.

The whole room is bathed in royal-blue light. Waverly sits in front of the judge's bench on a woven blanket surrounded by bowls and items hanging from a metal stand. Her eyes are closed, and she has her wrists resting on her knees, palms up. In real life, the actress graduated with a degree in Meat Science. That sounds like the furthest thing away from a wholistic healer, and she has gotten a real kick out of imagining how her former professors in the meat processing program would react to the character she's playing. She's impressed me with her dedication to the character. This sound bath event involves more than memorizing lines, and I am interested to experience it. I've never heard of a sound bath before and ask if Alex has. They have not taken their eyes off Waverly. They simply shake their head.

Waverly opens her eyes serenely and motions us in. "If you would be more comfortable in a chair, you may sit anywhere in the gallery. It is important that all present rescind any power they might hold. I rescind my power as a jurist for this cleansing. Judge Court will give up her seat at the bench and either sit with me on the floor or take a seat where any member of the community can sit. The same thing goes for our lawyers, plaintiff, and defendant. We give up all titles as we enter this space, our purpose to reestablish neutrality."

The lawyers are staring at each other, waiting to see where the other will sit. The defendant sits on the floor, and her lawyer follows. The judge, the court reporter, the bailiff, and then the plaintiff and his lawyer all find a spot on the floor, and the courtroom begins to take on the appearance of children's story time. Many of our jury take seats in the gallery, but Sarah boldly threads through to take a seat next to Waverly, so I follow and am happy that Alex settles in next to us.

This feels more like our rehearsals where the actors engaged with each other as equals, and I wonder if anyone else is worried about this pushing the boundaries of reality. I can't imagine a real judge sitting on the floor with everyone, but Alex hasn't said anything about this feeling weird, which honestly shocks me because this is the furthest we've pushed the boundary of reality so far. Maybe I'm extra sensitive because I would never voluntarily take part in something so woo-woo as this.

"If you're comfortable, cross your legs at the ankle and straighten your spine. Push your shoulders back and rest your hands on your knees with palms up as I have. This enhances receptivity, positioning you to be open-minded. The more receptive you are, the more positive energy you will radiate to the space. Together, our energy will remove the cobwebs of past generations that did not always view the people in the courtroom as equals. Before we begin, let's collectively take three deep breaths. If you feel safe, you can shut your eyes. Once I begin the sound bath, picture yourself as part of the energy. Maybe you will float on the waves. Maybe you will simply put out your hand as if you are extending it out of an open car window, feeling the energy flow around you.

"Breathe in.

"Breathe out."

With the first breath, I am still so aware of how awkward this feels to be sitting on the floor with my fellow actors.

"Breathe in.

"Breathe out."

With the second breath, I feel the whisper of Alex's shoulder against my own and peek at them. Their eyes are closed, and they appear to be utterly at peace. I look at Waverly. She is in her element. Instead of coming off as a performance, it feels completely legitimate. She emanates seriousness and focus. I close my eyes.

"Breathe in.

"Breathe out."

On our exhale, a sound begins, a low reverberation. I have to peek again. Waverly has a stick that she drags around the perimeter of the largest bowl. The sound touches my body and moves through me. I feel warm and safe. A new sound begins and merges with the lower note. The higher note gives me lift. Wavery says our lungs have more room to expand, and I try to gauge whether I'm actually taking in more air as I continue to breathe deeply, in through my nose and out through my mouth.

The room drifts away from me, but not the people. Waverly describes how our energy will connect and resonate together, something she calls entrainment, and I am trying my hardest to find a sliver of believability in the idea of a court case beginning with a cleansing. The notes Waverly shifts between could represent the voices we have heard. They are different, but I can see where neither is more powerful than the other, and they blend together. There's a new sound, and I open my eyes a smidge to see what it is. Waverly has her right hand extended high and is gently shaking a suspended bar with what might be dozens of ox hooves strung together. It is different than a rain stick or a wave maker. I try my best to imagine what sound this is supposed to be recreating—maybe wind rustling a forest canopy? But I'm utterly unsuccessful.

I can no longer lose myself in this experience, as authentic as Waverly has made it. I wish I believed it and could allow myself to stay immersed in it, but I can't see beyond this being a gimmick to make great television. How is Alex going to feel watching this? Are they going to feel duped? Is the audience going to be laughing at how ridiculous we are, pausing midtrial to sit on the floor? Or, as the producers hope, is it going to be one of many things that plants a seed that different is not automatically bad?

We are deceiving Alex, and it feels awful. I feel awful, like I'm about to throw up. How much longer will Waverly's sound bath last? I will her to open her eyes, so I can implore her to put a stop to it. My stomach lurches again when it hits me that the deception will continue after this particular stunt. The camera is panning the whole spectacle and stops on me. This scene will require a clip for me to explain what's going through my mind. Correction: what's going on in Vicki's head. I have to strategize like an actress if I am to figure out what will create the best material. Snarky is good, right? I should give them some side-eye and build on that later when we're filming the talking head. I explore a handful of possibilities. *My butt was cold and both of my feet were asleep… That's about the time I'm sure I heard Judge Court start snoring. I opened my eyes because I was sure it was about to go all* Ghostbusters *on us, and I wanted to see that shit go down.*

It isn't difficult to brainstorm what will work for an episode, but I also can't forget that Alex will be watching it, too. They stood up for Waverly. I try to remember their words, something about Waverly believing in her stones and being more open-minded about what we don't understand. I hope they feel the same way after the big reveal. I should pull out of the show, ask them to replace me with an alternate. I wouldn't be part of the manipulation anymore, but surely they'd pull me back in for the reveal, and then I could explain everything to Alex and hope that they are into me the same way they said they're into Vicki.

I'm going to need therapy after this for sure, and I'm in on the creation of the show. How bad is this going to mess with Alex's head?

Finally, Waverly sets down the weird thing she's been shaking and begins playing the notes more quietly until the last of the sounds cease and it is completely quiet. Waverly puts her hands together in front of her solar plexus and bows to us, and I freaking hope they made sure she's not appropriating from a culture or religion here.

From the floor, Judge Court says, "Counsel, are you satisfied to the extent that you can now call your first witness?"

Ms. Saqsaq hums a few bars of "Baby Shark," making me wish for more plain notes of the sound bath. She consults with her client for a moment and then answers, "I am, Your Honor. But may we please use the witness box?"

"We sure as sh—" Judge Court stops herself. "Yes, that would be most appropriate."

Sarah groans as she gets to her feet. "My joints are not happy with me."

"Mine are talking to me, too," I say. "How do you feel, Alex?"

"Like I've had the best nap of my life," they say. "It's brighter in here, don't you think? It does feel different."

I'm in a pickle. I don't want to disagree with Alex, but if I agree, I'm adding to the ways I've actively deceived Alex. I'm relieved when several other jurors agree with Alex, congratulating Waverly on clearing the room of patriarchal gloom.

Judge Court scowls at the chatter and assesses the room herself. I'm sure she's stalling as she waits for instruction through her earpiece.

"Your Honor," Mr. Patel says. "To continue now when the room is pulsing with female energy is unfair to my client."

Ms. Saqsaq rolls her eyes. "As if they have not been enjoying an unfair advantage this whole time. I move we continue."

Judge Court consults her watch. "Gather your things. We will reconvene Monday."

CHAPTER SEVENTEEN

Alex

"Wow, your brother wasn't kidding," I say when Vicki steps back to let me in, followed by the camera crew. I am hyperaware of them as they keep the camera trained on me as I take in the space. At least it takes away the question of whether Vicki and I are huggers. Remembering the awkward exchange when we were talking about pickleball, I hunch my shoulders to pass by her without touching. I wish I were here alone. I tell myself that if we were, I'd be able to say, "Look, I know this is the worst timing, but I feel this energy between us." And then she could either say there is or there isn't. It will hurt if she says there isn't, but at least I would have an answer. I think I'd prefer that to the limbo I'm in.

"You okay?" she asks, touching my forearm lightly.

"Yeah. Fine," I say, taking in the bare drywall that's been mudded but not primed. Her brother said she needed to do some painting. What had he said? Her place needed my help. "What year was the house built?"

"Fifty-five."

I nod. "Keep-your-woman-in-the-kitchen era."

"Exactly. The old kitchen was a cave designed by an architect who must've never cooked a meal and spent a lot of time in front of a fireplace with a great view of the San Gabriels."

"And now whoever cooks gets a fantastic view," I say, admiring the abundance of light that comes in from the north-facing windows. I rest my hands on the generous island, stools tucked into one side, perfect for perching out of the way while someone cooks and counter space to help chop. I wonder whether Vicki's almost-fiancé helped at all with the layout. Did they talk about cooking together?

"There was a pass-through here," she says, walking farther into a now open space. "It was a partial wall, so some light from the window came through, but there were pillars that made it seem like the kitchen was a jail cell. I busted that up. Literally. I'm no good at seeing the possibility in a space, but I'm great with a sledgehammer."

"Too bad I came too late to see that," I say, easily picturing her covered in dust with a sledgehammer slung back on her shoulder. Hair pulled up off her neck, skin sticky with sweat, a look that draws me like a magnet but one I must resist. In the fantasy, she'd insist she was too dirty to touch, and I'd agree that we absolutely should remove her dusty clothes.

The length of time we stand there, I swear she is reading my thoughts. Would it freak her out to learn how badly I want to kiss her? We haven't talked since I tried to bring up being interested in her. Her glance shifts to the camera. I'd forgotten we aren't alone.

She walks farther into the house, and I follow her and the camera. The partial wall on the right gives the feel of a dining room without separating the kitchen from it, and a partial wall on the left defines the living room space with a fireplace in the center of the far wall. "This room was walled in with an atrocious sliding door."

"What do you think of the paint on the fireplace?" I ask, walking through the room to get a sense of how many coats of paint cover the brick.

"Hate it. If I can get the paint off, I'm thinking this space should have warmer earth tones."

"To echo the mountains," I guess. "And as you walk through the house, you head toward something that feels more like the ocean. I love the blue tile in the kitchen."

"That's exactly what I was going for when I picked the color scheme in the kitchen!"

"It's nice," I say, making my way back through the stark space.

"I hear a *but* in your voice."

"For some reason I thought you wanted to paint one room."

"Oh, I don't expect you to do all three rooms! Cesar said it's important for me to get paint on the new drywall."

"Yeah, that's the priority. You don't mind that your place is so…"

"Messy?"

"No! No." My face flushes with embarrassment. I'm worried about going out on a limb. It's just that I was hoping to get more of a sense of who Vicki is by being in her space, but this in-progress makeover doesn't give anything away. There's no bookshelf to scan for queer titles, no artwork that might help me sort out what I'm reading from Vicki. She doesn't even have notes or pictures hanging on her fridge. "Bare."

This makes her laugh. She rests her hand on my arm, and that's all it takes for my whole body to flush hot. I am painfully conscious of the cameras and pray that they can't tell how much I'm affected by Vicki. "I'm not used to having all this space. I'm not in a rush to fill it all up."

"And even less so now, I'd guess," Nick says. "Since you're newly single?"

She looks at me before she answers, and something is off. I can't tell if it's because the camera is here, but I definitely get the sense that she can't say what she wants to say in front of them. I can't shake how little the place feels like Vicki—like anyone at all, really. Had I walked into this job blind, I would have put money on it being a property in the process of being flipped.

I'm grateful when Nick steps in to ask the question I've been pondering. "How long have you been here?"

"Just a few months," Vicki says. "Does anyone need a drink? Water?" She crosses the kitchen to open the fridge. Okay. So maybe she does live here.

"I've got a water bottle in my car," I say. "So I'll go ahead and get started. I can bust out the primer on the drywall today. Do you have the paint picked out, or should I bring in my color wheel, too?"

"Cesar picked up paint. Primer, too. It's just the labor part I need."

I nod. "Okay. I'll grab my tarps and brushes."

The camera tails me. I can't imagine that rooting around in my car is going to be interesting to anyone watching a show about jury duty, but what do I know? When I come back in, Nick and Vicki are both sitting on stools at the island. Nick snaps his phone up off the counter and takes it off speakerphone. He motions to the camera to keep rolling as he steps outside. Vicki holds up her phone as she moves toward the hallway and says, "I need to make a call, too," leaving me alone with the camera operator.

"You really think you'll use any of this footage?" I ask, arranging a tarp.

"The only way to get good unscripted stuff is to film absolutely everything," the camera operator says.

"Have you ever filmed something like the sound bath thing today at the courthouse?"

"Nope. That was a new one for me," he says.

"It feels funny to work with you in the room and not talk to you. If it's weird, I could put in earbuds."

"No, it's fine. The others should be back soon. How'd you wind up painting for Vicki, anyway? What happened with the car?"

"Oh, at the beginning of the week, my old Honda wouldn't start."

"And Vicki was around to help."

Was there something in his voice? I glance over, forgetting that he's filming. Great. Now it looks like I'm reacting to what he said about Vicki. Shit. I go back to taping. "She gave me a lift home."

"You two seem to have hit it off," he says.

"Yeah. We have," I say. I review all the times Vicki and I have been around the cameras. Today is the only time I can remember us being on camera outside of court. There's been a few times that the whole jury has been questioned, but most of the time the cameras are documenting the experience of the jurors who are serving for the first time. I'm being paranoid. "I think someday I'll look back on this experience and credit it as a major turning point in my life, you know? I told y'all about how the wrangler from California got me out of Kentucky with his twenty-mule team?"

"Yeah, I remember that story."

"It's like that was a domino that set off a chain of events. I was meant to be here for this trial. Maybe that sounds…"

Vicki strides through the kitchen as though she's on a mission, and she is definitely not happy. "I am doing you a courtesy to be talking to you right now, Malcolm. Can we please remember that?"

I've reached the bottom of the cabinet I'm taping and rip it free. Vicki must be talking to her ex. I duck my chin and move to tape around the window, keeping as low a profile as possible.

CHAPTER EIGHTEEN

Vicki

I don't know what Nick's plan is leaving the camera on Alex while they set up to prime the kitchen walls. I already feel bad posing in this house as if it's mine and have stepped out of the room to call Sarah because were it not for them including Alex painting here into the show, I could have been honest with them about owning the place with my brothers as an investment that pays off once we've cleaned it up and flipped it. Then I hear that stupid camera operator needling Alex about how helpful I've been, fishing for personal content. Not cool.

"Let me be clear. You made your decision, it's none of your business."

"What just happened?" Sarah asks.

"That may be true, but you were very clear about your priorities. That means what's going on at my address is no longer your concern." I grab a water bottle from the fridge and storm toward the living room area where I'm sure the camera operator will be able to pick up some of what I am saying.

"Something with Alex," Sarah intuits. "Do you need me to come intervene?"

"No. Absolutely not." I turn at the fireplace and make sure the camera is on me. Then I drop my voice and tip my chin down so I'm sure nobody can read my lips. "I'm worried that this wasn't about getting more of Alex's profession on tape. They're talking about how nice it was for me to step in and help Alex with the car. This cannot be about me and Alex."

"You know my position, that it would be best if you stayed with your fake boyfriend."

"I'm removing you from the account. I'm hanging up now and taking you off the account. Dude. Grow up."

I hit the end button and scroll through my phone to text Sarah that I had to hang up to make sure that the camera operator does not resume his conversation with Alex. I hope I've sold my fake fight with the ex. I walk out of camera range for a moment, take a swig of water, and then return to the kitchen where Alex has almost finished taping off an entire wall.

"Everything okay?" the camera operator asks.

"Where's Nick?"

"Still outside."

I will not look at Alex. I will not look at Alex. "I need to talk to him. I don't have the bandwidth for this tonight." I wave my hand around the space and hope that he'll take the message and stop filming. "Have you got what you need?"

"Well, I was hoping to film Alex painting in action."

I slump down at the island and put my head on my arms.

"I've got this wall taped. I could go ahead and start cutting."

"Works for me," the camera operator says.

"I'll get the paint," I say, but I keep my head on my arms. "This is good. It's good to know before you commit to someone that they're a creepy peepster, right?"

"Excuse me?" Alex is sitting on their feet and turns toward the island. "Creepy peepster? Did you just call your ex a creepy peepster?"

"He's been watching my Ring app and wanted to know who's here."

"That is creepy."

"Creepy peepster?" Nick is back. "What did I miss?"

I fill him in and ask if they can wrap up after they've filmed Alex doing their paintbrush and roller action. His eyes are gleaming as I'd known they would. My phone chimes, and I pull it out. The camera shifts to me.

"Who is it?"

"Malcolm." I glance up at the camera and add "The ex" with an eye roll for context. It's actually Sarah asking how things are going. My thumbs fly. I'm glad she's given me the opportunity to carry this a little further. *Fake fight was a good plan. Pretty sure they're trying to dig into the chemistry Hiroki picked up on.* "He's pissed that I cut his feed to the house."

"So, he did live here?" Nick asks.

Bad idea, Sarah replies. *You have to shut that down.*

I know, I text back. I toss the phone face down on the island and cross my arms. "No. We didn't live together. I was expecting a delivery when I was out of town one weekend. I put him on my account so he'd know when to stop by. I should have kept my eye on the porch myself and texted him instead. Hindsight is twenty-twenty, right?" I take another swig of my water. "I'll need something stronger than this tonight. Anyone else need alcohol?" I waggle my eyebrows at the camera operator. "You wouldn't let a girl drink alone, right?"

I swing around to grab a beer from the fridge. I extend one to each person in the room. No takers.

"All I need is paint," Alex says.

I twist off the cap, tossing it on the counter next to my phone. "Paint's in the closet there." I point with the bottle before I take a long drink. We all watch Alex work in silence, and I feel terrible for them. This is awkward for me and has to be triply awkward for them. I grab my phone and scroll through photos, trying to project pensive and angry. By the time I finish my beer, Nick has decided they have enough footage of Alex painting. I'm immensely relieved when they pack up and leave.

Alex is still working in silence, and there is so much I want to say, I'm having trouble figuring out where to start. "I'm having another beer. You want one now that the camera's finally gone?"

"No, thanks. I don't drink."

"Oh." Is it bad that I need more alcohol to get through this?

"But I don't mind if you do. Really. It's just something I've learned about myself. I make better decisions when I don't drink."

That makes me kind of snort-laugh, which brings such a sweet smile to their face. They go back to taping the ceiling, using a stepladder they must've brought in from their car. "Isn't that true of everyone? This is a terrible idea but not the worst I've had today, so…" I advise myself to pace myself through this second bottle. I'll need food if I hope to keep a grasp on rational thinking. Vicki is nursing hurt, so it made sense to drink when the camera was here. Why can't I stop now?

"Yeah. About that." They're studiously keeping their gaze away from me, and I observe how tight their shoulders are. They're upset. I straighten my spine.

"About what?"

"Was lying about having Ring the worst idea, or are there more to choose from?"

I gulp, terrified that I have given something about the show away. I can't find any words. They glance over their shoulder, and I can see it in the way they tip their head ever so slightly that my inability to answer confirms something for them.

"I paint for a living, Vicki. I take in details like what would need to be taped before painting." They hold up the roll of tape they're currently using. "There's no Ring doorbell in your entryway." They calmly go back to taping while I try to contain my panic.

Is there a way to not be this person? I can't outright stop lying to Alex, so I speak one truth. "I need to eat. Are you hungry? There's a good Thai place nearby. I could order in." I don't even wait for their reply. I pull up the menu on my phone, then walk to the ladder and hold it up for them.

"Let's Have The Best Thai Food?"

"I can't say whether it's the *best*, but I love their confidence! And it is good. I've had it before."

"I'll have a curry with tofu, whichever one is least spicy."

Their clipped response hurts because I could so easily fix things by coming clean. "Wait, are you vegetarian?"

"No. Remember the burgers?"

"Oh. Right."

They raise their eyebrows, and the tension almost starts to break, but then they turn back to their work.

"Did anything else sound good? I can get a couple of dishes to share."

They shrug. "Doesn't matter to me."

I want it to matter to them. I call in our order and pick a dish with cashew and tofu. "They said it'll be a half hour. Can I help?" I gesture to the roller.

"It's your place. Isn't it?" They meet and hold my gaze for several counts before they pick up a brush and start cutting.

"The thing is, I'm a trash painter. That's why Cesar was so excited when you said you paint."

"I don't need help."

They're right. There isn't a whole lot of wall space in the kitchen to begin with, and all they have to prime is the new drywall. They are fast and precise with the brush. There's nothing left for me to do but sit and sip on the beer I no longer want. I've been working through what I might be able to say to patch up the evening. Maybe it's easier to talk when I don't have to make eye contact. Their focus on the job gives me time to form my thoughts. "I didn't like how the camera guy wanted to talk about us hitting it off. That didn't feel right."

"Why?"

Because this is a show and they want all of you and you didn't sign a release for your whole life to be on camera, I wish I could say. "Because I don't exactly know what is happening between us, and sure, I understand that they are interested in learning about who we are, but they shouldn't get our personal lives. Boundaries. Am I right?"

"But you told them about your ex."

I wave them off. "Not the truth."

They stop painting. "What *else* have you lied about?"

I'm so close to telling them I lied about not knowing what's going on between us because I am absolutely aware of what's going on and what I'd like to do about it. "The high school girlfriend at the reunion."

They step down the ladder to move it to the left and shoot a glance my way before they step back up. "There wasn't a girlfriend?"

"That part of the story is true." I consider how this will sound when they've been told the whole story. But then I tuck myself back away and ask Vicki what is true. "But they are not back together. My ex is angry because of what I said."

"Is what you said to him the truth?"

I wait until they look over at me again and nod. "There's no spark there." This is only a lie because he's made up, but it's essentially true. What I felt when I first laid eyes on Alex has never happened before. With complete honesty, I say, "The first time I saw you, something happened. Something shifted, and now there's this pull that I can't ignore."

"And you told him that?"

I imagine being in a relationship and experiencing the zap of electricity I noticed when Alex walked into the room. I would have to confess that, wouldn't I? I run with that. "I can't ignore how you make me feel. It would be dishonest."

They pour primer into the rolling tray, taking care to catch any drips with the paintbrush. They swipe the excess from the rim of the can before replacing the lid. I can't decide whether to be annoyed or relieved that they keep working. They carefully saturate the roller. Once they're ready to apply the primer to the wall, they say, "But you said you were with him for a year."

"I did. But I have never felt this level of attraction for another person before. Ever."

They purse their lips, but it's to hide a smile. Their expression gives away a whole slew of emotions, and it hits me that I didn't say I'd never been attracted to a man or a woman. I said *person*, and it fits, and it's the truth. I've connected with Alex in a way I haven't with anyone before. It's like watching a child witness fireworks for the first time. My words have lit them up. They shake their head as if they can't believe it, which makes me laugh. They're laughing, and I want to cross the room and take them in my arms.

Of course, that's when the food arrives.

They become super serious. "I'm going to whip this out before we eat, okay? It'll only take a few minutes."

I nod and sign for the food. I place it on the counter and am about to grab plates, but I notice them swipe the roller across the bare drywall like the beginning of a cursive V before moving from ceiling to floor in swift, fluid strokes. I'm mesmerized and cannot look away.

CHAPTER NINETEEN

Alex

Vicki is watching me. And she's attracted to me. To me as a person. She didn't define her attraction by man or woman, which makes me feel fully seen in a way I so rarely am. So many people take in my short hair and start to check the mental "boy" box in their head. My face and height don't add up, though. When they don't pick up any trace of facial hair, their eyes drop to my chest. Depending on the day and how I am feeling in my body, my breasts either put them at ease, relaxing when they can check the "girl" box, or my flattened chest keeps their doubt suspended. Most people are uncomfortable with the in-between, and the in-between is where I am most myself.

This is where I am with Vicki. Under her gaze, I can be proud of my strong shoulders and unapologetic of my unbound breasts. As I told her, the rolling is super fast. Normally, I'd clean my brush and roller first, but they can wait while we eat dinner. I dampen a towel at the sink and drape it over the whole tray.

"Smells good," I say, washing and drying my hands before I sit on one of the barstools.

"I thought plates so we can share?" Steam puffs out from the containers when she opens them.

"Sure. I trust you." The serving spoon hovers above the steamed rice. "Your choice." I gesture to the smaller container. "The cashew dish you ordered looks amazing."

She rests the spoon on the container and pushes it closer to me. "Go ahead and start. I'll get you something to drink. Water okay? I don't have any soda."

"Yeah, water's fine. I can help." I start to stand.

"Please," she says. "Sit. You're fine. I know where the glasses are. Ice?"

Now that I'm facing Vicki instead of the wall, the conversation becomes awkward. "No ice." I want to ask her so many things, but it's difficult to find a starting point. She returns to the island with two pint glasses filled with water. We eat and talk solely about the food.

"Well? Is this the best Thai food you've ever had?"

"By far the best," I say. "It might be the best dinner I've had in California," I add.

"Be real," she says.

"Okay. It's a hundred percent the best dinner I've had in this state. But it might be the company."

"Oh, I see how you are." She's smiling, and I want to trace the curve of her cheek where it dimples. I want to rest my finger on her full lower lip.

"Do you?"

My question hangs in the air which crackles around us. I've dreamed about her lips on mine, yet I am utterly unprepared when she answers by placing her hand on my thigh so she can lean toward me and press her lips to mine.

They are so sweet and so warm and it has been such a long time since I have kissed anyone. Or, correction, since I have been kissed. I want so much more than the brush of her lips against mine, but I also have so many questions.

"I'm sorry," she says, pulling back.

I quickly grasp her hand, keeping it on my thigh. "Don't apologize." I stroke the delicate skin of her wrist with my thumb.

"You said before that you…You brought up attraction, being attracted to…people? What kind of people do you mean?"

She keeps her eyes on our hands. "So for me, attraction is not about gender."

It is so strange to hear her say what I usually have to explain to people. I nod, wanting her to continue.

"I'm attracted to people more for how they are than who they are. It's more about how a person interacts with the world. What I like about you…Can I use you as an example?"

My eyes flick to hers, and she's looking at me now. I nod.

"You listen. You don't exist in the middle of the room demanding attention. You're at the edge, taking it all in. But once you have something to say?" Here she straightens her own spine and kind of broadens her shoulders, which makes me laugh. Her face lights up, too. "Don't mess with you. You're not afraid to use your voice, and you don't apologize for doing it. That is very attractive."

I nod slowly. What she has said matches my self-perception, though her version comes across as more confident. "You say what you think, too, and I like that. I don't…I know that I present more masc, but I…I'm not trans, I don't…I'm not male or female. I don't identify as either gender."

"Is it okay if I ask how you identify?"

"Nonbinary."

"Somewhere in the middle."

"I don't know about the middle," I say. "I think of it as being outside of any box."

"I see that. And like I said." She rests her chin on the hand I'm not holding and studies me. "I find that extremely attractive."

"My ex said I emasculated her. In the beginning, she told me she liked how brave I was. And it's not that I associate being brave with being masculine. But I had to be brave, you know? To tell her I liked her as more than a friend. And it felt so amazing to be liked back, and the longer we were together, the more I felt like I could be myself. Who I am inside didn't change, but when my appearance did, all of a sudden…" I cover my face with my hands. "I should not be talking about my ex."

"Why not?"

"Because. Only an idiot would let themselves fall back into that mess when there's someone this beautiful sitting right in front of them."

"Well, you know about mine."

I rest my chin on my hand, eyes locked on hers. "And you really ended it?"

"I did. This jury, it's a temporary thing, and I was so scared that it would be over, and you would disappear. I had to tell you, but I had to be unattached to be honest with you. I don't cheat."

"You felt that much." I'm dumbstruck. I felt it too. It's why I told myself I could not sit next to her that first day. It just feels fantastical. How could the kind of connection I'm feeling, that she says she's feeling too… How can it be real?

"I did. And I do. And I really, really want to kiss you again. Even though I really, really shouldn't."

"No? What's stopping you?" I ask, still nervous about how recently she got out of a relationship, even if she does say it was her idea. Her hesitation has got to be tied to her almost-fiancé. I remember how she was talking to Sarah the day she said she got dumped. What advice did Sarah give her? I search her eyes. What is she thinking? That it's too soon? She is weighing something, and part of me warns myself to wait for her to answer, but desire drowns out sense. All I want is to kiss Vicki again. I stand and take her hands in mine. "Can I kiss you?"

She stands and rests her hands on my hips. How did I get here, from Kentucky to this kitchen, from Vicki being in a relationship to her being in my arms?

"Please," she whispers.

I bend, just slightly, and this time when our mouths meet, it is more than a press. It's an exploration of how her lower lip nestles between mine, her tongue tracing my upper lip, me answering with my tongue and nearly melting at that first touch. The hitch in her breath emboldens me, and I ask for more, kissing her more deeply. She answers, her hands moving from my hips to my shoulders to the back of my head, pulling me closer, demanding more, nipping at my lower lip with her teeth. We duel like that, me chasing her and then running to catch up when she abruptly changes direction. It is fun, and I can't help but laugh.

"You're laughing?" She presses her forehead to mine. "What about that kiss is laughable?"

"I have never been kissed like that before."

She wraps her arms around me and leans her head on my chest. When I encircle her with my arms, my entire body hums the way it did with Waverly's bowls in the courthouse. A note inside of me starts small and grows stronger and stronger until it fills me to the brim. I used to hear a sound like that when the wind blew just right against our front door back in Kentucky, making me happy to be exactly where I was. I close my eyes and breathe her in. Having her in my arms, I am home.

CHAPTER TWENTY

Vicki

"Something happened," Sarah says. "What happened?"

I shush her. "I'm trying to listen," I say, keeping my eyes on Chad, our jury colleague turned instructor for the day. He is talking about bounce rules. This whole pickleball thing must be a ploy for him to get more time on camera because Nick and the camera operator who was at the house yesterday are here filming again. I don't want to attract their attention. I am Vicki, fellow juror, here to learn how to play this ridiculous-sounding game.

"Fine time to listen now," she mumbles.

I shoot her my best side-eye, but she's not looking at me. Her eyes are on Alex, who is holding a paddle in their right hand. They hold their left hand held up like a dancer, bend at the knees, and execute a fluid, graceful swing. They take two steps and swing backhand, still bending low and swinging in a long arc. They must sense our eyes on them because they glance our way and stop.

When I turn my attention back to Chad, I spot the camera operator making the same motion. Caught. I will have to be more careful. Vicki can't be interested in Alex. I want to admire their short running shorts and the T-shirt with the sleeves cut off, allowing an alluring glimpse of their torso.

"It's all quite simple and probably easiest for you to learn on the court," Chad announces.

Right. Pickleball. I'm here to learn about pickleball. I can focus. I will not get distracted reflecting on what a good kisser Alex is. I will absolutely not recall how silky their hair felt under my fingertips.

Sarah taps me and points to the court. We're apparently a team. Sarah's wife, Jass, takes the court with Chad, and Alex seems to have volunteered to tap a ball around with Sarah and Jass's daughter off the court. Jass has her dark hair pulled into a ponytail that pokes out the back of a blue ball cap a few shades darker than her blue shirt. She's wearing white shorts and stretching out her shoulders, so I windmill my arms and jog in place.

"Your wife looks serious," I say, keeping myself in character. Vicki doesn't know Jass. Emelynn met and instantly clicked with her one afternoon when she waited for Sarah to finish a meeting with the director and producer prior to filming.

"She's very competitive," Sarah confirms. She's in yoga pants and a shirt with a rainbow and *Drag Queen Story Hour* in big lettering. Not seriously athletic but sportier than my yellow spaghetti-strap tank top and skintight black shorts.

"Vicki, you comfortable offering up the first serve?" Chad calls.

I nod, and both Sarah and I move to the back of the court.

"The camera appears to be tracking the energy between you and Alex."

"We didn't give them anything yesterday. They left before…" I should not talk when I'm distracted. Chad calls out the score and reminds me to serve crosscourt, which I do.

"Before what?" Sarah says. She steps forward and smacks Chad's return so hard it sails over Jass's head.

"This isn't baseball," Chad admonishes at the same time Jass hollers, "Home run!" while she chases down the ball. Their daughter cheers on the other side of the chain-link fence.

Jass returns to the court for her serve.

"Don't talk to me about Alex right now."

"Oh, so you wouldn't be interested to know that they're watching your every move?"

I return Jass's serve, and Chad easily keeps the ball in play. Sarah doesn't make it before the second bounce. "Maybe keep your eye on what's happening on the court?"

"That's not what I'm paid for." She raises her eyebrows and fixes me with a level gaze. She's not playing because she's interested in learning the game. She's here keeping an eye on Alex—keeping an eye on me, I realize. I crash from the high of kissing Alex. Yesterday, I convinced myself that kissing Alex was okay. I rationalized that turning the camera back on my own drama made space to be partially honest with Alex, and that was enough. But partially honest is still a lie. I am sucker punched by the likelihood that our kissing will crush Alex when they find out the truth.

I have to stuff this away where Sarah will never see it and I will not have to confront it. "We didn't even talk to each other when the camera was there."

"And when they left?"

"We had dinner."

"Only dinner?" she presses.

I point to our opponents, not because I need to focus on the game, but because her questions…no. I have to at least be honest with myself. It's not her questions that are making me uncomfortable. It's being forced to evaluate my behavior that makes me uncomfortable.

In no time at all Chad and Jass make it to eleven points to win the game. Chad motions us all to the net where we tap paddles. "Good game! Alex, you ready to rotate in?"

"I'll take Chloe," Jass says, looking from Sarah to me, echoing Sarah's investigative energy before jogging off the court where Chloe and Alex give her high fives.

"Mama won!" Chloe cheers.

Sarah retrieves her water bottle. "Didn't Chad say the most important part is to have fun? I'm having fun."

Chad's nodding enthusiastically. "So, me and you, Sarah, against Vicki and Alex?"

Alex is doing their adorable practice swing again.

"How about you and Vicki? Against me and them?" Sarah suggests, gesturing to Alex. Her expression is part mom, part therapist, and wholly intimidating. I'm not arguing with her.

Though I felt chastised by the reorganization of teams, I'm actually grateful during play because it gives me a legitimate reason to have my eyes on Alex, and they are surprisingly good, which makes Chad increasingly agitated. He's elated when one of his shots passes in between Alex and Sarah, calling out, "Oof. Gotta communicate over there. That husband/wife shot will get you every time. 'You got it? No, you got it!'"

He's too busy laughing to hear or respond to Sarah's comment about not having a husband, motioning for Alex to keep the ball in play. He might miss the paddle tap Alex gives Sarah for calling out the normative language, but I see it and am silently cheering for them. It doesn't take long for Alex to pick up on Chad's strategy and move beyond getting the ball over the net. Chad and I are, unsurprisingly, more often left staring at each other as the ball slices directly between us than celebrating our own clean shot.

With Alex in the game, the teams are more evenly matched, and Chad talks to me less and less, which is fine with me because I'm trying my hardest to hear what Sarah and Alex say to each other. I'm clearly a handicap for him and do my best to stay out of his way. Alex is poetry on the court, and they offer advice to Sarah, encouraging her not to defer to them even though they're clearly a stronger player. Chad manages to carry our team to a victory, but he's not smiling when we do the paddle tap at the net.

"Wow, are you good!" I say to Alex as we break for water.

"They are," Sarah agrees.

They beam. "I grew up on Ping-Pong and my family is very competitive. They got me in good shape for tennis. I played for my high school."

"That explains why you play so deep. For pickleball, you want to play the kitchen," Chad admonishes.

Alex shrugs. "But having fun is the important part, isn't it?"

"Oh, absolutely," he says.

Alex catches my eye. "You playing again?" They lean closer to me and whisper, "This guy needs to go down."

"Then you should partner up with Jass."

"No way," they say, holding my gaze. "We could take him. We'd make a good team, you and me."

Their words hang in the air, and the camera is locked on us. I would love to play this game with Alex. I also feel Sarah's eyes on me, asking if it is a good idea.

"Jass?" Chad asks. "You in?"

Alex and I lock eyes. Theirs sparkle with determination. They will win this game. They squat into a runner's stretch, showing off deliciously long and muscular legs. They lithely switch feet.

"Sarah? You good or you ready for another game?" Jass asks.

Sarah assesses me and Alex, and I almost roll my eyes like a teenager. What kind of trouble does she worry I'll get into? I'm not even thinking about kissing Alex because Vicki didn't kiss Alex. I kissed Alex. My stomach does a backflip. I kissed Alex! And I want to kiss Alex again. Now I can't look at Alex without giving away that something did happen. And I can't look at the camera because it's clear they want to exploit the chemistry between us. I'm absolutely not going to look at Sarah. I step away to grab my water bottle.

Sarah finally answers, "I haven't played with Chad yet. Do you mind if I stay in?"

"Not at all," Jass says. "You got this."

Sarah leans over for a quick good-luck kiss, and I've never been as jealous as I am of them right now.

"C'mon." Alex taps my shoulder lightly with their paddle and waggles their eyebrows at me.

"I hope I don't let you down," I say.

They wink. "You won't."

I take a deep breath. I hope that's true about so much more than this game.

CHAPTER TWENTY-ONE

Alex

I was having fun with this new game, feeling out the size of the court and control of the ball, but then this Chad dude started playing mean, which irks me. In his little lesson, he told any former tennis players to leave that attitude off the court. "Pickleball is about the community. It's about having fun, not about winning," he'd said. Unless you're about to lose. In that case, at least if we're going by this guy's rules, it's about playing mean.

"Okay," I say, walking to the south side of the court because of course Chad stakes first serve and is standing there ready to begin the game. "Here's the thing. This guy doesn't understand the meaning of fun. We all learned this game an hour ago, but he's playing like it's the nationals. That's not fun. It's mean."

"That's why we have to beat him," Vicki says.

"Exactly. If he's so good, he could be honing his skills. He could be trying to hit it to you so you can return it."

"Even if he did hit it to me, it's not like I have a strategy to hit it back like you do."

"You're a beginner. Don't try to be more than that. Don't try to make points. Just aim to get it back over. Every ball you return will make him so frustrated, he'll start to hit it out. That's your strategy, okay?"

"Okay. What's your strategy?"

I smile, ready to have some real fun. "I'm going to start trying." I waggle my eyebrows again and laugh at her shocked expression. She still has her eyes on me when Chad calls the beginning score, so I tip my head in his direction and get in my ready stance.

I purposely position Vicki in the spot that will give her first serve once we gain it. This guy needs to learn to read a court. I know players like this, and I don't get how pulling out all the stops on a clearly inferior player brings them joy. I'm all for competitive play, but watching Chad play Vicki and Sarah made my blood boil. I expected him to pull back like Jass did when they were six points ahead, but he kept on with everything he had until they won. He better be ready for a taste of that in this game.

Chad serves low and fast, and it sails part Vicki.

"I'm sorry," she says when she's returned with the ball.

"No more apologizing. Get mad. If he were as good as he considers himself, he'd be able to serve it for you to hit it, okay?"

"My serve," Chad calls out.

"Like I don't know," I say, winking at Vicki. "Let's have some fun." I extend the paddle, and she does the same, tapping it lightly. It's not even our bodies touching, but it connects us. I'm enjoying this. I like that we're doing this together. I could do without Sports Guy acting like an iceberg out to sink the *Titanic*, but everything else about this day is perfect.

This is why I accepted Tom's invitation to come with him to California. I cannot picture Jass standing courtside to cheer on her wife at a Kentucky park. And they're raising a kid on top of that. And Sarah's challenged Chad on his husband/wife comment. I have found my people.

I'm light on the balls of my feet, waiting for the serve. Again, it's low and fast, but I'm ready. I could play mean by playing exclusively to Sarah, the less experienced player, but that's not how I want to win this. I want him to lose it on his own with his impatience. I compliment Vicki on every return, and it's not difficult. She's got great reflexes, and they are even better the more she relaxes into the game. She won her game with Chad, but she hardly got to play at all. When we're in the lead, she's glowing because she's part of the win.

The game is evenly paced, but that contributes to Chad's frustration, and more often than not, he serves or smashes a return into the net. As I anticipated, it's those errors that cost him the game, and he's fuming by the time we meet at the net. He barely lets us tap paddles and he's collecting his equipment back and rattling off an unlikely story about an appointment he'd forgotten.

"You totally broke his game," Vicki whispers. She's leaning toward me, not enough to touch shoulders, but enough that I feel her warmth. She says it loud enough that the others hear and laugh.

"You're an amazing player," Jass says. "I wish we had our own gear. It would be fun to play another game."

"I feel bad you only got to play with the ball hog," Sarah says.

Jass throws back her head and cracks up. "Such a ball hog! Like, back off and give me some space!"

A flash of insight hits me. Jass could be talking about our court case. I can so easily map out how frustrating it would be to run a business with someone like Sports Guy. It would absolutely motivate a partner to break away to form their own business, but to have freedom, or to teach them a lesson? I start to match up the players on this court to those in the court we spent the last few days in. Vicki and Chad were partners, but I was the one who convinced her that we needed to take him down. Did someone do the same for Marlene? I wish I could ask the group, but I hear the judge admonishing us to not discuss the case outside of court.

"I'm so sorry you got stuck with him at the end and didn't get to win any of your games," Vicki says.

"No! Is that true?" I ask.

Sarah chuckles. "I lost playing with each of you and then against the two of you together. Clearly, you make the better team."

Vicki bumps her hip against mine. "I definitely had more fun playing with you. And it wasn't just because we won."

Even that small amount of physical contact reminds me of what her lips feel like on mine, and I feel my face flush. My mind is no longer on the game or Sports Guy or how it had me drawing parallels to the trial. All I want is to be alone with Vicki again.

Sarah's watching us, and I'm very aware that Nick and the camera are still here. I squirm under their scrutiny. Is it bad that I wish I could break away from the group with Vicki? Did she and I break any laws kissing last night? The judge reminded us that we were not to talk about the case outside of court before we left on Friday, but that was it. She didn't say we couldn't meet outside of the court schedule. To be safe, I don't return Vicki's hip bump.

"Thank you for being so patient, Chloe. Are you ready to check out the play structure before we go?" Sarah asks.

"Yes!" the youngster says, already moving in that direction.

Jass follows, waving and calling, "Nice to meet you!" over her shoulder.

"What's next in your day?" Sarah asks, gathering her backpack from the picnic table.

The way she studies first me then Vicki, I get the sense there is a right and wrong answer.

"You said you have the paint already?" I ask Vicki. "We could get that finished up?"

Wrong answer. I can tell by her face, but I don't know why there would be a problem with me and Vicki spending time together.

"You're still game if we follow you for a bit?" Nick asks Sarah.

"If you can keep up with a six-year-old," Sarah says, striding toward Jass and Chloe. She turns and, walking backward, says, "Be good."

"Did you tell her…" I ask Vicki when I'm sure they are all out of earshot.

"No!"

"Do you think there are rules about jurors not kissing?" I step closer to Vicki, though there is absolutely no way I'll risk kissing her here in the park, although I ache to.

"I've run through what the judge said over and over, and I'm pretty sure she didn't say a thing about kissing."

My stomach tightens with anticipation at the way she appraises me. "Okay, then."

"Okay," she repeats, raising her shoulder and her eyebrow.

She knows exactly how sexy she is in the cropped tank top she's wearing, and it is so easy to imagine pushing the string from her shoulder and kissing her sweet, warm skin.

CHAPTER TWENTY-TWO

Vicki

Cesar's truck is in the drive when we get back from the park. The expression on Alex's face when they climb out of their car is exactly why I had to get my brothers to come work on the house today. If I were here with Alex alone, it would be too easy to slip back into their arms. I can still feel the way they pressed their lips to my crown when they held me.

And how it felt kissing them.

It would be all too easy to pick up where we left off the last time we were in the kitchen together. We were barely getting started when it hit me how wrong it was that I was kissing someone who didn't know who they were actually kissing. It was the hardest thing to do to stop after such a small sampling, but I had to. From their perspective, there are no barriers, so I had to invent one because I cannot allow us to go there again.

"Hey, sis, 'bout time," Mateo says from his perch on the ladder.

"Alex, Mateo is our whiny little brother," I say. "Mateo, this is Alex. They primed the drywall yesterday, and they're here to paint the kitchen today."

"My idea. Because I helped with their bad-ass Honda. You're welcome," Cesar says, bowing.

"And you remember Cesar?"

"Yeah. I'll try to stay out of your way," Alex says. They start unfolding the tarp, and I hate how small they are making themself in this space.

"I'll grab the paint," I say, and the silence in the space is heavy.

"And then we need to talk about where to put the recessed lights in the dining area," Mateo says.

"How was the whole pickle paddle thing?" Cesar asks. I'm doing my best to keep my ear on the conversation while I dig in the closet. Alex is more kind than I would be in relaying the overview of our experience. Unsurprisingly, they don't say anything about teaching Chad a lesson.

"You should have seen Alex cream the guy who taught us," I say.

"Wait. You beat him at his own game, after he just taught you?" Cesar asks. "Classic."

"I played tennis in high school. It wasn't that different. Same ego-driven competitiveness," Alex says. "He's the guy who takes it as an insult if a girl beats him. And to be beat by someone who looks like me? Watch out."

Alex checks to see what my brothers think, glancing up for an instant. This awkwardness is my fault, and I hate it, but I would hate it even more if we were alone and I had to keep my distance from Alex.

Cesar, as he has often done in our lives, saves me. He raises his arms like goalposts, flexes, and then admires his impressive biceps before regarding Alex. "So you said, 'Bring it on!'"

"And he went down," I confirm. "Left with his tail between his legs."

Cesar nods his approval.

"Can you put away your muscles and help me out?" Mateo asks.

"You good?" I ask Alex, who has relaxed a little.

"Sure."

I almost reach out to squeeze their arm but stop myself, knowing my brothers will be curious about us. We map out where they'll put in the recessed lighting, the next step in preparing to sell the house. They are the ones who saw the property and came up with the idea to flip it. My part is to live in the house while they work on it, so they don't have to pay capital gains when the house sells. I get a place to stay, and they can take their time working on the improvements. They're being nice, especially Mateo, in pretending I have opinions about the remodeling.

With my brothers all set, I check on Alex to see if they need anything. I don't mean to pause—I have the paint on the fireplace to remove—but like yesterday, I am mesmerized by the way Alex moves while they work. I have never seen anyone move as quickly or as accurately as they do as they cut along the cupboards and around the window.

"It's nice of your brothers to help you out," Alex says.

"They are good guys. Would yours help you out like this if they lived close by?"

They continue their long, quick strokes with the cutting brush before answering. "Before I came out, sure. Now, though? They're relieved I moved all the way out here where they don't have to think about me."

I think about you, I want to say. Way more than I should. "Is there anything you miss about home?"

They're cutting under the window and rest their weight back on their heels, considering. They purse their lips. "Is it bad if I say no?"

"Not bad," I say quickly. "How big is your family?"

"Four kids. Three boys before my mom got the girl she'd been hoping for."

"No pressure or anything," I say.

They chuckle. "Yeah. No pressure. They wanted a cheerleader. My brothers all played football, and that was our whole world, so I would have fit in if I'd done cheer."

"Not okay to be good at your own sport?"

"Right. Football practice, football games, all of those were on the family calendar. Nobody missed. Tennis, though? It was always 'Can you get a ride with so and so?' 'Sorry I can't make your game because..." They are quiet as they set up the roller. "What about your parents? They support you?"

This is where I would love to be able to be honest with Alex and share how excited my parents are about me landing a part, but I can't. I have to answer from the perspective of Vicki. How would Vicki's parents react to the engagement falling through? Would her mom be supportive or worry that I'll never get married? Maybe it's that I am in my own home that I am considering my actual parents, and how I have never felt like I was in a competition with my brothers. I'm still trying to figure out what to say about Vicki's parents when Cesar answers.

"Dude. You should tell them about how you almost gave Papa a heart attack."

I try to catch his eye from across the room to tell him to shut his trap, but Mateo is already laughing. "Oh, yeah. Emelynn recorded this sex book..."

"It was not a sex book!" I interrupt, trying to put out this fire. "It was a romance, a regular, run-of-the-mill romance."

"No, no, no. It was steamy, like that *Fifty Greys* or whatever," Mateo says.

"Don't you even...You know how I feel about that book. And you didn't ever listen to it, so shut it!" I'm hoping he'll keep arguing about the details to distract from the fact that he slipped and used my real name.

"But Mama and Papa listened to it," Mateo continues. I want to throttle him so badly.

"What did your brother call you?" Alex interrupts.

The room is quiet, and then Cesar clears his throat. "We're ready to do the rewire here. Is it okay if we cut the power? We could mess with the breakers to isolate the dining room, but it would be easier if we kill the power."

"Fine." I wave him away, quickly forming a reason my brother didn't use the name Alex knows. "He called me Emelynn. It's the name I use for recording." That's true. I am not digging myself into deeper trouble here. As long as they don't search me up and start asking questions about my acting career.

"Emelynn," they say, as if they are savoring a sweet treat. "I like that. Would I like any of the books you've recorded?"

I love the sound of my name on their lips and would love to talk about the books I've recorded and whether they would like any, but I have to get us on safer ground. Thank goodness Cesar returns from flipping the breaker. I catch his eye and nod toward Alex's work. "Looks good, doesn't it?"

"Damn, you're fast, and it looks awesome."

"Thanks," Alex says.

Cesar grabs a glass and fills it with water. He downs half and says, "I meant to ask you. You free for a job? Because I got a client who needs interior work done."

"A recommendation would be great," Alex says. "I'm not sure how much longer the jury goes. I thought we'd be done this week. I'm sure I could take a look and give them a quote, though."

"Sure, sure. I can get your number from Vicki to pass along to them?"

I could kiss him for using the name Alex knows me by and for helping to keep the conversation off my real work.

"Yeah, great. I appreciate it," Alex says.

Cesar mouths *sorry* and scoots out of the kitchen, leaving me feeling more vulnerable. Having my brothers here means I'm safer to spend time with Alex without worrying what we might get into if we were left alone, but it also knits Alex into my real life in a way that worries me.

"Your brother is really great," Alex says.

"Yeah, I got lucky with Cesar. We do our best to put up with Mateo."

"You do know I can hear you, right?" he says from the other room.

"Kinda the point!" I say.

"First coat is done. You want to take a look at the fireplace? I brought something to help strip the paint."

"Watch out. If my brothers see how handy you are, they'll drag you along on all sorts of their jobs."

"Maybe I'm trying to get in good with them because I want to spend more time with their sister," Alex says.

"You're nice," I say vaguely, wishing the trial was over and I could hang out with Alex as myself. My chest starts to squeeze with anxiety when I think about the trial ending. Here I am imagining an aftermath where the two of us could be lounging by the fireplace, admiring the way it looks with the bare bricks and then exposing more of ourselves.

I slam the door on that fantasy.

Because what if it is only a fantasy? There is no guarantee that Alex will even want to talk to me after they discover that the show is all about them. A swell of anticipatory loss numbs me, and I stop abruptly.

Alex takes a few more steps before sensing that I'm not following. They double back to me and cup their hand around my elbow. "You okay?"

"Vertigo," I lie. The tenderness of their gesture nearly undoes me. "I must've stood up too fast."

"Should I grab a chair?" they ask.

I take three deep breaths to center myself in Vicki. "No, I'm good."

"If you're sure."

"Don't fall for her fainting lady trick. She'll try to get you to do all the work," Cesar yells.

"I work!" I say with indignance.

"So far, all I've seen today is Alex working, but okay…If you say so," Cesar says, and I can hear him roll his eyes.

Alex smiles at me. "You sure you're good? I won't tease you about how much work you do or don't do."

They are so kind and sweet that my heart aches with it all. This is their character. It's who they are and why I could so easily fall for them.

CHAPTER TWENTY-THREE

Alex

I have to pull over on my way home from meeting with the client Cesar hooked me up with. I called immediately after I left Vicki's and had an appointment set up for ten o'clock on Sunday to give them a quote.

They're as anxious to get their bathroom repainted as I am to get a more steady paycheck, so they hired me on the spot. I've spent the morning on the dirty grunt work of sanding and washing the walls and am on my way to pick up the paint I'll need when the view pulls me to the side of the road.

Does the couple who hired me take it in anymore as they descend the winding roads from their home in the Sierra Madre mountains? It's a clear spring day, and I can literally see the entire Los Angeles valley, including the cluster of skyscrapers downtown. It takes my breath away. Every state has beautiful cities. Louisville is only a three-hour drive from my hometown of Paducah. But it's more than the cityscape itself. It's the feeling of being on the fringes in the foothills of the San Gabriel mountains. Close enough to recognize the tiny bumps as the famed Los Angeles, but far enough that my life never intersects with the TV world my family is convinced I live in.

I snap a few pictures, and even though they capture exactly what I'm seeing, I stay longer leaning against the car and soaking in this feeling of expansiveness. So much feels possible. When I first rode out to California from Kentucky with Tom, I felt like I could finally breathe. From this vantage point on the mountain, though, I realize how I've basically been burrowed in a dark den, surviving but not living.

Vicki makes me feel alive.

She makes me believe I could have the life my parents said was nothing but a misguided dream.

I want to text her. All day I've been composing texts in my mind, but so far I've resisted sending any. I don't want her to see me as a lost puppy who has followed her home. I need to distract myself, so I pass over the texting app and open the app where I've downloaded a bunch of Sarah Cooper's podcasts. After I listened to her "Falling All In" episode about Jass, I listened to "Reimagining the Red, White, and Blue." Like the first episode I tried, Sarah shared all the things she struggled with when her family attended a Fourth of July event with her ex. I liked how she acknowledged both her anger and her sadness and how she was able to find peace.

It helped me identify and untangle some of the emotions tied to my own ex. I often steeped in the red anger I experienced at her betrayal. I had not realized or honored the blue sadness that came from losing the future I'd invested in. And we weren't even married like Sarah and Trisha had been! That she had found a way to smooth out her emotions and embrace a white peace flag had given me a lot to reflect on. Having moved from a red state to a blue state also made me see conflict on a greater scale and how there wasn't enough peace in our union. I filed the response away to talk to Sarah about sometime.

I scroll through the episodes that had caught my eye back when I sought out Sarah's podcast. "Out in the Wild," about running into clients when she was a braless mess; "You're Not in Trouble," about learning to praise yourself for what you do get done instead of punishing yourself for not achieving all you set out to do; and "Labels DO Matter," which seems like the most logical place to start.

My car is so old, it doesn't even have more than an ancient AM/FM dial, so I always have my phone playing music or, now that I've discovered podcasts, an episode as I drive to and from jobs. Sarah's voice welcoming listeners back and thanking them for their feedback on a podcast about using *y'all* instead of *guys* make me smile. I'll make a mental note to download that one later. It's still hard for me to believe that I know Sarah, that yesterday I was playing pickleball with her and meeting her family and that I'll see her tomorrow when I show up for jury duty again.

She opens with a story about making an appointment for her wife, and I echo her frustration when she shares how the medical staff respond by asking for her "friend's" birthday to look up her records. I find myself audibly cheering for her when she gives the man feedback about the importance of language and grit my teeth when he does not demonstrate any understanding of her position.

"I saw this, too, in a Facebook post about Nonbinary Parent's Day recently," she says, and I look at my phone as if it is actually Sarah who can nod her head in confirmation that I heard correctly. There's such a thing as Nonbinary Parent's Day?

"I didn't even know such a day existed until a friend posted about it. Naturally, I wanted to comment to support them…" Sarah's comfort with her friend's pronoun warms my soul. "As I scrolled down through the comments, one caught my eye. 'Labels don't matter. Parents do.' By the time I saw the post, my friend had already replied with a way more level-headed explanation about why labels absolutely *do* matter to them, but I was also disappointed that they were alone in the dialogue with this 'friend' and bemoaned the fact that they had to step into the role of educator on a day when they simply wanted to celebrate being seen.

"It fell on them to explain how invisible they feel in a world designed for men and women, in a world that celebrates

Mother's Day and Father's Day, and instead of replying with any kind of acknowledgment, the friend said they totally understood and wished there was a day for stepparents."

"I'd bet there already is," I say as if we are having a live conversation.

"By the way, there already is a Stepparent's Day…Anyway, I have endured this frustration when I pick up my child and hear the teacher say, 'Find your mommy or daddy,' so I've invited my friend on to extend the conversation about what we can do to make our nonbinary friends more visible."

I'm at the hardware store by this time and hate to pause the interview for the time it takes me to get an employee to prepare the paint required to finish the bathroom. As I wait for the color to be mixed and the paint shaken, I realize that when we were playing pickleball yesterday, I was not misgendered once. This is something I can ask Vicki about.

Random question. Did you tell Sarah my pronouns? I text. I'm relieved when I immediately notice the dots indicating that she's typing.

Depends.

I smile. I have no idea what she's been doing with her Sunday, but her immediate reply makes me hopeful that she's been thinking about me as well. *On?*

Whether you're mad.

Why would I be mad?

It's your identity, not mine.

I'm not mad. I have to make that clear.

Oh good!

I'm listening to a podcast of Sarah's, and she was talking about how exhausting it is to have to educate people about being nonbinary. I didn't have to educate yesterday. Tnx.

Sounds like a good topic!

It is. Do you listen to her podcast?

No. Should I?

I'm typing my answer when another text from her pops up. *Don't tell her.*

I have to erase what I was saying to type *Of course not!*

The woman at the counter pulls out my paint, pops the lid and dabs a bit of the blue on the lid. I retype, *There's so much I want to talk to her about having listened to a few shows!*

This is not what I want to be talking about, but I'm still happy to be firing texts back and forth. The woman has used the blow dryer on the dab and holds it up for me to approve. I compare it to the paint swatch and give her a thumbs-up. I wake up my phone as I exit the store to read the texts that came in.

I was just thinking about you.

She was thinking about me! I high-five the universe and stow the paint in the hatchback.

You relaxing today?

Working on the fireplace.

I settle into the driver's seat but don't turn the ignition. *Your brothers there today?*

Yes.

More electrical.

I tell myself that's good. I'm not missing anything, and by that I mean another opportunity to kiss Vicki, since her brothers are there. And this job helps my budget. And I'll see Vicki tomorrow. All this is good. It doesn't change my desire to see her right now. Good thing I have this paint job to finish.

Tell Cesar tnx for the job. Starting first coat now.

Sweet!

The bubbles continue to undulate, so I don't text again. The bubbles stop and then start again. Have they interrupted her, or is she wondering if I plan on working the whole day? It occurs to me that her brothers never misgendered me, either, and I start to type how I appreciate that, too, when her next text finally comes in.

See you tmrw

Ouch. It's okay. I have the podcast to finish. Still, I'd seen a whole conversation rolling out where I could tell Vicki how exhausting it is to always be on guard and how the two circles I was in with her yesterday allowed me to drop all that and simply enjoy being human. That is a real gift.

CHAPTER TWENTY-FOUR

Vicki

"Please state your name for the record," Ms. Saqsaq says.

"Marlene Menjivar."

"Just a moment, Counselor," Judge Court says. "Juror Three, what are you wearing? Are those pajamas?"

"I didn't sleep in them," Juror Three says.

"That was not my question," the judge says. "Would you wear that outfit to church?"

"Church?" Juror Three says, confused.

"Would you report to work wearing that?"

Juror Three plucks at the spaghetti-string tank. "I'm a student?" she says. "I'd wear this to school?"

"Are you asking me or telling me?"

"Telling you?"

The judge closes her eyes. She's probably counting to ten. Slowly. "All jurors, please take note. These are serious proceedings. Your attire should reflect your attentiveness. We are adjourned until Juror Three can return home or locate a store that will provide something appropriate for a day of service. The rest of the jury will wait in the jury room. I must remind you of the admonishment. You are not to talk about the facts of the case at this time. Bailiff! Escort them out." She bangs her gavel.

Today's goal is to test the limits of Alex's patience.

Chad gripes about lost time on the pickleball court.

"Such a waste of time," Juror Ten, one of the other male jurors, agrees. "It's bad enough putting my own work on hold when we're actually hearing the case. But now I'm falling behind at work so a woman can go shopping? Fucking ridiculous, isn't it?" He nudges Alex as he takes a seat next to them at the large table.

They shrug. "Anything with moving pieces takes a while to coordinate."

"Yeah, but the pieces could move just fine whatever people are wearing."

"It's part of our job to take this seriously," Alex says. "If the judge says it's important to dress respectfully, then we wait for Juror Three to come back in that mindset."

Juror Nine pulls a brown paper sack from his backpack and removes three hard-boiled eggs.

"You're not peeling those in here, are you?" Waverly says.

"Why wouldn't I?"

"The smell of egg makes me sick," Waverly says.

"Breathe through your mouth," he snaps.

"That's not very nice," Waverly says, putting her hand up to cover her mouth.

"You're the one who wore patchouli! You can't talk!"

"I haven't worn any perfume since that first day." Waverly crosses her arms like a petulant child.

"Maybe you could at least invest in deodorant. There are several people who could benefit from the miracle of deodorant." He looks pointedly at a few other jurors. "The judge should remind all of you about that. My personal hygiene shows I'm serious." He's finished picking the shell off the first egg. He salts it and takes a satisfied bite.

"I never realized how bad eggs smell," Juror Five says.

"Oh, please," Juror Nine says. "Are you going to tell the judge you can't complete the day because you're nauseated."

"Nauseous," Sarah says.

"You're sick, too?"

"No. She feels nauseous. The smell of the egg makes her feel nauseated. People confuse them all the time."

"You can stop with the judgy," Juror Nine says.

"I am not judging," Sarah says. "If I were misusing a word, I would want someone to tell me." She turns to Alex. "Am I'm being judgy?"

Alex scans the room. Everyone is waiting for their answer. They quickly thumb something into their phone. "Maybe? The Internet says that people don't differentiate between the two anymore."

Sarah huffs out her disappointment. "I have to voice that it doesn't bode well that you will not consider your fellow juror's feelings or ideas," she says to Juror Nine. "How will we deliberate when it's time to give a verdict if you ignore her request?"

"Like I would take any advice from you," Juror Nine says.

"What does that mean?"

Alex bristles next to me.

"Look at what you're wearing," he says.

Everyone eyes Sarah. She dips her head. "What's wrong with what I'm wearing?"

"This is the fourth time you have worn a white shirt."

"I beg your pardon? You have a problem with the color of my shirt?"

"Racist," he says under his breath.

"I'm racist for wearing a white shirt?"

"White shirt, white shoes. Your sandwich is made with white bread. I'm just saying. If anyone is prejudging the outcome of this trial, it's you. You'll obviously side with the plaintiff because he's white."

"That is so not what I expected him to rant about," Alex whispers to me.

"What did you say about me?" Juror Nine snaps.

"I didn't say anything about you," Alex says.

"Then you can say what you said to the room."

Alex's face starts to flush red. They don't repeat what they said to me. Instead, they ask how he knows Sarah wears white so often.

"I recorded it." He pulls out his notebook. "She mostly wears pants, usually jeans, and has never once worn a skirt. Of the women jurors, only three have worn a dress or a skirt."

"You're cataloging what we wear?" I ask.

"That and other information that might be relevant to the case."

"Like?" I ask.

"Pets."

"How in the world are our pets relevant?" Sarah asks.

He points across the table to another male juror. "He's always showing me pictures of his Chihuahua. Totally racist. I can't believe the plaintiff's lawyer didn't get rid of him. And have you heard how that lady almost lost her ear?"

She looks up, startled, and puts a hand over her ear as if he's threatened to rip it off. "I never told you about that."

"I overheard. A horse bit her when she was a kid." His tone makes it sound like she's a major threat to national security.

"That makes her racist?" Alex asks.

"Of course not," he snaps. "She'll try to hang the jury."

Alex whispers, "Is this guy for real? This is hidden-camera-level weird." They stretch the word *weird* out as they peer around the room looking for cameras.

"Can you please just finish your snack?" Waverly's voice is nasally because she's pinching her nose. "The smell is making me feel faint."

He makes quick work of the second egg, dramatically popping the entire thing in his mouth.

Waverly covers her mouth and runs from the room. Alex and I exchange another look. I cover my mouth. "Actually, I'm starting to feel…"

"Nauseous," Sarah says.

"Let's get some fresh air," Alex offers, extending their hand.

Hoping I don't get in trouble for allowing Alex to escape, I happily accept.

CHAPTER TWENTY-FIVE

Alex

"Shall we try this again?" Judge Court says when we reenter the courtroom. She levels her gaze at the jury. "Juror Three, please stand."

She does. She fidgets under the judge's silent assessment, popping the wrinkles from each sleeve by pulling at the cuff.

"I don't remember you reporting being a member of the armed services."

"I'm not."

Judge Court puts on her glasses and frowns. "And yet you are wearing Navy dress whites."

"You said to show up for a day of service. My mom was in the Navy, and she lives close to court, so I borrowed this from her."

"Your mother did not inform you that it is a misdemeanor for a civilian to don military attire?"

"No. She did not." In the silence that hangs in the air, Juror Three adds, "Your Honor."

"Juror Three, let me explain to you the idea of respectful attire," the judge says.

I bury my head in my notes, uncomfortable on behalf of Juror Three. Logically, I know that the judge is not talking to me, but my nerve endings and stomach do not believe me when I tell myself I'm not the one in trouble. Too often, I'm the one scrutinized and lectured for failing to wear the "right" attire.

"I still smell those eggs," Waverly hisses as the judge continues her lecture.

Before I can be annoyed with her fixation on the smell of eggs, especially as I agree there are some jury members who desperately need deodorant, there is the unmistakable sound of flatulence. I go rigid with the embarrassment of hearing one of my fellow jurors pass gas in the jury box. In public!

Juror Nine groans. "Sorry. I love eggs, but they don't love me."

Another jury member gags.

Then another.

Murmurs of disgust ripple through the jury, and then the smell hits me, like someone has cracked a spoiled egg open on my head.

We are all eyeing each other in confusion and disgust. Only Juror Nine and Three have their eyes on the judge. I pull my kerchief from my pocket and place it to my face.

"Is something the matter, Juror Eleven?"

My stomach is starting to turn from the smell. How is it getting worse?

"No, Your Honor."

"Why, then, are you covering your face? What is going on in the jury box?"

"Nothing." The smell has to dissipate. I breathe through my mouth into my handkerchief and try to conjure up the smell of night jasmine on an evening breeze.

Juror Nine farts again, so loud that I'm certain the judge will figure out the problem on her own. Many jurors are tittering, others gagging.

"Juror Eleven?"

I repress a shudder and lower the tissue, breathing through my mouth even though I swear I can taste the egg fart.

"Allergies, Judge…Your Honor." I blow my nose for effect, fold the handkerchief, and put it back in my pocket, careful to keep breathing through my mouth.

"Judge Court," Baby Shark says, humming her theme song for, what? Strength? Courage? Is she even aware of this nervous tic? "I object to this behavior. Clearly something is transpiring with the jurors. My client should be judged by a jury of her peers. Is she fidgeting in her chair? Suppressing laughter? No!" She searches the corners of the ceiling for more words, humming a few more bars. "I have yet to begin presenting my case and am quite certain this behavior will taint the way it is received."

The weight of the judge's stare settles on me again. Why me! I do my best not to fidget or show any discomfort.

"I warned you about those eggs," Waverly mumbles.

I clamp my lower lip between my teeth. I will not add to the conflict.

"The jury will disregard the morning's antics and hear the defendant's testimony with a clear perspective. Understood?"

"Understood!" Juror Three shouts.

I shoot her daggers. How can she think the judge wanted a response? It's like the jury box is filled with kittens and puppies. Only not cute or cuddly ones. Well…I catch Vicki's eye. One is cute, and I still hope to find out if she's cuddly.

"Thank you. Counsel. You may call your witness. Again."

The defendant is sworn in and asked to give her history with the plaintiff.

Like the plaintiff, she begins by describing the early days of their friendship that began in college. I draw a line down the center of the page and jot things that match what I remember the plaintiff saying on the left and new items on the right. She emphasizes that the company was struggling and that she suggested adding rides for the neurodivergent population to attract new customers.

"He wasn't interested. I told him time and time again that TheraPony needed to expand its services to stay afloat, but he told me to stay in my lane. He said he knew business and I only knew horses, and that was that."

Next, Baby Shark calls an accountant to the stand, who takes us page by page through the clients. I try my best to repress a yawn after forty-five minutes of listening to the comparison of client lists to establish that not one client left TheraPony to enroll with No More Stubborn Mules.

My attention starts to wander. I take notes to keep myself alert, but I'm not desperate enough to write down a list of names. They go on and on. I sneak a look at Vicki. She is blinking slowly, about to fall asleep. Being able to glance over at her during these long boring periods lifts my spirits. All sorts of feelings jostle inside me: the doubt spurred by her quick *see you tomorrow* text, warmth from being in the same room with her, and also the anxiety of what might happen when the trial is over. Is she thinking about that, too? The kiss we shared sparked feelings I long to explore after this is all over. I hope she feels the same.

"Totally different client base," the accountant says, finally bringing his testimony to a close.

Vicki's eyes snap open wide. She glances my way, catching me staring. She rolls her eyes, and we share a smile that makes me think something could happen beyond this trial.

"I have one more witness, Your Honor. I'm calling Rosehip Applepicker as a character witness."

The judge gestures for the lawyer to proceed. The witness's name brings to mind the way Tom will present a mount to its rider with a flourish, saying the name of the animal in the style of important guests being introduced at a ball. I lean close to Vicki and whisper, "What if they call a pony to the stand?"

"Could they do that? I mean, where would it sit?" she whispers back.

I cover my face, pressing my knuckles to my mouth, to keep the judge from seeing my smile. I don't want to get the jury in any more trouble today.

A blond woman in a blue sundress enters the courtroom and brings with her a breath of fresh air that revives everyone in the room. Everyone in the jury sits a little taller as she is sworn in.

"Please describe your relationship with the defendant," the defense attorney says, adding in a whisper, "Doo-doo, doo-doo, doo-doo."

"I have been besties with Marley since kindergarten, and let me tell you. You and the jury..." Here she turns her gaze to us, and the way she smiles, I think we could be best friends, too. "Marley does not have a competitive bone in her body. I do. All of my bones...How many bones are in the human body?"

Baby Shark hums for a moment. "Two hundred and some."

The witness pulls out her phone. She holds up a finger, asking us all to wait. "Hey, Siri. How many bones in the human body?"

"There are two hundred and six bones in the human body."

I'm pretty sure she's not allowed to use her phone in the courtroom. I'm relieved she's stowing it when it offers, "Babies are born with more bones than adults."

"Is that true?" a juror behind me asks.

Then Siri says, "Bones are stronger than steel."

"Hashtag strange things about bones we absolutely don't need," another juror grumbles.

"The hashtag symbol is technically called an octothorpe," Siri supplies.

"Counselor, your witness must control her phone."

"So sorry, Your Honor," Ms. Applepicker apologizes. "Let me turn it off here. Now. Where was I?"

"Doo-doo, doo-doo, doo-doo," Baby Shark hums before prompting, "Two hundred and six bones."

"Precisely! Every single one of my two hundred and six bones is competitive." She holds out her palms in a *wait till you hear this* gesture. "My dear friend Marley, on the other hand, does not try to pick the fastest line at the grocery store. She stands there without giving a single thought to whether another line is moving faster.

"In an Easter Egg hunt, she doesn't count how many eggs she has. In fact, the years I didn't get as many eggs, she gave me some of hers. If she's getting on the freeway when there's traffic and she has to wait her turn? She always lets the other car merge first, even if it's a total junker that takes forever to accelerate.

"What I'm saying is that she cares about other people, even when other people don't even deserve it." She glares at the plaintiff. "She loved TheraPony and would never have done anything to threaten its success. I mean…All you'd have to do is take one look at their setup and you'd know that Mr. Assha…I'm sorry, Mr. Aschbran. You'd know beyond a shadow of a doubt that he has not lost one cent to my friend."

After Rosehip Applepicker is dismissed, Baby Shark says, "Your Honor, as my last witness, I call No More Stubborn Mules."

Judge Court assesses her above the rim of her glasses. "Your last, last witness?"

"My final witness, Your Honor."

"And how do you intend to do that?"

"It's a mobile unit, Your Honor. I can have them here tomorrow morning." As the lawyer returns to her chair, I can hear her humming "Doo-doo, doo-doo, doo-doo."

CHAPTER TWENTY-SIX

Vicki

"Don't get comfortable," Judge Court says. "As you heard yesterday, the defense has called the mobile unit. We'll be convening on the lawn outside. Counsel, do you stipulate that the court reporter will not be required to take down what is said on this field trip? There will be no written transcript of what is being said."

"Agreed," both lawyers say.

"Bailiff! Show them out, please."

"They better not make us get close to the horses. I swear, I must look or smell like a carrot. I've never trusted them since I got bit," says Ripley, who I remember being one of the other first-time jurors.

"I wonder if we'll be riding the horses," Chad muses.

"Why would they make you ride the horse? Are you on the spectrum?" Ripley asks.

"Well, why did they bring the horses? To demonstrate, duh."

"But they help kids on the spectrum. Have you been listening to anything in there, or do you spend the whole time dreaming about pickleball?" Ripley says.

I'm walking with Alex, trying to get a read on what they think about the field trip. After their comment about calling a pony to the stand, the writers completely reworked the last day of trial material. After this, the lawyers will give their closing statements, and we'll be directed to select our foreperson. The one absolute of the day is that Alex accepts that role. Everything else, as usual, is roughly mapped out. We round the building where there is a generous patch of green, and I ask Alex if the horses are likely to make them homesick, given their background.

"Oh, no! I was a terrible barn hand. I'm probably as clueless as the next city person."

"Man! Look at the judge," Chad says.

We've only seen her in her robe until this point. Now she's wearing jeans with a sharp green polo shirt tucked in. She has what has to be a borrowed snap-back with the Dodgers logo perched very awkwardly on her head. She adjusts it, though no amount of repositioning is going to change the stiff, flat bill.

She stops and puts her hands on her hips. "Counselor!" she hollers. "Where are these horses?"

"They're here somewhere, Your Honor," Baby Shark says, fingering her hijab as if by doing so, she could fix the judge's hat.

An ancient truck and trailer sits at the curb, the doors already open.

The entire jury and all the court staff are gathered on the lawn. There is a small commotion in the parking lot that draws our attention away from the trailer. A mother and father are trying to get two young boys to follow them across the grass.

"You've done this a hundred times before. Today your lesson is at this nice park. Otherwise, it's completely the same," the man playing the father says.

"No it's not!" one boy says, trying to wrench his arm free from his father.

"This is what we've been practicing," the woman says. "Ms. Menjivar is going to be so proud of you when you show her you can ride the mule in a different place."

The older boy continues to pitch a fit, but the younger one smiles and yells, "Lurch!"

We collectively turn in the direction he's looking to see two animals grazing in the display of miniature roses.

"Ms. Menjivar!" Judge Court hollers. "Who is responsible for these animals?"

Menjivar stops short and says, "My girlfriend," at the same moment Aschbran says, "My wife."

A small thrill runs through me as I recognize this as the plan the writers created for confirming Alex's hunch that there was conflict about Marlene's college roommate. I'm not even acting when I turn my look of surprise to Alex, who mirrors my shock.

"Your *ex*-wife," Menjivar says.

Ex-wife, Alex mouths, eyebrows raised and lips shaped around an unspoken *oh*.

"I never signed the divorce papers," Aschbran hisses.

"So she stole his girlfriend and then his wife?" Alex whispers.

"Do you think she's the old college roommate?" I ask.

"I don't know. So many years ago? Hard to say, but damn." They stretch out the word *damn* and shake their head.

"Enough, enough!" Judge Court demands. "Get those animals out of the flower bed. They're eating my roses!"

Marlene runs toward the animals, which spooks them. They burst from the flower bed, kicking up whole plants with their hooves. Aschbran rests his crossed arms on his chest as Menjivar and her girlfriend try to cut off the animals. She is about to grab the bigger horse's lead when he shies away from her and trots back into the flower bed.

"My roses!" Judge Court shrieks. "Do something before they destroy everything!"

The younger boy breaks away from his parents and joins Menjivar and her girlfriend. The adults are able to block the animals while the smaller boy steps forward to grab the rope attached to the big horse. "C'mon, Billy. Come get Lurch."

"Get those animals out of there!" the judge yells again. "Or you'll be facing a fine for destruction of property!"

"We're trying," Marlene says. She's hopping through the garden, trying to avoid the miniature rose bushes. The girlfriend/ex-wife is trying to grab the second animal, but Marlene turns to follow the other woman, gesticulating wildly.

As they pass by the stunned jury, I hear the girlfriend/ex-wife saying, "It's not my fault I got a summons..." her head angled away from both us and Marlene.

"I hope this isn't how these therapy sessions typically go," Sarah says. "This does not seem like productive applied behavior therapy."

"The plaintiff's going to blow his top!" Alex says.

"Yeah, he is," I say, watching his lawyer grab him by the sleeve and pull him away from the cluster of jurists.

"Counselor! Why are we standing here watching these animals eat my roses?" the judge hollers.

"Yes, Your Honor!" Saqsaq scurries toward the garden, motioning for the other boy to follow.

Reluctantly, he does, and they catch the other animal. I lean close to Alex and whisper, "I wouldn't want to ride the one with funny long ears, either."

"It's a mule. That's why it has long ears," they answer, but they are not watching the demonstration of No More Stubborn Mules. They are watching the plaintiff seethe, his scowl never leaving the two women.

The cameras are trained on Alex, too, and I can visualize exactly how this will play in the final cut, pieces clicking into place for Alex. What will they see when they watch this? Will they even remember what I leaned over to whisper? How I wish I could grab their hand and swipe the horses...horse and mule, I correct myself...and ride away from this whole circus. I let myself imagine the cameras capturing that. We are so close to the end now, so close to seeing whether Alex will step up to help guide the jury toward a verdict. Only one verdict matters to me, though, and that's what they will think of me when the truth is revealed.

CHAPTER TWENTY-SEVEN

Alex

"Now that you have heard both closing arguments, you will retire to the jury room. I remind you that for this case, you will be deciding four issues. Was there a valid contract between the parties? Did the defendant breach the contract? Did the plaintiff suffer damages as a result of the breach? If so, what damages will be awarded to the plaintiff? Your first order of business will be to choose a foreman. This person will serve as the captain of the jury. Together, you will decide on whom you trust to make sure you reach a sound verdict. For a civil case, it is not necessary for the jury to reach a unanimous verdict. You must have nine jurors agree to reach a verdict. The bailiff will show you to the jury room." She bangs the gavel. Surprised by her use of the word *foreman*, I follow the others.

Once there, we sit in silence around the long table. After a week of jury duty, there are still some jurists I hardly know at all. A few have been so off-putting that I hope to never see them again. One feels like a friend, having listened to many of her podcasts. And one distracts me to the point of forgetting what we are doing here altogether. Everyone eyes each other as though this is a game of chicken and the first one to talk will get stuck leading the deliberation. Except Vicki, who is simply eyeing me with the hint of a smile at the corner of her lips. I'm hoping that, like me, she's already thinking about how much easier things are going to be once we've reached and delivered our verdict.

Part of me is tempted to volunteer to be foreperson—which of course would include explaining why is important to me to use foreperson in place of foreman. The old me would not have even considered it, but this me, the one who needed to get dumped to finally find the motivation to pursue my dream without any constraints, feels the tickle of interest. I came into the experience hoping to get a better grasp of who I am as an individual, without Lilian, and I am confident I have honored the duties of a juror and might be able to lead the deliberation.

I'm about to open my mouth when a juror who has not talked at all during the whole trial process raises his hand. He's built and has tattoos that give him a familiar feel, like he could be someone I'd meet on a job. "Not it."

Waverly sighs aggressively. "Normally, as an Aries, I would be happy to accept this leadership role. However, I have to disclose that Sun-Pluto opposition is dredging up unresolved conflicts from my past, which I fear will compete with duties and obligations required of the foreperson. For that reason, I cannot offer myself, nor should any Aries offer themselves for that role."

The woman who wore pajamas to court yesterday punches the air in victory. "Aries!" She points at the tatted-out guy and raises her eyebrows. "Not it!"

Juror Five, who complained about the smell of eggs yesterday, says, "The judge said that the foreman has to read the verdict. I have panic attacks if I have to speak in public. I'm breaking out in a sweat just thinking about it."

"Can I offer…" Sarah pauses, clearly considering her choice of words carefully. "It would not be appropriate for me to lead these deliberations, but as we continue, may I suggest we use the word foreperson instead of foreman."

"Not again with the judgy," Juror Ten, the one I've been calling Scooby Doo Fred, says. "Who cares whether we say foreman or foreperson?"

I am both swelling with appreciation for Sarah's words and boiling at Scooby Doo Fred's response. I do not want to explain the importance of language to this idiot.

"It matters if someone is nonbinary," Vicki says. I could hug her for backing up Sarah's statement.

"Shouldn't we all be nonbinary?" PJ Woman asks. "Or...I mean...are we allowed to have sides now about whether the defendant is guilty or not?"

"Nonbinary isn't the same as not being biased," Sarah says. "We should absolutely be mindful of our biases and make our judgment solely on the testimony we heard in the court."

"So what's nonbinary, then?"

"It's..." Sarah begins to turn her head in my direction and catches herself.

I could step in here, but I know from listening to her podcast about Nonbinary Parent's Day that she can field this question, and it's a rare luxury to be in a situation where I don't have to be the one to explain.

"You know how we can either say guilty or not guilty? There are only two choices for us as jurists?"

"Yeah."

"That's like the choices for biological sex. Male or female. But what if someone is neither? A person who does not identify as male or female is nonbinary."

"I don't see why any of this matters, and it's just making us sit here longer," Scooby Doo Fred complains. "The judge said foreman. It's a role any one of us could serve."

"Not exactly," Sarah says. "Saying foreman is to accept that the word represents men and women when it does not. I am not a man, so if we say foreperson, we're making room for the possibility that the person we choose may not be a man. It may be a woman..."

"Not you. I vote for anyone but you," Scooby Doo Fred says.

I can tell that Sarah is working to not roll her eyes. "Given my status as a public figure, as I said before, it would not be a good idea for me to accept foreperson. So our fore*person* might be another woman or perhaps someone who does not identify as either man or woman. The point is that the word is divorced from the patriarchal power imbalance."

"Exactly why we cleansed the courtroom," Waverly reminds us. Her brow furrows. "Maybe we need to cleanse this space as well."

"Not another cleansing!" Tattoo Guy groans.

"Can we get on with choosing our fore*person* so we can wrap this up and get back to our lives? I mean, we all know the defendant is…"

"Stop!"

I'm as surprised as anyone to hear my own voice. Everyone turns to me. "Before we deliberate, we should take an anonymous poll to see where the jury stands on the defendant's guilt or innocence," I say.

"And we have a foreperson!" Waverly says as if she's announcing the winner of a raffle.

"I wasn't saying I should be foreperson. I just think it's important to get a read of the room before any one person puts an opinion forward," I say.

"That's a very good idea," Sarah agrees. "And may I add that you would be a great leader for our group."

Foreperson. Even though I was toying with the idea, the reality of accepting settles heavily across my shoulders. Sweat trickles down my back, and I feel like I'm the one on trial.

But I'm not.

Marlene Menjivar is, and she deserves a fair trial.

"Do you accept?" Sarah asks. Her voice is particularly gentle. Does she understand how intimidating it is to accept that responsibility?

I take a deep breath and survey the table. Nobody is arguing. Nobody is volunteering. As I meet each juror's eyes, they nod their encouragement.

Marlene Menjivar deserves our careful consideration of the facts. Recalling the comments from the beginning of the trial where many were deciding the defendant's guilt based on her appearance, I find that I don't trust many of my fellow jurists to mediate a fair deliberation.

"I accept."

Palpable relief fills the room, which feels oddly gratifying. They've put their faith in me. I rip a couple of pages from my notebook and tear them into smaller pieces to distribute to the group. "The issue at hand is whether there was, in fact, a legal contract for the defendant to breach. If there is a contract, the defendant can be held responsible for breaching it. So let's start with a vote of contract or no contract. How does that sound?"

Nobody challenges me, and it feels amazing. I surprised myself with my ability to sum up our vote. I understand all this legal stuff way more than I thought I would! "Okay. When you have your vote, fold it and push it to the middle of the table." One by one, they all follow my direction. The image of Tom coaxing twenty mules rigged together comes to mind, and it's almost like I feel the momentum of our group as we begin this journey of deliberation.

I take a deep breath and pull all the papers in front of me, mixing them thoroughly before I tally the votes.

"Contract. Contract. Contract. No contract." I hear sighs as I start a new pile. "Contract. No contract. No contract. Contract. Contract. Contract. No contract. Contract." I count each pile. Eight people have voted that the document we were presented in court qualifies as a contract. "Wow. Okay." We're one vote away from establishing that the plaintiff has presented a solid case. I'm disappointed. Not surprised. The things I've heard people say have hinted toward opinions about the case, but there is no way I believe that the defendant has violated something that meets the definition of a contract.

I scan the table once more and wait for someone to say something, but they are all silent. Waiting for me, I realize. Okay. Time to step up. "So I guess…" I hear how uncertain that sounds and start again. "Let's review the evidence and discuss what is necessary to deem the document submitted by the plaintiff a binding contract."

CHAPTER TWENTY-EIGHT

Vicki

"Look," Juror Ten says. "I'm just saying that Islam is not compatible with democracy."

I am so glad that I'm one of the jurors already voting that that the paper we were shown is in no way a contract. I could not believably deliver an argument like that. From the expression on Alex's face, they are having a hard time believing it as well. As the foreperson, the whole room turns to them for a response. Their eyes meet mine, in need of support. I side-eye Juror Ten in a "what can you do when you're surrounded by idiots" way.

That seems to help. Alex appears to be a fraction less anxious. "Please remember, we're talking about the defendant, not her lawyer," they say.

"Excellent point," Sarah says.

"Why does she wear that thing on her head? What's she hiding? This is who the defendant hired, so I can only assume it means she's hiding something." Juror Ten continues to prod.

"It's a hijab," Waverly says. "Obviously, if you don't know what it's called, you don't know what it is and that it's a symbol of their religious values. Would you question a nun for wearing a wimple?"

"Are we talking about wiffle balls?" Chad jumps into the circus ring with an absurd redirect. "Pickleballs are not actually wiffle balls." He rummages around in his bag and pulls out a yellow ball. "See, this ball, first off, is yellow, and it has holes all the way around which slow down…"

I groan and slouch in my seat. My part today requires exuding boredom, which is easy when folks are throwing out such absurdities.

"Thanks, Juror One, but we're not talking about wiffle balls or pickleballs or hijabs," Alex says, trying to regain control of the conversation.

"But the hijab is relevant!" Juror Ten says. "How can we trust what the defense presents when she's represented by a terrorist sympathizer with a blurred sense of morality?"

"For the last time," Alex says with a new level of firmness in their voice. "The lawyer is not the one on trial. Marlene Menjivar is. We will supply a verdict that is grounded in the facts that were presented by both sides, not based on the opinions we may have about the individuals." They scan the table to see if anyone else is going to support the attack on the defendant's lawyer. "Good. Let's talk about the contract first. Does anyone have any comments about the contract itself?" They walk to a side table that has the evidence and hold up the stained paper we saw during the trial. "Remember, the question is whether this is a legally binding contract."

"It absolutely is," Juror Ten says. As if his words weren't clear enough, the way he slumps against the back of the chair conveys that he is not interested in engaging in a discussion with any of us.

Alex leans forward. "Because?"

"Because it says right here in *all caps*." He raises his voice so we all visualize the letters. "*In it together or not at all!* And the defendant wrote it. She said so herself."

Several people around the table nod in agreement.

"There's no signature," Sarah says. "From either party."

"Doesn't matter. Remember how the plaintiff's lawyer said that even a handshake is binding? There's no signature on a handshake, but it's an agreement." Juror Ten taps the table, pleased with himself. "That makes this paper an agreement in my mind."

"I don't think it is?" says Juror Five, the one who complained about the smell of eggs yesterday. "What's the antecedent? My sister's girlfriend is taking an English class, and the teacher is always asking what 'it' stands for or…"

I yawn without covering my mouth and rest my chin on my hand. I have to remind myself to appear disengaged, especially when my interest is piqued by the breadcrumbs of support the writers have suggested. I can see how a simple gesture such as a nod to a woman being partnered with another woman translates into allyship for Alex. It's a subtle shift, not like going from crumpling under the ultramasculine delivery of Juror Ten's opinion to standing up to him. They have kept Juror Ten contained despite how hard he pushed with the hijab diversion. I try to put my finger on what has shifted, how Alex can look both more relaxed and stronger at the same time. I hope that when this is all over, they can understand how fully the cast and crew has supported them.

The woman taking us into the weeds of ambiguous pronouns continues to speak in the apologetic style of ending every sentence on an uptick that makes it sound like a question, and I can already visualize the episode edited to highlight the stark contrast between masculine and feminine argument styles.

My stomach tightens with the realization that we are nearing the end of filming. All we have left is the deliberation and delivering the verdict, where everything will be revealed. The nature of the show puts Alex at the center of everything here, but even beyond the filming, I feel their gravitational pull.

They don't understand why I have distanced myself since Saturday. I sense it when our eyes catch. As Emelynn, I wanted to answer their texts and spend more time with them, but as Vicki, I had to construct a boundary, flimsy as it is, to protect the show and to protect what I hope is still building between us. I yawn again and slump my upper body on the table. "I don't need an English lesson," I groan. "I need a break. We've been stuck in here for hours."

"It's only been thirty minutes," someone says. I don't see who because I've shut my eyes.

"Is any of this even changing anyone's mind even a tiny bit? So far, I haven't heard or seen anything that makes me believe that piece of paper is a contract."

"*No has estado escuchando*," Juror Four grumbles.

"I am listening, thank you very much," I snap back. "Is any of this changing your mind?"

"With all the words on the paper, I agree that 'it' has to mean the business," Juror Four says. "'In it together' means they'll start the business they did. 'Or not at all' means that they can't open their own business independently."

"I disagree," Chad says. "If you look at it that way, if she leaves, he shouldn't be able to operate the one they opened. I don't see him saying he's shutting down the one they started because she left it."

"Good point. We haven't considered that," Alex says. "Does that sway any of the folks who find the defendant in violation of noncompetition based on the document being a legal document?"

The juror who was sent home for wearing pajamas is scrolling through her phone.

Alex rests their hands on the table. This is clearly making them uncomfortable. "Juror Three…Do you need a break?"

"Oh, no," she says, still absorbed by her phone screen. "I think this is going to help. Here it is. *This* is a contract." She slides the phone to her right and it circles the table. When the phone is in front of me, I scroll a bit. It's pages and pages of tiny print. When I reach the bottom, there is a place for a signature. I pass the phone along, and when it gets back to Juror Three, she waggles it. "And that's just for one streaming service. I don't think something is a contract unless there's a bunch of lawyer mumbo jumbo, so much that you don't even read it all. Well, they would probably have read it all, but to be binding? That piece of paper doesn't cut it for me."

Sarah seems like she's contemplating something important. As she searches her thoughts, she taps her finger to her lips. Finally, she says, "I remember when my first wife and I created a contract releasing our donor of all parental rights. He said that he wouldn't ever challenge our rights as the legal parents, but we had a document drawn up. Even if we had not hired lawyers who, as you describe, wrote mumbo jumbo that I couldn't even comprehend, I would have written down my conditions in sentences and had both of us sign the paper. As a small-business owner, I was sensitive to the plaintiff, but this convinces me that the two did not create any kind of formal contract."

Alex's eyebrows shoot up in surprise, as if they didn't imagine Sarah would be one of the jurists who considered the document a legal contract.

The egg-eater grunts and mumbles, "Figures."

"Thank you for sharing your thought process with us, Sarah." The muscles in Alex's jaw jump as if they are struggling with how to respond to the egg-eater. "Would you like to respond to Sarah?"

"She's divorced, that means the marriage contract holds no meaning, so why would this contract? She was the one saying we shouldn't bring our personal biases in here. That's biased."

Juror Ten raises his hand. "I agree. This guy has lost everything. The defendant stole his girlfriend back in college and now did the same with his wife. The guy deserves a settlement."

CHAPTER TWENTY-NINE

Alex

Scooby Doo Fred has his mind made up, and his posture says he's ready to nail the defendant to the wall. Still, we don't need a unanimous vote here. As long as nine people believe it's not a contract, we can submit our verdict, but we were in a solid minority.

I scan the table, reading body language to see how Scooby Doo Fred's statement lands. We were split eight to four on the first vote, and, it being anonymous, I thought that Waverly, Vicki, and Sarah were the other three voting with me. Sarah floored me when she said the discussion had changed her mind. Crossing my fingers that the no contract side has gained more than just Sarah's vote, I say, "Maybe this is a good time to take another vote?"

Scooby Doo Fred agrees. "Let's get this over with. I'm beyond ready to wrap this up."

When nobody contradicts, I say, "Show of hands for the plaintiff proving there was a contract to breach."

Scooby Doo Fred of course raises his hand, as does the egg-eater and Juror Two. The men don't surprise me. The guy has been wronged and they have this drive to help avenge him. All have offered criticism of the defendant that focused more heavily on who she is than on the law we have been told to apply. I review my notes. Juror Four, the one woman voting that this is a contract, is the one who is reading the IN IT TOGETHER OR NOT AT ALL absolutely literally.

That this vote has flipped the script gives me a glimmer of hope. Now the no contract side needs to convince only one person that this is not a contract. But who? If the grammar lesson we were all subjected to hasn't convinced Juror Four, I don't know what would. That leaves the three men. I need one of them to change his mind, but I don't have the first idea of how to go about that and search the room for an answer. Waverly smiles encouragingly at me. Vicki looks like she's about to die of boredom. I catch Sarah's eye. She has so much more life experience than I do and hosts a podcast. She probably has strategies for mediating this kind of discussion.

I close my eyes and try to scare up confidence I don't have and remember listening to her talk about the importance of honoring voice and how difficult it is to speak up for what's right and not parrot popular opinion.

Sarah tips her head as if she's reading what's in my head. When we first met, I parroted the criticism I'd heard about her before I'd even listened to her podcast. Once I'd listened for myself, I formed my own opinion. Everyone on the jury has heard the same evidence, yet I hesitate to say that my understanding of the case is more valid than anyone else's. I scan the table, wondering how it is that the folks who think that there is a contract for Marlene to violate are so confident in explaining their position.

Together, we are supposed to serve as a jury of Marlene's peers, but having watched this process of the lawyers vying for who sits in the box makes me doubt how fair our justice system can ever be.

"I don't know where we go from here," I say, canvassing each juror in turn. "Maybe we should take a break."

Vicki surprises me by groaning. "We've been here so long already, and we only need one person to change their mind. A break is just going to prolong the agony."

The way everyone looks at me makes me feel itchy.

"I'm not the boss here. I can't make anyone change their mind."

"That's true," Sarah says calmly. "But you have valid life experience that makes you an authority. Maybe you can share how you view the evidence and why, after hearing those who argue that there is a contract, you stand by the idea that the plaintiff does not possess a contract that could be violated."

I shuffle the pages of my notepad to stall. My reasoning is so personal, which makes me doubt that it's valid.

"I'd like to hear why you believe there's no contract?" Scooby Doo Fred leans forward and rests his arms on the table, more of a challenge than concession.

That makes me chuckle inwardly because it's his argument that bothers me the most. "Actually, I keep recalling how you say the plaintiff deserves a settlement because of the things he's lost."

He nods and motions for me to continue.

"I'm guessing that each one of us here has lost something. The bigger the loss, the worse the sting, and I know from experience that the loss the plaintiff suffered stings something terrible."

I wipe my sweaty palms on my pants. Thoughts line up in my head like parachuters waiting for the signal to jump. That's what it feels like talking to this group, like I'm about to jump from a plane. A few of the people at the table feel like a safety net, but even after a week, most are vast unknowns. Would any stand by with indifference and let me plummet in free fall to the ground?

Only one way to find out.

Jump.

"About a year ago, I got dumped. I ended up in California because a cowboy friend of my parents said that it's no coincidence that people talk about getting dumped by people and horses. It can come out of nowhere, and it hurts. Even if you don't break anything visibly, it still wounds your pride. When your pride is wounded, it's real common to strike out. You want the person who hurt you to hurt, too.

"My girlfriend dumped me. Let me tell you, that was a tough fall. She was the first person I trusted when I was coming out. That's even more scary than starting a business. I risked losing her the minute I told her that I liked girls. Being with her made me believe I could do anything, be anything. She gave me the courage to be myself..." I look at Sarah for a confidence boost and plow ahead before I can chicken out. "Neither a man nor a woman. And then she dropped me. I would have loved for her to pay for my hurt and for my humiliation. So it's not hard for me to imagine the plaintiff, ass in the dirt, looking for a way to feel better and thinking that suing would help. He can't inflict the same hurt by taking her partner, but he can hit her in another way by taking away her business."

I pick up the document the plaintiff entered as evidence of a contract.

"This isn't a contract. It's a brainstorm of a dream in the roughest form. To call it anything else is to fall for a desperate person's strategy to regain his self-esteem instead of picking himself up and walking away. He was hurt. I agree. I was hurt, too, but I didn't stay in my hometown brewing up a way to get back at my ex. Should the defendant have to pay for that hurt? We saw in his financials that it's not a loss of business that's making him miserable. He's broke because of treatment he has sought for heartache. It's not really the defendant who caused that heartache—not with her business, anyway. He can't sue his spouse for breaking his heart, so he's using this piece of paper to go after her new partner. That's the way I look at it. That's why I say it's not a contract."

The room feels suspended in time. I'm shaking a bit after revealing what I did, waiting for someone to say *What do you mean, not a man or a woman?* but it doesn't seem to faze them. They are the same group I've become accustomed to. Sarah has a fist to her chest and taps it above her heart. I've touched her, and that fills me with warmth. Juror Two, sitting next to her, is as dismissive as ever, but it doesn't feel personal. The others who considered the document a contract may be contemplating. But contemplating the case. Not me. That in itself feels like a win.

"I don't know if that changes anything. Should we do another vote?"

Scooby Doo Fred clears his throat. "Can we do the next vote on paper again?"

Hope surges in me. Has he changed his mind? There is a reverent kind of silence as I pass out what I hope will be a final round of papers to the jurors. Each tosses their folded paper to the center, and when there are twelve, I pull them to me again. I take a steadying breath and start to unfold the papers, stacking them as I read, "No contract. No contract. No contract. No contract. No contract. No contract. No contract. Contract." I start the second pile, forcing myself not to glance at Juror Two. I'm sure my words did not sway her vote. "Contract." Two to seven. We need two more for a verdict. Just two more, with three slips left.

"No contract."

We only need one more.

I unfold the next slip of paper. "No contract. That's nine, folks!"

The room erupts in cheers and fists pumped into the air. One slip of paper remains in my hand. Scooby Doo Fred chins toward it. "What was that one?"

It doesn't matter, and yet, there is charged air between us. I unfold it and read the words. I meet his eye again when I say, "No contract."

He nods once and raps his knuckles on the table.

I convinced Scooby Doo Fred—the most vocal opponent, Juror Ten—to reject the idea that the brainstorm was a contract. I can hardly believe it. I convinced him plus one of the others, and it feels right. It feels like we have done something important together. I've never felt this kind of pride before, something collective like this, and I'm excited to share it with Vicki. I smile in relief. This is almost over, and I'm prepared to see her mirror my excitement.

She's smiling, but there's no joy behind it. I'm confused. She wasn't one of the four who wanted to hold the defendant liable, so why isn't she happier?

"I'll tell the bailiff we're ready to deliver the verdict," someone says.

I can't explain it, but those words echo in this weird, suspended space. Anxiety spikes through me as I realize that means I will be reading the verdict. I'm not the one on trial, so why does it feel like delivering this verdict will change everything?

The jurors stand and stretch and start to chat about inconsequential things. Vicki stays seated, arms resting on the tabletop. She is isolated in a world of her own. As if she feels my eyes on her, her expression shifts, like she's put on a mask, and she raises both thumbs. I am so ready to put this whole jury experience behind me and sink into her arms. That's what I'm thinking about as we file back into the courtroom for the last time.

I'm careful not to look at the defendant or the plaintiff, but even so, I can feel their eyes on me. I'm truly happy with the verdict we have agreed upon and nervous as all get-out as we wait for the judge to enter. I remind myself that only the jury knows I agreed to be foreperson. It's ridiculous to worry that they somehow know. At least this will be short and sweet. Once we deliver the verdict, that's it. I'll be free, which is a relief because I am so incredibly uncomfortable being in the spotlight.

CHAPTER THIRTY

Vicki

"My bailiff has advised me that the jury has reached a verdict. Who was elected foreman of the jury?" Judge Court asks. She's doing her best to appear indifferent, but like all of us, she is jittery with excitement. In a matter of minutes, Alex will know. Everything will be exposed.

I will be exposed.

Alex raises their hand. "I was elected foreperson, Your Honor."

"Fore*person*." The judge stares at them over the rim of her dark-framed reading glasses. The way Alex corrects her almost makes her break into a smile. "My apologies. Have you reached a verdict?"

"Yes we have, Your Honor," Alex says. I can hear both pride and anxiety in their voice.

"Please hand the verdict form to the bailiff."

Alex fidgets while the bailiff walks the form over for the judge to review. When they glance my way, I try to give them a reassuring smile. We hold our breath collectively until the bailiff returns the paper, and the judge instructs Alex to read the verdict.

"We the jury, in the case of Aschbran versus Menjivar, render the following verdict. To the question of a legal contract with a noncompetition clause existing between the parties, we find that there was no legal contract. Therefore, there can be no breach of contract and no damages, financial or emotional."

The defendant looks stunned. Her lawyer leans forward to whisper in her ear, and the defendant throws her arms around her, tears streaming down her face. The plaintiff argues with his lawyer, but the judge is smiling broadly. This is all going according to plan.

Alex starts to lower themself to their seat when Judge Court motions for them to remain standing. "Just a moment, Juror Eleven." She shuffles through the papers in front of her. "Alexandria Verita."

"Yes?" Alex says, a question in their voice. They obviously thought their job was finished.

"You said this was your first experience serving on a jury."

"I did."

She removes her glasses, carefully folds them, and sets them on the bench. "I didn't mention it as the trial started, but this is also my first experience as a judge."

Alex turns their gaze to the jury, and it is so difficult to keep the neutral face I must as the truth is unveiled.

"You see, while you believed you were being filmed for a documentary about what it is like to serve on a jury, the subject of this show is really you."

Alex looks from defendant to plaintiff to bailiff to each of us in the jury box. The cameras are trained on them as the moment draws out.

"Every person in this room is an actor. None of what we have done in the past week was real. The case was fictitious. The lawyers? Actors. The courthouse? Well, it was a courthouse once, but it has not seen a real case in years."

Alex takes hold of the wall of the jury box in front of them as the truth settles in. The moment they compute what the judge's words mean about me is painfully clear.

"Actors," Judge Court says as Alex's eyes land on mine.

"Actor?" they whisper so softly I can barely hear them. Sarah rushes to Alex and tells them they can sit. I reach for their hand, but they snatch it away.

The judge continues, "And though none of this proceeding was real, humanity was on trial this week. We live in a time of apathy. People draw conclusions of innocence and guilt largely based on appearance, yet you rejected that. Your keen attention to detail kept our writers on their toes as they scripted the court case."

Instead of enjoying the praise the judge delivers, the words seem to pain Alex.

You lied, they mouth.

"Alex," I whisper.

It's like my voice stings them. They take a step away from me.

"She hasn't gotten to the best part," I say, trying to take their hand again, trying to hold them in place. They step out of my reach. Their breath is coming fast, and I'm afraid that they are going to hyperventilate.

Everyone in the room begins to applaud and cheer. Alex wavers on their feet, and Sarah is there to stabilize them.

"I need to get out of here."

This isn't what the producers had in mind at all. The next shot requires Alex to take the stand and accept the prize the show has for them. Even we're not privy to what that includes. Cash? A car? Luxury vacation? Judge Court doesn't have a chance to invite them up. They slide past me, giving me as wide a berth as possible. Sarah stays close, her arm under Alex's elbow.

I stand to follow, but Sarah extends her hand. "I think it would be best to give them some room."

I am helpless as Sarah ushers Alex out. The courtroom has gone from raucous applause to utter silence.

"Shit," the judge says. "What just happened?"

"Should we keep filming?" one camera operator asks.

Most folks on the set have an earpiece and are listening to the behind-the-scenes crew discuss what the next step is. We learn that Alex and Sarah have left the building. A crew member is positioned by the door to alert the film crew when they return, so the camera operators remove their headphones and walk away from their equipment.

My fellow jurors are staring at me, and what am I supposed to say? *Uh-oh. I guess I messed that up!* Best to stay in character and pray that Sarah can talk Alex back into court. "What?" I say, channeling my character's boredom with the whole process.

"What did she say to you before she freaked out?" Chad asks. "What's wrong with her?"

"Nothing," I say, though I clearly hear Alex's mouthed words *You lied* on loop. "And it's they/them. Alex uses they/them pronouns, remember?"

Chad rolls his eyes. "It's not like she's here to notice."

"*I* notice," I growl. "I gotta pee."

As bad as I want to find Alex and explain, there's no chance the crew will let me outside. I visit the restroom even though I don't need it and stare at myself in the mirror. Sarah warned me not to get close, but did I listen? No. I can't even meet my own eye.

Of all the brainstormed scenarios, the worst is playing out before me. My gut warned me that this was likely to happen, but I convinced myself that the connection between us would override hurt or anger. I allowed myself to imagine surprise, dumbfounded laughter, or them throwing their arms around me. I've imagined a scenario that would allow us to talk, so sure of myself that I've rehearsed what I want to say to them. My heart sinks as that opportunity leaves the building with Alex.

I tell myself they'll understand when Sarah explains.

But what if they don't come back in? Could that happen? Could they give the middle finger to the show and refuse to come back? Probably not. They have to finish the show, but if they come back solely because they legally have to, they'll probably be pissed.

I pull out my phone and pull up our text exchange ending with my *See you tmrw.*

I'm so so sorry.

I hit send.

Can we please talk?

I hit send and return to the hallway to wait. I'm so badly tempted to go after Alex and Sarah, but I have to listen to Sarah. She would summon me if Alex wanted to see me. *Please, please, please, please, please,* my brain whispers on loop. Please talk to me. Please listen. Please understand. Please don't push me away. Please don't let this be the end.

CHAPTER THIRTY-ONE

Alex

I can't stop moving, like I need to stay in motion to avoid being a target. That's how I feel, like I'm a target. I've been a target for the last week.

It all makes sense now. How did I not see it? All the stuff that seemed like I was on a freaking reality TV show. Now I find out that I *have* been on a reality TV show. I'm sure it was in the fine print of stuff I filled out at the beginning, the fine print that nobody reads.

This is irony, isn't it? That the whole case was based on whether the defendant—fake defendant!—had breached a contract, which was nowhere near believable. It was never meant to be. How stupid am I? And I'm sure I've signed papers that say I am going to see this thing through, and I never want to step foot in the courtroom again.

"I'm not going back in there," I say to Sarah. I'm holding on to my head with both hands, which must look ridiculous. I stop and examine my surroundings, my heart rate spiking. Are they filming this, too? I don't see anyone, so I resume my pacing, hands holding my head because if I don't, it might float right off my shoulders.

"Take all the time you need," Sarah says in her soothing therapist voice. "It's a lot to take in."

I turn to face her. "You knew about all of it. You're an actress?"

"No. The show reached out to me because of my podcast. They were cognizant of the possible psychological effects and hired me to ensure that no ethical boundaries were breached. Your emotional health was always at the forefront."

"Even when you were manipulating me?" I ask.

"Me as an individual, you mean? Or me as part of the production?"

"You, Sarah. You manipulated me when I was ready to call for a break. You told me to walk everyone through how I saw the evidence. You encouraged me to share my life experience."

"But it wasn't predetermined. We were not told at the beginning of filming who would win."

"You were told to make me foreperson, I'm guessing."

She purses her lips. "Yes. That was manipulated. It was important that your morals and values drove the verdict."

"For a completely fake case." I pull at my hair. "God, I'm so stupid! All of you must have been laughing at how gullible the Kentucky hick was for the past week. I can't believe this!" Has Vicki been laughing at me? What has motivated her this past week?

"No one is laughing at you. Everyone on this project admires you greatly. The judge will explain how influential you were to the trial."

I can't go back in there. I can't look at Vicki when she's been acting this whole time. A memory from the weekend flashes in my mind. Her brother called her Emelynn. How did I not see through her explanation? How was I that stupid? "What happens if I don't go back in there?"

Sarah pauses so long that I wonder if she's waiting for instruction. I flush cold and then hot. "Are you wearing an earpiece? Are they talking to you right now?"

She lifts her hair and turns her head to both sides to show me that there isn't anything in either ear. "Many of the actors have them, but I took mine out when you asked me to talk to you. I am essentially your therapist."

That helps me start to relax. But then I remember Vicki. Emelynn. I shake my hands, trying to get rid of the tingly feeling.

"Why don't you want to go back in?"

"I already felt like everyone was staring at me. I told myself that I was crazy, and now I know I was right. Everyone *was* staring at me, and when I go back in, they're all going to be staring at me, and now it's even worse because I left. Doesn't that ruin everything?"

"I'm sure they can fix it when they're editing. They can't possibly use all the hours of footage they have."

"A freaking TV show. Unbelievable."

"You responded to the call for a documentary about jury duty. So you were okay with the idea of being filmed, yes?"

"That part, sure. I wasn't exactly comfortable with the cameras, but I thought that we were all normal people listening to a real case. But none of it mattered? And everyone is an actor working with a script I don't know about? I thought I was doing my civic duty, not being duped into a spotlight I never wanted."

Honestly, that it was a documentary was part of why I replied to the summons. I mean, who in the world watches documentaries? The possibility of anyone ever seeing or hearing about it seemed close to nil. I couldn't imagine anyone being interested in watching a documentary about what it's like being a juror, not a single person. I thought maybe a law class somewhere would use it, but even in that scenario, I felt sorry for the audience that would be forced to watch it.

Now I'm imagining my family finding out about this, the people in my town. Lilian. I feel sick.

"I completely understand," Sarah says. She sits at a picnic bench and crosses her legs. She doesn't behave like she's in a hurry to get me back inside.

I continue to pace, my mind spinning on Vicki being an actress. Has her flirting all been part of the script? I pause, turning to Sarah. "If you're essentially my therapist, does that mean that stuff I tell you is confidential? Or do you have to tell the director or producer because they're the ones paying you?"

"Anything you say is confidential," she assures me.

I want to tell her about Vicki, but I'm also embarrassed, and I'm not sure I can trust her.

"It's understandable that you are feeling guarded right now. It's a lot to digest. You can give yourself time."

I imagine walking away today. I have my car keys in my pocket. In minutes, I could be gone.

But where would I go?

And if I leave, none of these people can finish their job. Because of me, everything would grind to a halt. If I suck it up and go back inside, it can be finished, and I can walk away for good. I realize that the longer I wait, the more difficult it will be to return.

I feel utterly alone in this moment. I thought I was alone when I moved to LA and knew exactly one person, Tom. In the last week, many of the people on the jury had started to seem like friends. To lose that is a huge blow. I wish I could talk to Vicki about it, but Vicki doesn't exist.

"Fuck," I whisper, sitting down next to Sarah. I rest my elbows on my knees and my head in my hands. "Fuck. Who the fuck am I supposed to trust? Welcome to LA."

Sarah rummages in her bag and hands me her business card. "I already wrote my personal cell on the back. I don't expect you to trust me, but you can. I'm on your side and have been from the beginning. You can call me anytime, day or night."

I sit up and study her. From the podcasts I've listened to, I think she's trustworthy. I want to trust her. But I also trusted everything that the "judge" and "lawyers" told me. "What's left today?" I ask.

"I'm not sure," she says. "I could find out."

"No," I say quickly. I can't wait out here alone knowing I'm going back in. I don't want to give them a chance to try to get information out of Sarah, even if she did say that our interactions are confidential. I smooth my sweaty palms on my pants. "Okay. Let's go. The sooner I go back in there, the sooner I can leave?"

She nods and stands. As I turn, she touches my arm gently. "Is there anything else, Alex? Is there another reason you are reluctant to go back to the courthouse?"

She's studying me so intently that I have to look away. She must know about Vicki. Just as I thought I'd hit bottom, the world shifts under my feet once again. "No. Nothing," I say flatly, turning away.

"Okay," she says, but she doesn't seem convinced. "Day or night, you can talk to me about anything."

I won't be talking to Sarah Cooper after this, I vow to myself. I won't be talking to anyone.

CHAPTER THIRTY-TWO

Vicki

I am so relieved when Alex and Sarah return to the building. I know that Alex saw me sitting on the bench by the courtroom, but they turn away too quickly for me to convey anything. Sarah's expression says plenty but nothing I am eager to own. She's not alone in thinking that Alex's reaction is tied to me. I can't face that right now. I need to talk to Alex, but the way they avoided looking at me doesn't give me a whole lot of optimism.

The bailiff sticks his head out and points to me. "Showtime."

I join the rest of the cast for take two of the reveal. It's eerily silent in the courtroom as I make my way to the jury box. I try to make eye contact with Alex, but they've withdrawn deep into their protective shell.

"Alex," Judge Court says. "First of all, let me introduce myself. My name is Jennifer Fisher. Let's pick up where we left off, me having told you that humanity was on trial this week. Are you feeling better?"

Alex nods.

"Okay. I know this is all a shock. If you could stand again, we'll pick up at humanity being on trial." She pauses and glances at each camera operator to make sure everything is on track before going back to the script. "We live in a time of apathy. People draw conclusions of innocence and guilt largely based on appearance, yet you rejected that. Your keen attention to detail kept our writers on their toes as they scripted the court case.

"It was your question about the plaintiff's girlfriend in college that gave our writers the idea to bring in his ex-wife as the defendant's girlfriend, which dovetailed perfectly with the theme we wanted to explore. How many times are trials decided by which party belongs to the dominant gender, culture, or sexuality? When Waverly—her name is Jean by the way…"

Jean smiles and waves at Alex. They nod in acknowledgment, but their gaze purposefully skips me. I get it. They didn't want to be in the spotlight. It must be taking all their strength to sit and listen to the things the judge wants to share for the wrap-up episode.

"Jean's character pushed to equalize the genders, and you defended her. She made up all sorts of things about the stones in the room, and you defended her. You even called me out and convinced me that I should honor her knowledge of the energy my stone contained." Judge Court removes the blue stone from her pocket and then returns it. "Defending her beliefs was more important to you than getting in trouble with an authority figure. I appreciated that.

"You didn't rat her out as the one wearing patchouli when you had just met, and you didn't even sacrifice Juror Nine for his fart bombs!" She goes into detail about how they managed both the audio and olfaction to replicate the fart.

"And now I'm sure you'd love to see behind the scenes," Judge Court says with her practiced authority.

Alex agrees. They still look shell-shocked.

"Okay," the judge says. "Before I adjourn court for the last time, I do have one other formality to wrap up, if you'll join me at the bench."

They have no idea how much they are asking of Alex. I am about to step in and tell them that it would be better for Alex if they quietly collect footage unveiling the hidden cameras and staff and let Alex go, but I can't draw more attention to myself, to us.

The bailiff directs Alex to the witness stand. The judge leans down to pick up one of those ridiculous human-sized checks. They hand it to Alex and work with the camera operators to get the best shot of her, Alex, and the check for fifty thousand dollars, money that I hope will be a game changer for Alex.

With the thumbs-up from the camera operators that they have the shot the writers want, Judge Court starts clapping, and everyone in the courtroom claps with her. The defendant and her lawyer approach as Alex leaves the stand, gushing thanks.

"You absolutely saw me," I hear Marlene say to Alex before she hugs them. Remembering how Alex asked me if they could hug me, I want to run interference and tell her to ask for permission, but it's too late, and Ms. Saqsaq is hugging them too. Everyone starts clapping, and Alex looks utterly miserable. I push my way out of the jury box and over to Alex before anyone else can even think about hugging them.

I am standing so close I could touch them, but I keep my hands to myself and settle for breathing in their mountain scent. It's similar to what I smell when I manage to get away on a hike and escape the city pollution: morning sunlight warming dewy sage.

They look at me. Finally. I will them to hear the loud and clear *I'm sorry* in my head that I don't dare mouth, knowing how close the cameras will be on every single reaction Alex has. I am not a breath of fresh air for them. Their expression conveys that I am part of the pollution they would like to escape as quickly as possible.

In a beat, the moment is over, Judge Court ushering us into the next courtroom, which resembles the control room of a studio show. The ten people in the room stand up and push their headphones from their ears. They clap as well, and Alex grows even more stiff, another layer of armor clinking into place. They invite Alex to peruse the feed they have from the many hidden cameras around the building that have been collecting footage in addition to the cameras we all accepted as being part of the documentary. As the group follows the judge to the holding room where Alex and I first met to check out where the cameras are hidden, Sarah falls in stride with me.

"What's going on?" she asks me.

"Nothing is going on." That is strictly the truth. I have been super good about keeping my distance since Alex and I kissed.

As everyone files into the holding room, Sarah takes hold of my elbow to keep me in the hall. "The way you're evading the question most certainly means something happened, which you know you should have divulged to the team."

"I can sort it out with Alex when we break for the day. I'm sure we'll be able to sort it out."

Sarah doesn't believe me, and why should she? I've made an utter mess out of this. I convince myself all I have to do is get through the end of this filming day and then I'll have a chance to explain how I never intended to hurt Alex, but as the day and the filming continues, Alex evades me.

I check my phone.

They haven't answered my text.

This day is not about me, though. It's about Alex and how much everyone wants to cozy up to them. It's not because they want to latch themselves to Alex because they are a star. It's because everyone who has worked with them this last week has recognized what a special soul Alex has. I can feel the collective admiration when we are corralled in a room they've set up with seats in two rows. Since this mimics the setup of the jury box, we naturally take the seats we've been sitting in for a week.

At first, the actors clamor to share what it was like from their perspective, the times they worried that they had blown the show's cover. "I had my speakerphone on," Juror Five says, "and my boyfriend asked how much longer I'd be on set. I was sure you'd heard."

Alex shakes their head, the fakest smile I've ever seen glued in place.

"How are you processing all of this, Alex?" Nick asks.

"Um…" Alex scans the actors who surround them as though they're seeing them all for the first time. "I know Sarah's name has to actually be Sarah, but Chad? Waverly?"

"Our names for the show," Jean answers. "Mine is supposed to go with my woo-woo energy." She lifts her arms and sways them like she's listening to a love song at a rock concert or communing with nature in a hilltop meadow.

"So all that stuff about not being able to sit next to a Virgo? Or balance the energy in the courtroom? Is that really your jam?"

She cackles. "Oh, no. The writers had a lot of fun with that." Jean is beaming. "They wrote all that stuff about energy and crystals. I'm not even vegetarian."

Everyone laughs. Do they even notice that Alex doesn't?

To Darren, who they knew as Chad, they ask, "Do you even play pickleball?"

"I learned for the show! It's fun, isn't it? I got so into it, I bought my own paddle."

Alex simply nods as the revelations of all the show has crafted is unveiled. The more they reveal, the sicker I feel. How are they unfazed by Alex's clear discomfort? I want out, to have never taken part in this show and the deception. But if I hadn't done the show, I wouldn't have met Alex, and I'm absolutely certain I was meant to meet Alex.

Even though I'm sitting right next to them physically, every minute pushes me further away, like they have become the superstar the show set them up to be, someone untouchable. This is not the only crowd that will be clamoring for Alex's attention. When the show comes out, there will be plenty more people jostling for their attention. Will they even consider the time we spent together when the filming is over?

CHAPTER THIRTY-THREE

Alex

I am so done with this nightmare, but it refuses to end. I thought it was bad when they started pointing out where they'd hidden cameras. They pointed to corners and mirrored windows where they filmed so much more than I ever imagined. Every break we took when I thought I could relax off camera has been captured. From multiple angles. I start to sift through my memories from the week, trying to remember if I revealed anything terribly embarrassing, but I can't deal with the overwhelming possibilities.

They wore microphones to record conversations I thought were private.

Knowing that Sarah didn't have any wires on her when we spoke outside keeps that seed of anxiety from taking root. And they can't have placed a camera in the bathroom, which gives a tiny bit of relief, but it's a small comfort compared to the enormity of the revelation that the entire show has been focused on me.

This isn't what I wanted. I left Kentucky because I was tired of the way I stuck out, tired of being looked at, and now everyone is gawking at me like I'm a hero for using common sense with the information they spoon-fed to us in the trial. How hard is it for people to make a decision based on facts and not prejudice?

In our sit-down rehash, Nick clued me in on the level of fucked up manipulation involved. I'm supposed to be proud of myself for not letting the jury find in favor of the plaintiff just because he comes across as a respectable, middle-class white dude represented by his clean-cut model minority.

We're supposed to be celebrating the fact that I didn't allow the verdict to be skewed by Islamophobia or homophobia.

"You were so unfazed by Fatima's hijab that we had to think fast to create another way she'd come across as less competent."

I bite my tongue before I lecture them about how stupid it is to set up boys against girls with the assumption that boys always win. This doesn't feel like a victory. It feels fucking depressing that I'm still living in a time where they can fairly anticipate that the typical American will need to be convinced that a woman isn't guilty. That whole thing about innocent until proven guilty only works for dudes. And on top of that, they're piling on how surprising it is for a woman to be competent at a "man's" job.

"We do regret having her sing 'Baby Shark.' It got stuck in everyone's head every time she hummed it!"

Everyone is laughing again, basking in how much fun this has been for the actors and film crew. I'm sure it will make for great TV, especially with the bewildered Kentuckian at the center, trying to talk some sense into the bozo Californians.

I think the worst of it has to be over when the recap is finally done, but Nick doesn't let me go with the others. Instead, he informs me that there are a few things I need to sign before I leave for the day.

How can this not be over?

"Alex!"

I sit down across from yet another person I've never seen before who has been watching me for a week. Had Nick not said I was signing papers, I would think I was meeting an actress from the way she sweeps her hair behind her shoulder and smiles at me with perfect white teeth.

"We could not be happier with how this all turned out. I have to tell you that all my staff was rooting for you when we prepared the packets of applicants. We loved your little hometown in Kentucky, and that little note you wrote about having an option to check a box to decline to state male or female on the form was so perfect! Whether you were advocating for yourself, or even better, you were so moved as an ally that you would stick your neck out and speak up? I knew that would translate into your taking the case seriously."

My feelings have been stretched and pulled and stomped on to the extent that I don't even know how to react to this. "Or even better, if I'm moved as an ally? Does that mean that it makes for better TV to have someone straight standing up for the LGBTQ-plus community?"

"You must be exhausted," she says, waving off my question. "I realize it's been an extremely long day. Before you leave, we need to review the contract you signed and the next phase of filming."

"Filming?" I ask. "I thought this was it. I thought I was done today."

She giggles. "No. Now we go into post. The editors will reach out when they are ready for your reflection on content. It won't necessarily be with the cast. It depends on what content they want to flesh out with how you were feeling in the moment. That can be done in solo talking-head interviews. Once it airs, though, you'll be one of the cast members who tour to promote. We're hoping to generate interest that will get interviews."

"But I didn't sign up for that."

She quirks her eyebrows as if she can't believe what I said. "Yes, you did! It's in the contract. Like Casey said, nobody reads the fine print! And down there in the fine print, you'll find the clause that says your prize money is contingent on filming the remaining content as well as participating in the promotion."

I'm never signing anything else in my life.

I'm sure they can't imagine anyone walking away from fifty thousand dollars, but I am sorely tempted. The extra cash would be nice. That's why I signed up for the documentary in the first place, but that was before I had Cesar to recommend me for jobs. Now I don't need this money. I could walk out of here and back to my life. As soon as I think this, I realize it's not true. Whether I walk right now or not, they will air the footage of me they have. How successful is the show likely to be without their big finale? The show's success matters to Vicki. I correct myself. The success of the show matters to Emelynn. I can't have the show bombing on my conscience, so I nod. "Okay. Now can I go?"

"This is the last thing for you to sign." She swivels a piece of paper around on the table to face me. "Until the show is public, you cannot utter a word. You cannot tell your friends or your parents. No social media. The only people you can talk to are those who are already affiliated. The other cast members, Sarah Cooper, needless to say. She is on our payroll in a professional capacity and has said that you can meet with her anytime. She was adamant when we brought her in that you have a way to process this experience. Any questions for me?"

Until she said I couldn't talk about it, I had no urge to talk to anyone. Now that I'm trying to review the document she's asked me to sign, one that has more words than anyone could read and understand in the amount of time she expects me to slap on a signature, I want to call someone immediately.

Then I weigh all I would have to explain. Even without this restraint, I can't imagine trying to describe what I've been through.

So much for never signing anything ever again. I'm ambivalent about signing, but putting this day behind me takes priority. My stomach leaden, I add my signature and push it back to her.

"So excited to see how this shapes up!" She's not even looking at me as she tucks the papers into a manila envelope. I laugh silently when it hits me that she didn't even introduce herself.

I'm relieved the hallway is empty when I step out. I keep my guard up, happy to be able to nod and smile at the few people I don't recognize, people I would have ignored yesterday, thinking they were in the building for another trial, who I now realize are part of the behind-the-scenes crew.

Evening has already muted the day when I leave the building. I easily spot my orange car in the parking lot. The way the day unfolded, I imagined Vicki would be leaning against my car, waiting for me to finish the paperwork, an apology on her lips.

I pause at the curb, disappointed but also relieved, because what am I supposed to say to her? I haven't even read the texts that came in when I was talking to Sarah. That's a clear message that I need space. It stings a bit that she didn't try harder. I can't be surprised when I don't even know if anything I've learned about her is real or not.

It's only when I'm unlocking the door that I notice her car parked several spaces down. She's in the driver's seat, her eyes on me. I sling my backpack to the passenger seat and toss my keys on the driver's seat. She waited for me. The gesture makes the back of my throat tighten. I do not want to be emotional in front of her. I cling desperately to my anger. She knowingly lied to me for an entire week. She invited me to her home and lied to me. I have so many questions, but I'm not even sure I want her answers.

CHAPTER THIRTY-FOUR

~~Vicki~~ Emelynn

Alex is standing by their car, and it's all I can do to stay in mine. I will not pressure them. I don't even know if they've read the texts I sent. After everything that's happened today, I won't force them to talk if they're not ready.

I silently will them to want to talk to me, even if it's to yell at me. It's too painful to consider the fact that they could get into that Orange Beast and disappear from my life altogether. Unlikely, since the show requires more work, but I have to prepare myself for the very real possibility that they will hate me for my part. There is no smile when they drop their keys into the front seat and walk to my car, but my heart swells nonetheless, and I step out of my car to face the music.

They stop out of my reach, hands buried in their pockets.

We stand in silence in the soft evening light, and they are exhausted. It's apparent in both their posture and expression. This has been a long day for me, and I came in prepared for the reveal. They must be reeling.

I opt to skip asking how they are. I don't want to ask for too much. I say, simply, "Hi."

They bob their head in acknowledgment.

There is so much I long to say. I want a chance to explain everything, but I worry that every word I utter could be used to build a wall between us. When the silence has stretched to the point of painful, I know it's up to me to speak first. I've already texted that I'm sorry. As bad as I feel and as much as I want to explain, I realize this isn't actually about me. It's about them and the impact all of this has had on them. "I hurt you. I was part of this thing created to manipulate you, and I regret participating in something that hurt you."

I itch to touch them, even to rest my hand on their shoulder, but I have no right to be in their space like that.

They suddenly turn to scan the parking lot. "Can they film out here? Is this part of the plan? They thought it would be fun to put in a love interest?"

"It was never like that," I'm quick to assert. "Some of the writers…" I falter. I'm reluctant to admit that I'd been tempted to let what was developing between us happen on camera.

"Some of the writers what, *Emelynn*?"

The way they say my name punches me in the gut. I remember how it sounded in their mouth when Cesar accidentally used my real name. It was only four days ago, but the tone in their voice makes it feel far removed.

"Some of the writers picked up on the chemistry between us and wanted to script around it," I admit. I cannot hide anything, as hard as it is to be honest. "But Sarah said no way."

"Was that before or after you kissed me?"

"Before," I say quickly.

"And you did it anyway."

"I did. And I know it sounds messed up because you thought I was Vicki, but it was absolutely me kissing you. Emelynn."

They arch one of their perfect eyebrows.

"I know. I was in character. I know how it sounds, but I tried as hard as I could to be honest with you."

"That's why you broke up with your fake boyfriend."

"Exactly! I didn't want you to believe I was the kind of person who would fool around on her boyfriend."

"So do you date guys? Or was it your character who dated guys?"

"I date…whoever. Gender isn't my priority. I got rid of Vicki's boyfriend because I couldn't lie to you. That storyline was supposed to get fleshed out by the relationship advice you could offer, but I couldn't do that. What I told you about breaking up with my boyfriend because I was developing feelings for you, that was true. I forced the writers to let my character be closer to who I really am. Essentially, I'm still the person you got to know over the last week. Only my name is different."

"Cesar said you could do better than your boyfriend. Is he talking about a real person, or was he in on this whole charade?"

"He knows we're working on a show, but nothing specific. The producers have kept a tight lid on it."

"How could I have met Emelynn if even your brothers knew you were playing Vicki? Your brothers knew. So they'll lie for you. Not exactly comforting, Emelynn."

I'm trying to convince myself that it's a good thing that they keep saying my real name, but I can't deny how bad it looks that the lie extends to my family. "I wanted to help you."

"Or you saw a way to get more screen time and grabbed it. I'm guessing them filming me at your house was your brilliant idea? You'll be quite the star."

"I wanted to spend time with you. It had everything to do with you and nothing to do with the show."

"You lied to me. You went along with every idea they had to make a TV show. Do you have any idea how messed up that is? And the only people I can talk to are the ones who trapped me here. And you know who I want to talk to? Vicki. I really liked her, and she doesn't exist, and I can't trust the person who does exist. I don't trust you, Emelynn."

The past tense hurts, but I can't argue with a thing they've said. "Thank you for talking to me. I already texted you, but I wanted to make sure you heard me say I'm sorry. I'm so, so sorry."

"Yeah." They sound exhausted. "I am, too."

I am helpless as they turn and walk back to their car. It's

too dark to see if they even check the rearview mirror as they drive away, leaving me standing alone. I hiccup as the painful realization that they may never forgive me settles in my gut. Tears prick at my eyes, and I press my palms against them. I will not cry. At least, not here in the parking lot.

I am not exactly up for driving, but on the off chance that Alex is correct about cameras being on the parking lot, I have to get out of here. They don't get tears from me. Since there's a good chance Cesar and Mateo are still working on the house, I keep driving, taking random turns, each one reminding me of the choices I made to put myself here. "Fuck," I curse myself. I could have avoided all of this if I'd helped Alex call a tow truck instead of volunteering my brother.

But they looked so lost that day. I had to help. But I didn't have to include them in dinner. It's Cesar's fault they ended up painting at the house, but I sense that he was right, that it would have been harder for Alex to accept help with their car without being able to do something in return. I get the sense they would feel uncomfortable being indebted to me or my brother.

I should have listened to Sarah and let them put in an alternate when Alex caught us talking about how I had crossed a line. I let this alternate version play out where Alex finishes the jury experience without me there. The filming would not have left the courthouse. Maybe that would have contained the sense of betrayal. In that scenario, had I been waiting in the parking lot, would they have approached me, relieved that it was all over?

"I couldn't stay," I would have said in the alternate version. "I couldn't tell you, either, but I couldn't keep pretending because I care too much about you."

"It's so fucked up," I imagine Alex saying.

"So fucked up. But it's over now."

And they would wrap their arms around me, and everything would feel right again.

CHAPTER THIRTY-FIVE

Alex

A whole weekend goes by without any contact from Emelynn. I'm both relieved and disappointed. It makes sense for her to give me space to absorb everything, but it makes me feel completely alone. I try not to ruminate on how differently I imagined the weekend after the trial going. I'd hoped the end of the trial would bring us closer together, not push us miles apart. I could contact Sarah, but she has to know what happened between me and Emelynn during the filming, so I can't trust her.

Monday stings even more. I miss the routine of showing up to jury duty to spend the day with the same people, even Scooby Doo Fred. Damn. It felt like such a victory to sway his vote, and it wasn't even real. Another reason to be grateful I don't have to report for the fill-in filming yet, but it leaves me at loose ends. I felt so alone when I first moved to LA, but this is staggeringly worse. At least when I first arrived, if I'd wanted to call someone back home, I could have. I rarely call my parents or even turn to them for comfort, but knowing I cannot call and tell them how scrambled my brain is makes me want to call them.

Everywhere I go, I'm convinced the camera crew has followed me. I suspect that the checker at the grocery store is extra chatty with me because she's trying to lead me into revealing something about my life. I sense hidden cameras everywhere. When I tank up my car, I stand to the side of the pump, sure that the freaky screen that comes to life would record my every move.

I try to tell myself that I'm being paranoid, that nobody gives a fuck about me pumping gas, but then I remember the number of times that I felt uncomfortable filming jury duty and told my gut to shut up. I don't trust my own judgment anymore.

The worst part is not being able to talk to Vicki. Having confided in her the most during that week, my instinct is to reach out to her when I feel like a camera is following me. I pull up her number and scroll through the messages. It's like pulling a Band-Aid off an abrasion and finding it unchanged, still raw and painful.

I hear her saying that Emelynn and Vicki were essentially the same people, and I toy with the idea of changing her name in my contacts. Would that make it feel less like the floor has dropped out from underneath me? I wonder if Sarah knows Emelynn well enough to be able to confirm or deny that I essentially met and interacted with Emelynn, just under the name Vicki.

Didn't I ask for this same kind of grace from Lilian when I cut my hair short and started binding my chest? I argued that presenting more masc didn't change who I was on the inside. The thing is, I wanted to share with her a more real version of who I am. Emelynn willingly shaped a false version of herself. I'm supposed to feel happy that she broke up with her fake boyfriend?

Again, I have to wonder if breaking up with her fake boyfriend was merely an angle to develop a storyline that involved her more. She is an actress. I'm certain that she'll benefit from the exposure of the show. As much as I would like to believe that she was motivated by genuine affection for me, I can't allow myself to be stupid on top of being gullible.

These notions compete throughout the week as I work on a job I got through a contact of Cesar's. I methodically cut the edges and start rolling in the details, filling in dueling narratives, one defending and forgiving Emelynn, and the other cautioning and shunning her. I am both physically and mentally exhausted by the end of each day, which is typically good as I can crash out without my thoughts keeping me awake.

Friday evening, I'm completely wrung out by the time I finish packing my gear in the back of the station wagon and the car won't turn over. Again.

"I'm going to use my prize money to buy a new car," I snap as I slump against the steering wheel. I rest my forehead against it, remembering how Vicki came to help me with her shiny black car. That was the breach where Vicki strayed so far from the script that she had to rewrite her character. Would I feel as betrayed as I do now had she offered to sit with me as I waited for roadside assistance to come tow my car? I have so many questions and I know I'm not strong enough to resist Emelynn if I ask for answers.

I'm so freaking far into remembering when I started to fall for Vicki that I even hear her tapping at the window. I don't know what made me think I was strong enough to move to California and strike out on my own. I want to be home where Daddy can drive out in his truck and get the old car going.

"Alex! You passed out in there?"

My head snaps up. Someone is standing outside my car. So many emotions rush through me when I recognize Cesar. Relief that he can fix my car and has magically appeared when I need him. Shame that I'm driving a car that refuses to start. Embarrassment that Emelynn is sure to hear about this. I want to disappear.

"Oh, good. You're not dead." He angles his phone toward me. "I was about to call…Em…my sister and tell her you were passed out."

Since I still can't trust my window, I motion for him to step back so I can get out of the car.

"Didn't I tell you to bring this to me? You need to replace the carburetor and an old car like this?" He's shaking his head. "The ducting is probably all torn up or broken. I can replace all that, but not out here on the street."

"You did, but I can't."

"Are you serious right now?"

"I'll bring it to you when I can afford it. Maybe. I don't know. It might be time for a new car." Or to go home, my inner voice supplies.

The way he studies me makes me miss Emelynn's gaze. "Pop the hood and turn on your flashlight for me."

"Cesar..."

"Stop. You've got to get home."

"What are you even doing here?"

He motions toward the house before busying himself in the engine. "Edgar ran into something tricky with the electrical inside and asked me to check it out. I promise I'm not spying on you."

I cross my arms. I'm about to ask if Emelynn has told him what happened, but she has to have signed a nondisclosure clause as well. Am I allowed to ask how she is?

He glances at me on his way to his truck to retrieve some tools. "You okay? You look all shook up."

I can't tell where I intersect with Cesar. Who does he think I am if I call his sister Vicki?

He steps back from the engine. "Try it again."

I pull the choke, depress the clutch, and crank the engine. It sputters but doesn't catch.

"This would be easier in my garage."

"I'm sorry."

"No. I get it. I don't know what's going on, only that my sister says she signed some paper and can't tell us anything. It's probably the same with you?"

"It is."

He tinkers around a bit more. "You still working together?"

"For a while longer." I think I'm okay to say that much. "Does she talk about it at all?"

He tips his head side to side, considering. "She says this project is going to be big. That we'll like it. Or, that's what she said when she first got the job. She seems pretty mad about it now, which is why I was wondering if you're okay. I thought maybe the director was being a dick or something."

"It's kind of more than the director."

"You hoping it launches your acting career, too? That why you moved out here from Kentucky?"

"No. I'm no actor. I kinda fell into this. I'll be glad when it's over."

"Is that why she stays in character when you two hang out? She's mentoring you?"

Shit. If he thinks that Emelynn is mentoring me, that means he thinks that Alex is the character I'm playing on the show. Which I am, because I'm playing me. He obviously doesn't know that Emelynn had to stay in character to keep me from finding out it was all fake. Why would she do that? At this point, I'm confusing myself and decide it's easiest to agree and hope the car starts, so I can get out of here before I say anything to reveal things I'm not supposed to. "Yeah. She's mentoring me."

"So is her character into yours? Is that why you didn't like the boyfriend she was supposed to have?"

"Oh!" My mind is spinning.

"Sorry. I'm so curious, and she says I can't ask her stuff, but it seems like she was into you. Or that's the part?"

"I'm sorry. I can't say."

"No, no. My bad. It makes sense you can't say, either." He scratches his head. "Go ahead and crank it again."

This time it turns over and relief floods through me. Cesar drops the hood back into place. "Thank you, Cesar. I owe you again." This isn't good because I don't know who to be around Cesar.

"I get the whole starving actor thing. I see how many side hustles my sister does to keep her head above water, but you have to have a reliable car. This car is going to leave you stranded again if you don't bring it to a shop. Look, I get that you're new to California and you probably think you don't have any connections here, but that's not true. My sister wants to help you, so I do, too. My brother, too. We want things to work out for you."

"I'll probably be able to get a new car when we finish filming. There's a tipping point, isn't there? When it's not worth it to keep throwing money at an old car?" I don't understand why he is so interested in helping me out when he has only met me twice, and the way things went with Emelynn, I don't see why she or her brother want to spend more of their energy on me.

"I'm probably the worst person to ask about that," he says. "A car is more than a method of transportation for me. A car is like a member of my family, so it's a priority to keep it running, no matter what. You take care of them, they take care of you."

I nod, though the concept doesn't quite mirror my family's sentiment. Theirs is more along the lines of behave as we've taught you to behave, and we'll keep you.

"Let my sister know if you want me to pick up the parts you need for a full tune-up, okay? And drive this thing straight home. If you stop for an errand, I can't guarantee it'll start again once you turn it off. Promise me that you'll set up an alternate mode of transportation until you either buy a reliable vehicle or bring the Orange Beast to me."

I thank him for getting me going again and give him my word even though I don't know how I'm going to keep any of those promises. I wish I was in a position to ask him more about how he thinks Emelynn likes me. Would she risk the show by extending the scheme into her real life because that's actually true? Or because she sees it as a way to be seen?

And just like that, I'm back into my brain circle of doubt.

CHAPTER THIRTY-SIX

Emelynn

"You should text Alex about bringing that Honda over. It needs work," Cesar says when he comes to work on the house Tuesday.

I'm feeling so high on the fumes from the solution I spray onto the paint to remove it from the brick around the fireplace that I think Cesar's talking about Alex, but why would he be talking about Alex? I am certain that I've imagined it because I can't stop thinking about them. I spend every waking minute trying to call up a magic phrase that will help them believe that they know the real me despite the fact that I was playing Vicki for a week.

"Would she sell it? I'm sure I could find a buyer for a cool old car like that. It's in super good shape for a seventy-six."

"I haven't talked to *them* about the car since you said to bring it by."

"Oh, right. Damn. I hope I didn't use the wrong pronouns. I don't think I did."

It takes me a few minutes to realize what he's said. I drop my tools and run to the other room. "You saw Alex? You talked to them? When? Where?"

"They were stuck at Edgar's jobsite. They're lucky Edgar needed another pair of eyes on the breaker box upgrade."

"Why didn't you tell me?" I am furious that I'm only finding out the day after.

"You never said you were friends. You're just doing some show together that you can't talk about. Right?"

"Cesar! They have no family here!"

"Relax, sis. I adjusted the carb, so the car will probably limp along okay. I told them not to put off bringing it in any more, but they listen about as well as you do." He grabs a glass from the cupboard and fills it with water, watching me as I take out my phone and then reconsider my instinct to text them. "You like Alex, don't you?" he asks.

"I already explained this to you. I met them on this project, and they have no support system. I feel bad for them. That's all. It was your idea to get some painting done in trade."

"You know what I'm trying to figure out?" He crosses his arms and leans against the countertop.

"Why you care so much about a car that's not yours?" I'm doing my best to appear uninterested in this conversation. The last thing I want is for him to think he can help get me together with Alex. My brother is a fixer and definitely regards my being single as something that needs fixing.

He smirks. He is a dog with a bone now. "I'm trying to figure out this whole Vicki thing, because when you told me to call you that, I thought you were practicing for a part. And you said you and Alex work together, which is why they'd call you Vicki—but then, wouldn't Alex be their part? So did I meet Alex, or is Alex a character? Because it's Alex's car you asked me to fix, right? So is it that Alex is really Alex, and Vicki is someone you think Alex will like better than who you really are?"

"You're working way too hard on this," I say, setting down my phone.

"What kind of show you work on that you can't say anything about? Are you doing porn now, and you don't want Mama and Papa to know?"

I flush red at his question. "I am not doing porn."

"You're doing porn. Is there even such a thing as queer porn?"

"Are you kidding me? Why wouldn't there be queer porn? You think that the porn industry solely churns out stuff you want to watch?"

"That's not what I mean. I get that there are a lot of different audiences and...tastes..."

"Oh my god, Cesar. Seriously? Are you gay-shaming right now? Don't you think that there are people who need validation that their desires are absolutely normal?"

"I get that. I'm not saying it's bad, I mean, well, you know how Papa reacted to that book you read. He will literally die if he finds out you're filming porn."

"Well, I'm not. Can we stop talking about this now?"

"This doesn't answer why you're in character and they are not."

"No. Because I'm not answering any questions about Alex," I snap. I don't mean to, but every day that passes that Alex doesn't talk to me is more sand under my skin.

"Because you like Alex."

"Of course I like Alex."

"I mean you *like* Alex, and you don't think they'll like you back if you're not Vicki."

How is my brother this perceptive? It hurts me that I can't talk to Cesar. I want to pour out how awful I feel, but that would not solve anything. My brother likes Alex so much that telling him about the show will only make him angry. Instead of having someone to support me, I'd have another person angry with me. Suddenly the weight of what it will be like when the show airs hits me in the gut. There is a real possibility that people will be disappointed in me after they find out about the show. I think I'd rather everyone find out I've been filming porn than know about *Civic Duty*. "We're going to stop talking about this now."

"Why won't Alex like you if you're not Vicki?" He's trying to find something plausible, but there's no way he can imagine the deception I've deliberately subjected Alex to.

He doesn't make any move to get back to work, so I try to get our conversation back on that track. "I'm finishing stripping the fireplace today. What do you think about ripping out the paneling after that?"

"I think you're dodging my question, and I want to know why when Alex likes you back. At least they liked whoever you were pretending to be, but honestly, it didn't seem very different when you were pretending to be Vicki."

"Maybe you could tell them that," I mumble.

"Aren't the two of you still working together?" His arms are crossed over his chest, accentuating the biceps he works so hard on. It's an intimidation move, like he's finally realized that my feelings are raw and he's ready to protect me.

"We're still filming the same show, but not likely at the same time anymore. We're going into post-production."

"Well, they can't ignore you forever."

"What makes you think that?"

I am anticipating a remark about how great of a catch I am when he says, "That car won't hold out forever. Unless they sell it and get a new car, they need me, and I come with you." He surprises me again when he crosses the small space of the kitchen and wraps an arm around my shoulders. "No matter what."

His words touch me so deeply that the back of my throat tightens up too much for me to say thank you. I bump my hip against his and press my head into his shoulder. He's taller than I am, and in this moment I'm comforted by his protectiveness. I want to ask him how Alex seemed when he saw them, apart from frustrated with their car, but to do so would prolong the conversation I've only now been able to squelch. I want to talk to Alex, even if it is for them to yell at me, but that is a selfish desire.

I go back to the slow task of removing paint, baffled as to why anyone would paint brick or install dark wood paneling. It is easier to think about other people's dumb choices than it is to face my own.

CHAPTER THIRTY-SEVEN

Alex

I'm not thrilled about the idea of hauling my painting gear into my room every night at the end of the day, but it beats the possibility of the Orange Beast breaking down again. Cesar's words about cars being part of the family come back to me. I'm so used to the opposite attitude: if it's not working, ditch it and get something new. Am I defensive about the car because it reminds me of all the time I spent trying to make my relationship with Lilian work? At the end, I had zero to show for all of the emotional energy I devoted to that relationship. It still stings.

It also sucks to return to Tom's ranch and admit that I need help. I want to be able to say I'm fine on my own. At least I don't have to call my parents. I slow at the last turn of the half-hour drive where pavement turns to dirt and immediately hear the heartbreaking sound that is neither horse's whinny or donkey's bray. It's somewhere in the middle and sounds like they are about to throw up a lung. It perfectly captures how I have felt since the end of the trial. I park by the house but don't bother knocking when I spot Tom pushing a wheelbarrow full of hay toward the corral.

"Want a hand?" I ask when I reach him.

"I never say no to help," he says.

I'm happy for the distraction the task offers and grateful Tom doesn't believe in small talk. My family would be grilling me about what I've been doing in Los Angeles, asking if I've seen any famous people or been offered drugs or taken up surfing. I haven't even been to the beach in the year I've lived in LA. Realizing this reminds me of how shocked Vicki...I still have to correct myself...Emelynn and Cesar were when they found out I had never been to In-N-Out Burger. If I'd told them I'd never set foot in the Pacific Ocean, no doubt they would have driven me out and made sure I put my feet in. It is too easy to imagine hanging out with Emelynn and her brothers.

I follow Tom's lead and toss flakes of hay into the feeder, enjoying how bits of green leaves fall onto the mules when they stick their faces in. When we're finished, I mimic his posture, leaning my elbows against the fence and soaking in the peaceful grinding of the mules digging into their supper.

"This sure doesn't feel like LA," I say.

"Thank god for that."

"This isn't what anyone back home pictures when they think about me being in LA." This is my speed, far, far away from Hollywood and its cameras and deception. And yet, Tom isn't my tribe. I don't fit in with the barn rats and cowboys. I figured I would continue to hang out with Emelynn and Sarah and Jean after the trial concluded. Hell, I would have even enjoyed meeting Darren on the pickleball court every once in a while.

"Nope. Nobody thinks about the ordinary people living their simple, dirty lives."

"At least, not the dirt that's all over you. I'm sure they think lots about the morally dirty Hollywood crowd."

"I got as far away from that as fast as I could," Tom says. "I did a fair share of work on the set early on. Good money. None of it worth it."

This brings to mind the wranglers who provided the animals on our set for the No Stubborn Mules "demonstration." It didn't seem much different than providing a pony for a kid's birthday party. Or providing the mules to pull a historic wagon. "How is it different than what you do with the twenty-mule team in the parade?" I ask.

He considers my question a beat before he answers. "Parade people are a great crowd. You come down the street, and they cheer for you. On the set, there's no celebration. You're there to do a job, but it's the animal that's the star, not you. You're either invisible or in the way, or you're fucking up the whole shot because the animal didn't perform during the same take that the actor did it right, but they can't take it out on the star. And then you've got this animal that can do incredible shit, but no other studio will consider using it and then the goddamn actor thinks they've bonded for life and says they want to buy him. What kind of life is that animal going to have after some asshole actor buys it?"

"Not a working one, I'm guessing."

"Bingo. If it's lucky, it'll get turned out to pasture, but a horse or mule smart enough to learn that level of stunt work wants to work."

"So, the animals are great, it's the people who suck?"

"Always, it's the people who suck." He studies me, and I do my best not to squirm under his gaze. "You doing okay out here? Or do people suck?"

"I'm doing okay." I want to tell him I was doing fine at avoiding people who suck for the most part until I answered what I thought was a legit jury summons, but there's no way I can work through that tangle with Tom. "I made a contact recently who hooked me up with a new contractor."

"Good. Good." He's resting his chin on his crossed wrists, but I can sense the shift in conversation even without his eyes on me. "So, you're here because you missed the smell?"

"I'm here because my car keeps dying and it has no pickup and the car fairy said unless I get it fixed for real, I have to stop driving it."

We're quiet for a long time, but I'm used to that with Tom, so I wait him out.

"You need dinner?"

"No. I'm good on everything except reliable transportation."

"Your parents warned you about buying that old car."

"I didn't want to be indebted to them. And I don't want them to have the satisfaction of being right. I'm finishing up a job that I hope is going to pay well enough to buy a new car. I think it'll only be a few weeks."

"Sounds big."

I realize in the way he's eyeing me that saying I'm thinking about buying a new car sounds suspicious when I've been broke for so long. "It's legit," I promise. "Nothing illegal, I swear."

"Your parents would never forgive me if you started selling drugs or…"

"It has nothing to do with drugs. I'd tell you about it, but I signed papers saying I wouldn't."

"That doesn't sound suspicious at all."

"I know. I'm sorry. I wish…" I stop myself. Even if the studio would let me talk about it, if I talked to Tom, he'd have to tell my parents, and I don't want my parents to know. "I know it sounds sketchy, but it's fine. I'm fine." I rest my forehead against my arms. I know it's not good to keep wrestling with it on my own. I should call Sarah, but if I do, my feelings for Emelynn would inevitably come up, and I'm too embarrassed to admit how deeply I cared about her in the space of a week.

"Yeah, seems like it."

"I'm sorry to just show up and ask for a favor—well, two favors, I guess—because I would really appreciate it if you didn't tell my parents about needing a vehicle. I've gotten lucky twice, and the guy who helped me said that it's going to leave me stranded. I thought it would be better to drive it here than call you and ask you to pick me up on the side of the road. I can't ask this friend again."

"Is this friend part of the thing you can't talk about?" His shoulders tense like he's worried Cesar is a threat to me.

"Sort of? He's a great guy, but I work with his sister, so if I call him…It's complicated."

"Ah. Women are always complicated," he agrees. "Let's get you set up with something reliable. Take at least one worry off your plate."

"Thanks for saving me again, Tom."

"Day or night, kid. Call me anytime. I can tell you're almost as twisted up now as you were over that girl in Kentucky, but I don't have another escape plan for you."

"I know. I'll figure it out." He looks about as convinced by my words as I am.

CHAPTER THIRTY-EIGHT

Emelynn

"My name is Emelynn Rivas," I say when Nick motions for me to begin my interview on Wednesday. I had hoped to see Alex today, but there's no Orange Beast in the parking lot. I'm hoping that doesn't mean they have asked to shoot on days when I'm not on set.

"I played Vicki on the show. I was a big fan of *The Truman Show*, so when I heard about this project, I wanted in."

In retrospect, I understand that in the movie, Jim Carrey knew that he was playing a character who discovers his whole life has been filmed. It was created for a full cast to create a world of fiction. Nobody was duped, so the ethics of the project were never an issue. I realize now how far away this is from what *Civic Duty* planned for Alex.

"How much of yourself did you bring to this character?" Nick asks.

I picture Alex watching this and think this may be the chance I have to convince them that essentially, I'm the person they got to know on the show. "Quite a bit. My character doesn't want to do jury duty and tries to get out of it with a story about her boyfriend. The boyfriend part wasn't real, but I would absolutely try to get out of jury duty with a story like that. My character is pretty bored by the whole process. I know that the writers provided a lot of filler to take the emphasis off the more absurd stuff they threw in, and it was extremely effective in boring me to death. To their credit, Alex never complained about being bored, no matter how far out into the weeds the writers went. Me? I barely stayed awake filming most of the court scenes."

"What was it like working with Alex?"

"I have never met a better human than Alex. If I had to be in court for any reason, I'd want a dozen Alexes on my jury. They took their job so seriously. It was really inspiring, like faith in humanity, you know? To think that someone would invest their whole heart for a stranger…I've never seen anything like it. Honestly, the depth of their values made the whole reveal very difficult to participate in."

"Cut," Nick says. "Emelynn, you know I can't use that kind of material in the footage. It undermines the whole project."

"Don't you feel bad? They walked out, Nick. Don't you worry about whether this has fucked with their sense of right and wrong?"

"They knew they were being filmed. The amount of what we filmed outside of the 'documentary' material they already knew about was minimal. I stand by the project, and it doesn't look good if I have actors saying what we did was unethical."

"I never said it was unethical."

"That's because I stopped you. I would, however, like to talk about the chemistry that led to you breaking up with your boyfriend. It would be great to have a clip of you explaining your motivation. Do you want to watch the footage we have for that?"

"Footage? I didn't have that conversation with Sarah in the jury room."

"You know that we have cameras in the dining area as well. From how you positioned yourself, it certainly seems like you chose to stand there with a reason."

"I had no idea there were cameras in the kitchen area."

"Well, that's neither here nor there. We have a great clip of your heartbreak when you tell Alex that your boyfriend has broken up with you. I've got it cued up if you'd like to watch it, or if you're ready, you can jump directly into explaining why you decided to change your character's trajectory so dramatically."

"I'd like to watch it," I say, partly because I'm speechless and need some time to think about what to say, but also because I want to see Alex, even if it's just on screen.

Nick clicks a few things on his laptop before swinging it around so I can see the screen. Sarah and I enter the small kitchenette. From a viewer's perspective it does appear that we strategically stand in front of the cameras. I watch myself divulge spending time with Alex off the set. "Is Alex going to see this part?" I ask Nick, my mouth dry as I listen to Sarah tell me that I should allow my character to be written off the jury.

"We'll need to keep the part about the chemistry you feel. We want to play up that angle. It's great to balance out the content, so it's not too court heavy."

"Have you run this by Sarah yet? I'm guessing she didn't know about this camera, either. Is she okay with you using this content? Because I'm not. Having Vicki break up with her boyfriend was not about trying to date Alex."

"But the two of you! You have to see the expression on Alex's face when they see you and Sarah hugging."

I watch the interaction with Sarah, my stomach tight. It sucks to be caught in the half-truths I offered the team after I admitted that I was attracted to Alex. I try to keep my face neutral as I watch, especially when I see the flash of emotions flit across Alex's face as they took in the embrace. There's no way that they won't use the tape. Alex's eyebrows shoot up in utter surprise and confusion, but the crease in their brow is pure jealousy.

Their expression shifts to concern as I explain about being dumped. My body responds as I watch them warmly lay their hand on my shoulder. They were able to intuit exactly what I needed. In the moment, I was more aware of Sarah's disapproval and focused on her when Alex went to get me chocolate. Watching it now, I stay focused on Alex and see a flash of relief. Just before they disappear from the frame, they glance briefly back at me, and the longing they feel is unmistakable.

"You said clear as day that you are attracted to them. And that look? It's so obvious they feel the same way. Why wouldn't we capitalize on that? Can you imagine the reception the show will get if the two of you promote it as a couple? That shit's golden." He motions for the camera operator to roll. When he has a thumbs-up, he turns to me. "The scriptwriters had a whole plan for the boyfriend storyline. What was running through your head when you decided to ditch it?"

He's not angry. I know how interested he is in promoting an Alex/Vicki angle. I am trying as hard as I can to control my reaction to the film he's shown me, but his question sends my mind directly to my kitchen with Alex's soft lips on mine. *I want Alex.* That's what was going through my mind when I flipped the script. "From some of the things Alex said, I guessed that they had experienced a bad breakup. I thought that if my character also got dumped, that would put me in a position to talk to Alex about what they had experienced."

Nick smiles brightly. "That's not what your expression says. How much time did you spend with Alex off camera? Enough for deeper feelings to develop between you two?"

I am so glad that Alex isn't on set today. This would be a hundred times harder to bear if there was a chance that Alex was listening. "Alex is my friend," I tell Nick. "There is nothing more between us."

"I don't buy it." Nick shakes his head and wakes up the screen on the monitor next to us and pointedly studies it. "That's not what I see in their expression, either."

"To be fair, you're viewing all this footage with the biggest of ulterior motives."

He harumphs. "Don't try to tell me that you won't benefit if the show is successful. Why wouldn't you do everything you can to help it?"

"Alex walked off the set after the reveal. I'm far more concerned with their emotional well-being than I am about the impact it might have on my career."

"And if their well-being would be positively impacted by exploring their feelings for you?"

"For Vicki," I correct. "There's the rub."

"Ah." He points at me like I've scored on him. "That takes us back to what was going through your head when you broke away from the boyfriend script. I'd argue that was your way of introducing Alex to Emelynn. You said yourself that you would not be excited about serving on a jury, so after you ditched the boyfriend, was your time on set acting, or biding your time until the project ended?"

I need a snappy comeback for this, but my mind is a complete blank.

"Cut," Nick says.

"Wait, that's it? That's all you need from me?"

"I'm sure we've got what we need." He taps the edges of his papers on the table. "We'll be in touch about whether we need you for any more filming. If not, you'll hear from us about promotion in a month or so. We've got to move fast on this."

I exit the room numbly. I want to talk to Sarah about this interview, but it doesn't look like she's on set. In the parking lot, I scan one more time for the Orange Beast. It's still nowhere in sight. It may be months before I see Alex again, and I have to accept that they may not even want to do promotional events with me.

CHAPTER THIRTY-NINE

Alex

I slouch down in the ranch truck I've borrowed from Tom and watch Emelynn cross the parking lot. She looks amazing in formfitting black slacks and a red top with spaghetti straps. Her hair is up in a genie ponytail, giving her an air of playfulness. She scans the parking lot, so I make sure to duck below the window until I hear her car start and pull out of the lot.

It takes long enough for her to leave that I feel like a complete idiot for not talking to her before she left the set today. My phone pings from the bench seat, but I don't sit up to retrieve it until I'm sure she's gone. When I do push fully up in the seat, Sarah fills my driver's side window.

"Holy shit!" I gasp.

"Sorry to startle you," she says, glancing at the street. "Have you talked to her since the trial ended?"

"The fake trial," I remind her. She inclines her head, and I appreciate that she doesn't defend the show. She waits for me to answer her question. "No. I haven't talked to her."

"I was hoping to hear that you had since you haven't called me. There's a lot to grapple with. You need to talk to someone about it."

"I know." I glance at my phone. The timing of my notification makes me hopeful that Emelynn is texting me.

"You have somewhere to be?"

"No." I snap my attention back to her. "Sorry."

"You don't need to apologize." Her voice is gentle, but I'm keeping my guard up. I know that the producers have her on the payroll to make sure I don't lose my shit and ruin everything. "I was hoping to hear you didn't have plans. I was on my way to play pickleball, and my wife texted that we lost our fourth player. Would you be interested in joining us?"

I am pretty sure she's set this up to lure me out to talk, but remembering how good it felt to play during the trial, I agree.

"Super. Same park. Meet you there in fifteen?"

I agree and watch her pull out her phone, no doubt to text her wife, before she leaves the parking lot. It's only then that I pick up my phone and check the message.

It's from Emelynn, which sets off a string of firecrackers in my chest.

Not the same on set without you. Hope you are doing well.

No begging forgiveness. No guilt-tripping. Just an observation. In the tape I viewed today, I watched her carefully, asking whether I was seeing Vicki or Emelynn. I want to believe what she said about who I met essentially being Emelynn. I studied her face closely when they showed me the first day on set, my skin set atingle when I see myself notice her for the first time. I did not do a good job of hiding how taken I was with her. Watching the tape, though, I witness her studying me as well.

I try seeing it as an anonymous viewer. Through that lens, it does look like two people instantly attracted to each other, exactly what Emelynn described the night we kissed. A voice at the back of my head asks what people would think if they knew that she kissed me when I thought it was all real. I'm sure this is why Sarah has invited me out. There is no point mulling over it on my own. I read Emelynn's text again, trying to decide whether I should answer it. My mind is too cluttered to trust myself to answer. Hoping that hanging out with Sarah can help settle it, I set my phone down and drive to the park.

Sarah is already on the court with Jass and their daughter, Chloe. I chuckle inwardly. I've been set up.

"Hi, Alex!" Jass hollers as I walk to the court. "Great to see you again. Chloe, give Alex a paddle."

Chloe has been warming up with a paddle in each hand. She looks from the green one to the red one and then to me.

"Either one is good for me," I say.

Reluctantly, she hands over the red one. Sarah motions for me to join her on her side of the net. "Need a refresher on the rules?"

"Nope. I've got it. Three bounce rules, no volleying in the kitchen," I say, gently returning the ball to Chloe.

I was worried about how vigorous of a game we could have with three adults and a six-year-old, but she's surprisingly fast on the court, and I find myself laughing and relaxing for the first time in a week.

When an ice cream truck pulls up in the parking lot, Jass and Sarah have a wordless exchange that results in Jass asking Chloe to take her to the ice cream truck.

"You're a grown-up." Chloe giggles, obviously used to this kind of humor from Jass.

"I'm pretty sure you need a kid with you," Jass says seriously.

Giggling, Chloe grabs her hand, and they run to the truck, Jass jogging backward to ask if Sarah and I want anything. I sense that the correct answer is no and wave off the offer before turning to Sarah. "Thank you for bringing me out here. I had so much fun playing pickleball with your family and Vicki..." I have to look away when I correct myself. "And *Emelynn*. I thought I was making friends. That was one of the worst parts of finding out that the whole trial was fake."

"Oh, Alex," Sarah says, hand over her heart. "I would love to be your friend, as would Jass and Chloe. It was Jass who suggested we invite you to play today. It's an added bonus that it gives me a chance to see how you are doing."

I eye her warily. I don't believe her.

"If you don't want to talk about the show, we will not talk about the show. That is completely up to you."

"If I talk to you about the show, that means we can't be friends, doesn't it?"

"If you were a client of mine, I would not be able to be friends. But nothing about this is normal. I do not take clients I've worked with, and essentially, we worked on that show together. Will I be using my professional training if we talk about the show? Absolutely. I'll be honest with you, I get in trouble for doing that all the time." Her gaze turns toward Jass, who is standing in line by the truck. Then she chuckles. "Actually, it's my ex who will tell me not to 'therepitize' her. Jass is substantially more receptive when I offer professional insight. And it goes both ways. Being with her has taught me so much." She turns back to me, and I can practically see wheels turning in her mind. "You remind me of her."

I wrinkle my brow. "How's that?"

"You stretch my thinking and help me see the world in different ways. That's why you were such an amazing pick for the star of *Civic Duty*. Imagine the impact your observation about how people respond when they are hurt could have. So many people strike out with a misery-loves-company attitude instead of letting go of the hurt, dusting themselves off, and simply getting on with their lives. That's good stuff!"

"I got a lot of that from listening to your podcast." Her life view is so different from most of the people back home. Living in California and meeting people with different attitudes made me feel like I was finally getting planted in a place where I could thrive. The idea that people across the nation will be watching me makes it feel like I'm being scattered like breadcrumbs.

She touches her heart again. "That's very kind of you to say."

"You make it sound like I'm going to be some kind of hero, and I'm terrified that people will only see a gullible dimwit."

"It's quite difficult to turn off the part of your brain that worries about public feedback. I understand completely. I can see that you are in a different position, that I had control of my narrative. I chose to put myself out there in the public eye where you've been thrust into it, but what I've found is that the benefits far outweigh the downside. I've faced a fair share of criticism. People have also told me that I helped them take control of their life. That's what I hang on to."

I nod. That helps turn down the volume on my insecurities. "Thanks. That helps me wrap my brain around the show part of things."

"What's the other part you're struggling with?"

I could kick myself for showing my hand. I should have shut my trap after I thanked her.

"Is it what happened with Vicki?" she asks gently.

A wave of embarrassment crashes over me. "She told you?"

Sarah holds up her hands. "She told me the two of you had dinner together. That's it." She's studying me carefully.

I take several breaths before I say, "She didn't talk to you about…anything?"

"She has not confided in me."

All I can manage is, "Huh." I'm literally scratching my head. I thought for sure Emelynn would have talked about our kiss. Whether she told Sarah directly or told only the producers or directors, Sarah would know. My mind clears for a moment. Emelynn said I kissed her, not Vicki. She said I got to know the real her. In her mind, there's a difference, but I continue to see someone who willingly lied to me.

"Trust is a scary, scary thing," Sarah says. "I'm not sure how much of my story you know. When Jass and I first got together, she didn't tell me she knew who I was. I had a very difficult time accepting the choice she made to keep that information from me. She said it wasn't relevant, and I can see her point. I wasn't dating at the time. But then…fireworks that neither one of us could put out. I can see the sparks between the two of you. I watched Emelynn struggle with how to handle them, but she never shared what she did with me."

"Have you talked to her since the trial ended?" I ask.

"I have not. I'm available for you. The producers factored in how the reveal would impact you. In no way did they factor the possibility of fireworks into the outcome."

Suddenly I feel really sad for Emelynn. I know exactly how isolating it is to not have anyone to talk to. It hadn't occurred to me that she would feel as muted as I do.

Jass and Chloe return, Chloe finishing up an ice cream sandwich. I'm glad they are back because I don't know what else to say to Sarah.

"Thanks for joining us today," Jass says. I can see from the look she exchanges with Sarah that Sarah doesn't interpret their coming back as an interruption.

Jass says, "I thought maybe you'd bring your friend. She seemed to enjoy playing last time."

"Oh!" I turn to Sarah, unsure of what to say.

"Maybe she'll come next time."

There is significance in the way she says this. She wants me to reach out to Emelynn. I love the sound of more pickleball with Sarah's family, but that next time could include Emelynn as well? My body overrides the concerns I ruminate on and buzzes with excitement at the possibility of seeing Emelynn again. I gather hugs from Sarah and Jass and a fist bump from Chloe and try not to remember how right Emelynn felt in my arms.

CHAPTER FORTY

Emelynn

My thoughts keep returning to the empty parking lot, and it's difficult not to catastrophize and see that as a sign that I won't hear from Alex again. Given how slimy I felt after talking to Nick, it's easy to create a narrative where Alex's anger grows to the point where they will refuse to talk to me again.

I thank the gods of good timing for the fantasy series that landed in my email in the last days of the trial. Nothing compares to getting lost in a competent and creative writer's world-building to offer my mind a distraction.

It doesn't stop me from spinning a more hopeful fantasy. After all, Alex has been to my house, so it's not difficult to imagine them showing up at the door. I close my eyes to give myself over to this more favorable outcome. I invite them in. We stand in the kitchen unsure of what to do with our bodies at first, studying each other for what words will help push us over this hump of awkwardness.

"Can I be honest with you?" I imagine saying. "I can't think beyond wanting to kiss you again. All I thought about during those stupid last days of the trial, all through the deliberations, was kissing you again."

"I was hoping we could skip right to that part," Alex would say, closing the distance between us. I want them to thread their hands in my hair, lean in, and kiss me. Gently at first, followed by all the desire we held back during the trial. The movie my mind offers spikes my pulse, and my tummy flutters, remembering how Alex's soft lips felt on mine. My skin hums as I allow the fantasy space to expand. My whole body is taut with desire when my phone pings me back to reality.

My phone! I scramble to check the screen.

Alex texted me.

I rub my palms on my pants, working up the courage to see what they have to say.

Not the same without you on the pickleball court. Played with Sarah's family. They asked about you.

I set the phone on my table to keep myself from replying too quickly. I don't want to give them the impression I've been sitting by my phone waiting for them to text. I read the text again, focusing on how they said Sarah's family asked about me. Not Alex. But they're reaching out. That has to be good, right? My response can't be overeager. No *Wish I'd been there!* If they'd wanted me there, they would have texted. I go for neutral.

That sounds fun!

That's fine, I tell myself. But I continue to stare at it without hitting send. My thumb hovers over the delete button. Maybe I should say I'm glad they got out, aim for support without pressuring them to include me. That's better. I delete what I had, but another text from Alex comes in before I can type another response.

They said they would like to play with you again.

And Alex? Would they meet up with Sarah and Jass again if they knew I would be there?

And me.

I'd like that, I tap out.

Now I'm riveted to the phone, willing them to say more. Nothing comes for so long that I begin my bedtime routine. I remove my contacts, wash my face, and finally climb into bed. I close my eyes and picture Alex in their space. If the show was about us, this would be a split-screen shot, both of us in bed thinking about the other. After a few more texts, one of us would say we should FaceTime. We'd sink lower and lower as we talk until each of us has the phone propped on the pillow, so it's as if we're lying next to each other in bed. Smiling. Laughing. Talking about our days, filling in all the little details because it's painful to be apart for even a minute. It is so easy to imagine them next to me in the bed, their hand brushing my hair back from my face.

My phone snaps me awake, my fantasy having lulled me to sleep.

Do you think it would be okay to talk rn?

I push myself up, scared I might still be dreaming, this being what I have wanted to hear for days.

Of course, I quickly text back. *Text? Call?* I've barely hit send when my phone rings. I close my eyes. *Do not fuck this up*, I tell myself.

"Hey," Alex says in the exact tone I imagined.

"Hi." My mind spins out all sorts of conversational possibilities. I want to tell them I've been hoping they'd call, that I've been wanting to talk to them. But I don't want to make them feel guilty for the time they have needed. "How are you?"

"I'm..." They take a deep breath. I can picture their hand on their head as if they're trying as hard as I am to pick out the right thing to say. "It's crazy. Intellectually, I know that the cameras were only at the courthouse, but I'm so paranoid now. The checker at the grocery store asked if I was doing okay, and I had to stop myself from looking around for hidden cameras."

"I'm sorry."

"No. Don't be," they are quick to assure. "I'm not saying that to make you feel bad. I just...You asked how I am. I'm paranoid, I guess. And I'm also...I don't know...Last week I couldn't wait for the trial to be over. I wanted to spend more time with you. And then the bombshell. And I can't talk about it, which is hard. Is that hard for you, too? Sarah and I talked a little bit after pickleball, and I was sure that you had been talking to her, but you haven't."

"No. We haven't talked since the trial ended."

"Who have you talked to?"

"Cesar, but not really because I can't tell him anything, so now he's convinced that we're filming porn."

"Porn!" They guffaw with surprise.

"I know."

"As if porn is synonymous with shame."

"That's essentially what I told him." This brings a smile to my face. I like being on the same page as Alex.

"Seriously?"

"Yeah. He basically recycled the old story Mateo pulls out to try to make me feel bad for recording romance novels. Older protective brother syndrome. It's real, even when it's only by minutes."

"Wait. You're twins?" they say, completely unguarded. "I had no idea!"

"Yeah, he worries over me. He's trying stupid hard to figure out why you knew me as Vicki."

"Yeah. I saw him when the Orange Beast died on me again. He was fishing for why I call you Vicki, and I got all sorts of confused about whether he thought Alex was my on-set name and…oh my god…he thinks you're mentoring me on a porn set."

They erupt into laughter, and I follow. This is the best I have felt since the trial ended, and I laugh until I cry. I don't understand what's happening. One moment I'm laughing with tears streaming down my face, and then I'm only crying.

"Emelynn?" Alex says. "Emmy? Are you okay?"

I'm trying as hard as I can to keep the light mood we had, but all the emotions from the week have slammed down on me. I reach for a tissue and remember Alex's handkerchief in my pocket. This, along with the endearment Alex used and the gentleness in their voice, simply undoes me, and all I can do is let the tears fall until I'm spent. "I'm sorry," I say when I can catch my breath. "I'm so sorry."

"I know," they say.

I hiccup. "I'm so sorry, Alex."

"I know," they repeat.

"Where do we go from here?"

"Well, I've never shot porn before, so I don't know where to even begin. As my mentor, maybe you can make a suggestion."

This makes me chuckle again. I am thankful for their levity but also at a loss for what to say. I'm the actress. It should be easy for me to jump into this scene Alex is offering, but I don't want to play with Alex. I want to be real.

Thankfully, Alex continues as if they have read my thoughts. "Maybe it would make more sense to talk about that when we see each other again. Right now, I'd rather hear more about you and Cesar being twins. Do the two of you have a secret twin language?"

"No secret language," I say. "But we read each other insanely well. When we're together, he'll bring me a snack before I even realize I'm hungry. But even when we're doing different stuff, he'll call me when I'm starting to come unraveled and ask if I'm overwhelmed. When we were kids, I had a hard time falling asleep when our mom moved us into our own beds. In the morning, she'd wake up, and Cesar would be in my bed again with all his stuffed animals. He'd chuck all his animals out of his bed, carry them over, and chuck them into my bed before crawling in to comfort me."

"That sounds super sweet. Were you in the same classes together?"

I lean back and start telling stories about being in class together, remembering how much it bothered me when teachers would ask who was born first and then treat Cesar differently because he took his first breath before me. We talk for another hour, going back and forth sharing stories about our families, comparing California to Kentucky. I'm reminded of how late it is when they yawn in the middle of a story about a crush they had on their babysitter.

"We should get some sleep," I say, wishing again that Alex was next to me.

"Okay." They sound disappointed.

I am about to thank them for calling me, but I want to hold on to this uncharged mood. I want to believe that we can be friends again, so instead of apologizing or thanking them, I simply say, "Good night, Alex."

"Good night, Emelynn."

I fall asleep replaying the sound of my name on their lips.

CHAPTER FORTY-ONE

Alex

"Early in the filming, you said that this felt like reality TV. Viewers are going to want to hear how we were able to pull this off without you figuring out that it wasn't a real court case," Nick says. He's leaning back in his chair, elbow hanging off the back. It's been a week since the reveal, and while I'm experiencing much more anxiety, the frantic energy he had when I knew him as the director of a documentary he worried could implode at any minute has been replaced by this smug Hollywood stereotype.

"Yeah. I'm sure kicking myself for overriding my gut whenever I was internally saying *What the fuck?*"

"Let's begin by having you explain how you became involved in the project."

"You want me to explain how I was stupid enough to fall for fake jury service on camera."

"That's not what I'm saying at all, Alex. Our intent was never to make you feel stupid in any way."

"Whether you intended it or not, that's how it feels."

"Okay. I will grant you that. Can we set that aside for the moment, so we can discuss on tape how we selected our star?"

I shrug. It pains me to call up the memory of the summons I should have seen as a fake. "Something came in the mail that looked like a legit jury summons. There were instructions on how to report, but then there was an extra section for people who would be willing to take part in a documentary project. There was a QR code you could scan if you were interested in applying."

"What led you to apply?"

"The summons I got said that if you were selected for the documentary, it paid more than typical jury service, so I thought, why not? I was between jobs and needed the money."

"Did you talk to others in the jury selection room about the documentary?"

"No. Waverly was asking everyone for their sign and figuring out where everyone had to sit. Wait. Can we go back to the jury summons? If that was from the show, does that mean I haven't served on a jury?"

"That's correct. This was all entertainment."

"Shit. So I could get called for legit jury duty?" I ask.

"I'm afraid so."

"It just gets better and better, the more I learn about this whole messed-up project. So how many people fell for the fake jury duty summons?"

"We sent the mailer to five hundred random addresses within a ten-mile radius of the courthouse we found for filming. We got a hundred and thirty-six responses and chose ten people to screen, and of those ten, we chose you."

"Why'd y'all pick me? Was it because I'm from Kentucky?"

"A few people pointed out that it would give the show a wider appeal. It certainly made you stand out. But the staff were really impressed with the note you left them about needing to update the form—a form you assumed was government issued. You said it should have an option to decline to state gender."

"Sex," I correct.

"Sure. Obviously, it's not something we had considered at length, but we knew we wanted the show to examine right and wrong, and that note gave us insight into your ability to scan for things that are not right and take a stand, even if it isn't popular. And we chose perfectly! We could not be happier with how it all came out."

I sense that he wants me to be as excited as he is. I'm doing my best to honor my contract. I hope that the affect I manage continues to portray me as the country bumpkin stunned by all the big city lights.

"Would you like to share how you feel about the project now that it's all over?"

"What do you want me to say?" I ask. "That I'm excited that I saved a fake person from paying a fake settlement?"

"Maybe you're excited about the cash prize? That's a great angle."

"I never wanted to be an angle."

Nick threads his hands through his hair, arranging it precisely even though it's me on camera, not him. "I understand that. Try to see this from our perspective. Think about what the last episode wants to do to leave the viewer feeling good."

I cross my arms, unmoved by his reasoning. My thoughts drift to Emelynn, though, and how excited I was to arrive and reluctant to leave because it meant I wouldn't see her until the next day.

"You looked slightly less mad for a second there. What are you thinking about?" Nick asks.

"I met a few people I hope to stay in contact with, so I'm grateful for that," I say honestly because I do enjoy Sarah's company as well.

"Ah, perfect. You were just remembering Waverly talking about signs, and that is footage we wanted to highlight. First day on the set and all." He smiles cheerily as he clicks around on his laptop before turning it to me.

I watch myself enter the room, and I recognize the exact moment I saw Vicki for the first time.

Nick pauses the tape. "Let's talk about what you were feeling when you first walked in. I'd like to know what flashed across your face just now."

"I was not aware that I was being filmed in the…What is that called? The jury pool room? It makes me feel really uncomfortable watching footage that was filmed without my consent." He holds up a finger, and I wave him off. "I know I technically consented in the paperwork I signed. You know what I mean."

"Okay." He's frustrated, but I'm not about to let that trouble me. "What was going through your head when you first came into the room? Do you remember?"

Of course I remember. "I'd like to watch more."

He sighs and pushes play. It doesn't take long for the view to shift to a camera trained on the empty seats next to Vicki. Through the camera lens, I'm offered a view of her seeing me for the first time. The way her eyes sweep over my frame shows unmistakable interest. Even when Sarah comes in and is supposed to distract people with her fame, Vicki's eyes stay glued to me.

This sends such a thrill through me that I forget the straight face I have been so careful to keep in place. I forget how angry I am with Nick and the show and smile. If this had been a dating show, everyone would have put the two of us together after seeing that look.

After seeing how Emelynn looked at me.

Because that wasn't Vicki. The truth of that hits me in my solar plexus. What Emelynn said about most of the interaction between us being me and Emelynn is true. Vicki wanted out of jury duty. Vicki was devoted to her boyfriend. Vicki was never supposed to fall for Alex. It wasn't a dating show. It was jury duty.

"I need to go," I say.

"But you haven't answered my question about what you were thinking when you first came into the room!"

"I thought there should have been more chairs," I say, standing.

The second I exit the building, I call Emelynn.

"Hey!" I can hear the surprise in her voice. "Everything okay?"

"Who were you during deliberations?" I ask.

"Who was I?"

"When we were deliberating. Were you Emelynn or Vicki?"

There is no pause. She doesn't have to think about it. "Vicki."

That one word makes everything fit. "And that day I asked you about the podcast, you were Vicki that day, weren't you? When you texted *See you tmrw*, it stung so badly because I couldn't understand why you were so cold all of a sudden. But that was you trying to not be Emelynn?"

"Yes."

Again, her reply is immediate, and I have to look at my feet to make sure they remain on the ground because I feel like I'm floating. "Okay. Wow." That's all I can say for several beats. I have so much to rethink. "That's a lot. It's probably not fair to do a hit-and-run call like this, but…"

"It's okay, Alex. Take your time. I get it."

"Really? Just like that?"

"Really."

"Okay. I appreciate that." I sign off, tapping my phone against my leg. What does it mean if it's Emelynn who likes me? It doesn't change how the show and all the actors manipulated me, but would I have been able to do differently if my role was reversed with Emelynn's? If I'd been the actor and felt what I did when Emelynn walked in? I lean my hands against the bed of the truck in a runner's pose, trying to settle my thoughts in order to sort them. The more I try, the more I confuse myself. I need to talk this through with someone, but not Emelynn. I pull out the card Sarah gave me with her personal number. She said to call anytime.

I take a deep breath and dial.

The phone rings a long time before I hear a cautious "Hello?" from Sarah.

"Hi, Sarah. Alex here. I hope it's okay to call."

"Alex! Are you okay?"

I smile at how similarly she and Emelyn answered my call. A voice in my head whispers that they both care about me. I wasn't lying to Nick when I said that I am grateful for this.

"Can I brain-dump on you? I just had my interview with Nick today, and I learned so many things, and I'm not sure what to do with all the new information."

"That's what I'm here for. Are you comfortable talking where you are now, or would you like to come to the house?"

"Am I…Is that allowed?"

"Coworkers, remember? We'll talk through what you learned today."

She gives me her address. It's not far, though it takes a few minutes longer because I have to navigate around a bunch of peacocks that have congregated in the middle of the road.

Sarah's house is a stucco a year or so away from needing new paint. The maroon shutters are showing some wear. Sarah greets me at the door with a shoulder squeeze. "Let's chat out by the pool. It's such a nice evening. Do you want something to drink? Water? Lemonade?"

"I want lemonade!" Chloe hollers from the living room where she and Jass sit on the couch with gaming controllers in their hands.

"You've had so much lemonade, you're going to float away," Sarah admonishes.

"Water would be nice," I say, not wanting to take lemonade away from her daughter.

She guides me through the dining area to an outdoor furnished patio, beyond which is a sparkling blue pool. "We can sit here or dip our feet in. Wherever you're comfortable."

"Of course you have a pool," I say. Her backyard is the definition of California.

"Thank goodness. Otherwise, I might never have met Jass."

We kick off our shoes and dip our feet into the water, and I try my best to lay out the tangle of ideas about Emelynn and the show. "So, I don't know what to do now," I say, kicking my feet gently in the cool water. "I kept telling myself that I could pursue Vicki after the trial ended. Being able to identify Emelynn from Vicki kind of helps remove the hurt that caused me to walk away, but we're never going to be free of the show. Where does that leave me and Emelynn?"

"What would you like to happen with Emelynn?"

I open my mouth and shut it again, embarrassed by where my imagination immediately takes me. Obviously, that's not what she's asking, but it's too late to tell my blush response. Sarah notices. How could she not? I bury my face in my hands as she laughs. "I want to be able to ask her out like two normal people, but if Nick is right and this show blows up, we won't be two normal people. We'll be in the spotlight. I never wanted the spotlight."

"I hear you. And that's something Emelynn wants."

"This is a huge opportunity to launch her career. I can't stop that."

"You can't stop it for yourself, either. That must feel scary."

"So scary. I want for it to be over. I want to be able to put it behind us and pretend that it didn't happen, but I won't ever be able to do that." The enormity of how I'm forever stuck with this sits like lead in my stomach. Sarah doesn't try to placate me with words about how it will get easier with time, which I appreciate. She rubs calming circles between my shoulder blades with her palm.

"You won't," Sarah confirms. "But you are a resilient person. When it hurt you to be in Kentucky, you came here. You made a life that is comfortable for you, knowing how much more important that is than trying to build a life that's acceptable to someone else. As long as you are still comfortable being you, I'm sure you'll be able to manage the spotlight and stay true to who you are. I'm in the spotlight, and occasionally that includes Jass, but it's not a comfortable space for her, so she largely avoids it. It's a little like the first time you jump in the pool in the springtime." She kicks her feet in the water neither one of us hesitated to put our feet into when we first sat down. "It can be a real shock, but you get used to it."

"Or you get out!" I say.

"Or you get out," she acknowledges. "And people might comment on that choice and try to pressure you to stay longer, but it's up to you. Ultimately, what matters is what feels right to you."

"We don't have to be in the pool together, is what you're saying."

"Exactly. Whatever the pool is. For me, it's literal. Jass and Chloe love being in the water. Me, not so much. But the entertainment 'pool' is a space that I acclimated to when I saw the value it offered me as a tool."

Since the reveal, I have become unmoored. Sarah's words offer a sense of control I feared I had lost. Just as quickly, thinking about the reveal spikes my anxiety again, and my skin flushes hot remembering the shame of how I fell for everyone lying to me.

"I don't know how to stop feeling angry every time I think about the show. And when I think about Emelynn, I think about the show."

Sarah continues to splash her feet in the water, and I'm ready for her to say more about staying in the water and getting used to the cold. "Maybe when you think of the show, that can be Vicki?"

She leans against me, and I'm grateful that it doesn't seem like I owe her an answer. She's giving me permission to sit with all of this and see how it settles.

CHAPTER FORTY-TWO

Emelynn

I'm certain that I said the right thing when I told Alex to take their time, but that doesn't keep me from kicking myself in the week that follows.

If I had told them not to hang up, could I have convinced them to confide their feelings to me? As the days without a response stretch out, I agonize over whether I should have told them how much I struggled to stay in character. I convince myself that the perfect words would have shown Alex that they do know the real me.

I tell myself to be patient, reminding myself that the adjustment to real life is easy for me since I knew all along. Alex has a lot to figure out. It would be unfair to pressure them. Still, I check my phone constantly, hoping that they will reach out.

They don't.

After a whole weekend of silence, my body stops reacting each time my phone pings. Once I finish making my notes on the first book of the fantasy trilogy and begin recording *Love Song for Windalore, Last of the Goblin Queens*, the days go faster and less painfully. Everything in my backlist of audiobooks has been voicing humans. This is my first time creating voices for different kinds of fey and working with the author on the pronunciation of her invented language, so I hardly have any brain space left at the end of the day after mapping out my recording plan.

It's also my first time recording with Bryan Productions. They've got their own editing and mastering team, so I am able to lock myself in my makeshift closet studio and lose myself in this mystical world. An added bonus to recording is being able to tell my brothers they can't swing by whenever they want. I need the house quiet when I'm working, and in the hours I'm not recording, I remind them that I have to rest my voice and leave them to their current project.

Wednesday, a few folks from *Civic Duty* start a text chain to plan a meet-up at a nearby brewery on Friday. One of the actors I didn't interact with very much has a gig with her band. I check the list of recipients. Alex's name isn't listed, so I largely ignore the string of messages from people accepting or sending regrets. I do note that Sarah, unsurprisingly, sends a regret. It's tempting to be able to talk freely about the show with the other actors, but I also know they will want to talk about the reveal, and that still stings. A lot. I'm reticent to explain and own the impact of why Alex was so hurt by me in particular.

I use my current job as an excuse, typing out that trying to holler over live music would throw off my recording schedule.

Cesar comes by to tape paint chips up in the living room, which we've decided will be green.

"Mateo likes this one best," he says, feeling my presence behind him. He's taping a deep forest green chip to the wall. He's brought several degrees of light to dark options as well as variants of cool and warm tones.

I hum a noncommittal response. It feels too dark to me.

"You okay?" he asks, his back to me.

"Sure," I say. "Why?"

"I dunno. You look constipated."

"Asshole," I say, going back to my recording studio. I can hear him chuckling.

I eat my breakfast in the living room. Mateo's dark chip seems okay when the morning light hits it, but evening light confirms it's too dark.

Each time I take a break the next day, I examine them again, ruling out the minty one that is an appropriate color for ice cream but not walls. I'm partial to the warmer tones, but cooler ones can make smallish rooms feel more spacious. I want to ask Alex what they think. I reach into my back pocket and take out the handkerchief they gave me at the courthouse. I picture them reaching for it and remember them giving it to me. I hope they don't regret it.

It's my favorite time of day, the sun slanting through the west window as it sets. The cast—minus the queer people—will be gathering at the brewery. I'm finished recording for the day and back in the living room with the paint chips when Cesar comes by. I hear him creep down the hallway to make sure I'm not recording before he trucks in and out to carry in equipment they've been using on other jobs during the week that they'll need for the weekend work here.

A good fifteen minutes goes by when he pauses on one trip to look into the living room. "Punk! You've been here the whole time?"

"You didn't say 'hi' either."

"Because you *could be recording*," he says in a terrible imitation of me.

"Done for the day."

He comes in and lowers himself to the floor to sit next to me. I hand him the bowl of salsa I've been snacking on and shove the chips toward him. He eats a few before he says, "Recording going good?"

"I'm happy with how it's coming along."

"You bummed to go back to audio after the acting gig?"

"Not really. I kind of missed my recording studio and being in charge of my own workday, my own morals. Acting..." I shake my head.

"You know that absolutely confirms for me that you were filming porn, right?" He pushes against my shoulder, and I try to laugh at his attempt to lighten my spirits. "Seriously, though. Did something happen with Alex? Or not happen?"

I can't look at him. If I look at him, I'll tell him, and I can't tell him.

"Em..."

I will not look at him.

"I know something's up. I almost said so to Mama today."

"Cesar!"

"I didn't, okay? But she asked if you're good, and I paused."

"I hate you so much right now." The weight of what the show did to Alex pushes on me so hard, I can hardly breathe. Tears prick behind my eyes, and I whisper, "And me."

"Who do you hate more?"

"Definitely me," I admit.

"Oh, Em. What did you do?"

I tell him, not in detail, not enough to compromise the show, but enough for him to understand I purposely lied to Alex.

"Shit," he says when I finish.

"Yeah." I rest my temple on his shoulder. Telling him is a bit of relief, but I am also sick to my stomach waiting for him to respond.

Finally, he says, "That paint chip Mateo liked is too dark. What do you think about the one two to the right of it?"

"That one keeps catching my eye."

He nods. That's it? He's not going to help me at all? I'm about to sock him when he continues.

"I can't say one way or another because I'm biased. I already liked that one. But you've seen them throughout the day over the course of a bunch of days. You know with paint chips you've got to look at 'em in all kinds of different light."

"Why else would I have been sitting in here when you got here?"

"To save yourself the heartache of making the wrong decision."

I study him, unsure about why he's talking about heartache. "It's just paint."

"It's more than that. It's an investment of time and money. Nobody wants to get a whole wall in and realize they made a bad choice, and chances are, if you choose based on one thing, especially if you pick what looks good at the store? It's not going to look the same once you get it home."

"Why are you telling me all of this?"

"Because Mateo said the chip we like was the worst one at the store. He said it looked like snot. But in this light, it looks pretty good."

"How could anything look good under fluorescents?" I ask.

He frowns at me. I'm missing something, but I don't know what. "How could anything look good on a TV set? You said you didn't like how the director pushed your morals."

He's still looking at me, not the paint chip.

"Wait. Are we talking about paint here, or are we talking about Alex?"

He rolls his eyes. "I was talking about *you*."

"Oh."

"Based on what you told me, you look pretty shitty right now. But now you're not on the set…"

"So maybe they'll see me differently."

"Exactly. Like this paint chip here. Give it some time…see it at different times of day…" He leans against me more solidly. "Or season. You could come out looking better."

"How are they supposed to see me differently when they're not around me at all?"

"You hope they're remembering all the great things your brother did for them and weighing that in?" he offers.

"There's nothing to do but wait, is there?"

"Nope. Can't rush it. You're in that stage where it looks really bad and all you can do is wait for it to dry and hope it looks better."

We sit as evening turns to dark. In the fading natural light, the chips are harder and harder to tell apart. When the sun sets, the only light in the room comes from the light he left on in the front bedroom.

He pushes himself to his feet with a grunt and pulls the chip we've settled on from the wall. Even in this light, he can pick it out. My chest tightens. Even when I've done something that doesn't put me in a favorable light at all, I've got my twin.

He holds out his hand to pull me to my feet, and I accept.

CHAPTER FORTY-THREE

Alex

I am not a mirror person. All the years that I wore what my mom bought and kept my hair long for her trained me away from them. It hurt to look at my reflection and not see myself. One of the reasons I had to leave Kentucky was to get away from the people who still saw the girl I was, not the person I am.

The show has reawakened my anxiety about what people think about me, so I've taken to swinging by Tom's to talk to the horses. I googled whether pony therapy is actually a thing, and they didn't lie about that. I'm not supposed to talk to anyone, and for a solid week, I get around that by slipping into the corrals when Tom's not home. I run a brush over the mules, who take it all in with their enormous ears. I'm more likely to run into him on Saturday, but I don't have a job, and I can't sit in my rented room all day, so I risk the inevitable run-in.

"The more you're here, the less I believe that everything's fine," he says, joining me in the corral.

"Maybe I'm here for my car."

"Uh-huh. The horses are too clean for me to believe that."

He starts picking up hooves, talking to the mules about who

needs new shoes before they hit the parade route again, which of course involves my hometown parade.

"Do you think I did the right thing coming to California with you?"

"Your mom finally got you to pick up?"

I'm not surprised my mom tried calling Tom when I didn't pick up. I put her off as long as I could. I had so much spinning around in my mind I thought I'd blow a fuse up there if I picked up, but when she started calling multiple times a day, I gave in.

"She said she wants to see me, either me going out there for the parade or them coming here."

"Yup. What did you tell her?"

"That I'm still getting settled here in California."

"You're already settled." He's working his lower lip over his mustache like he does when he's mulling something over. "Why don't you want to see them?"

"I don't want to explain myself again."

"What if they're not asking for that? What if they want to get to know you as you?"

"I don't know if *I* know who I am well enough to be around them."

"Sure you do."

"What makes *you* so sure? I mean, you barely know me, and you didn't even think about it."

"I don't know you? Bullshit. I watched you grow up from just a little thing."

"You saw me once a year when you came for the parade. That's hardly knowing a person."

"You don't have to spend any time at all watching a herd to know the pecking order. You were a live wire when you were a kid, before your mama cared about whether you were a girl. You were like a curious colt tearing around a pasture, getting into all sorts of trouble. Taking off at the parade and scaring your folks half to death. And I watched the life go out of you the older you got. I watched you get quiet and cautious, crawling further and further inside of yourself."

"You could see all that one weekend a year?" I'm astonished. Not that he has memories that go back to my childhood—I've known him practically my whole life, but it never once occurred to me that he paid any attention at all to me. His description is painfully accurate. Everything about puberty hurt. Having to shave my legs but not being allowed to have short hair. Wearing dresses. Leaving the outdoor chores to my father and brothers. Before I met Lilian, it was smothering me.

"In Kentucky, you were the horse at the bottom of the pecking order, always jumpy, waiting for the next person to kick you. I got to worrying about what another year would do to you and if you'd survive it."

"Did you talk to my parents about it? During the year, I mean. Would you ask?"

"I'm not much of a phone talker."

That makes me chuckle. I honestly don't know if I've ever heard Tom say as much as he has in the last twenty minutes in all the years I've known him. We spent a lot of quiet hours in the truck together hauling the mules back from Kentucky. "You saved me."

"I got you out of a bad pasture and turned you loose, hoping you'd be able to remember yourself, who you were before you acted the way your parents expected you to. You're still watchful. Alert. You take in everything around you, but you're not guarded anymore. Your feet are more solid on the ground. There's more of you, like you've found yourself in the herd. So I don't need to see you every day or know what you're doing to know that whatever it is, it's done you good."

What he says about finding myself in a herd reminds me of playing pickleball with Emelynn, and Sarah's family. *Emelynn?* I'm surprised that Emelynn's real name is the one that comes to mind with a memory from jury duty when she was supposed to be playing Vicki. Meeting all of them has made me feel more grounded.

And yet, there is that undercurrent of doubt that comes with remembering Vicki and the deception Sarah participated in, and I feel foolish for trusting it all. And naïve. I hate feeling naïve.

"Trust yourself, kid. I don't know what's got you out here looking for answers with the mules, but I do know that even though your parents did everything they could to make you someone you weren't, your heart knew better. It pulled you in the direction of who you are. It sounds to me like your parents are interested in meeting you where you are now. They want to know you. Why do you need to push them away?"

"It can't be that easy. All of a sudden she's fine with this different version of me? What changed?"

"Nothing changed. They love you."

I recall the conversation I had with my mom. She never said she loved me. She said she was still having a difficult time letting go of who she thought I was but could not live with the hole my leaving had left. It makes me hyperconscious of the hole I've created by not talking to Emelynn.

I stay a bit longer to help feed the stock. The easy labor allows me time to examine this parallel of hurt and forgiveness. For years, I acted the part my parents wanted me to play because I knew it would keep my family whole. I accepted the role of their daughter like Emelynn accepted the role of Vicki.

I understand now that it was as hard for Emelynn to keep playing the role of Vicki as it was for me to continue playing the role of the daughter my parents scripted. The show being over allowed her to leave Vicki behind like the girl I left behind in Kentucky. So is it really naïve to trust her? Or, like Tom was saying, can I trust that her heart guided her through a time where she couldn't be truthful in order to keep the show whole?

Tom's offer to bring me out to California was terrifying. There were so many unknowns, and yet I threw what I needed into a duffel and climbed up into the cab of his eighteen-wheeler. Imagining trusting Emelynn is equally terrifying. I don't know where it will take me, but I sense that being with Emelynn might keep me on the path of being myself. I have felt more myself spending time with her than I have with anyone else.

As soon as I get home, I rub my palms on my cargos and pull up the last conversation with Emelynn on my phone.

Hi. Is this Emelynn? This is Alex from the jury pool. I hit send and mentally buckle in for whatever this road ahead holds in store.

CHAPTER FORTY-FOUR

Emelynn

I'm about to sit down to dinner when my phone chimes. Cesar was just here dropping off the paint we agreed on, so I'm sure it's him texting to say he forgot to tell me something.

But it's Alex's name that flashes on the screen.

My heart bounces in my chest like a small rubber ball, and I swipe open the message. *Is this Emelynn?* What?

I glance at the top of the screen, confused because I was sure it was Alex's name that flashed there. I am still puzzling over their text when another message pops up.

I hope you don't mind my getting your number from your brother after my stupid car died. Thank you again, by the way, for coming to my rescue.

Now I'm really confused. They're going back to before the trial? Unsure what they're doing, I thumb out, *You're welcome.*

I was hoping we would end up on the same trial. You would not believe how weird the jury I ended up on was. Did you end up getting called for another one?

Oh. We're starting over. They're giving me a chance to be seen in a different light. My mind is racing along with my heart now. Should I have been on another trial? I decide no. Otherwise, wouldn't we have bumped into each other at the courthouse? *Got out of it this time around. Yay!*

Jealous! comes the quick reply. *So…What's keeping you busy?*

I've been recording a new fantasy trilogy. Did I tell you I'm a voice actress? This is my chance to be me. Even though it feels dangerous, I embrace this chance to tell the truth.

Actress! they text. *You do TV work?*

Not really. I thought I wanted to do live taping, but I'm not sure it's my thing.

You don't have big Hollywood dreams? they ask.

Oh, I have dreams, acting isn't the top one rn.

Dots appear, and I wait, poised for the next text, but then they stop. Was that too much? Too close to the truth? It's too late. I've said it, and even if I could take it back, I wouldn't. I want to be completely real with them.

I'd like to hear about your dreams. Maybe we could explore another one of LA's musts? I don't want to embarrass myself again by admitting I haven't been to somewhere like In-N-Out.

I close my eyes tight, my dinner forgotten, as a list of things I would like to show Alex forms in my mind. I start to type out a question of what level of investment we're talking about—famous strawberry-filled donuts at The Donut Man or a day riding roller coasters at Knott's Berry Farm—but quickly ditch that idea, deleting what I've typed and replacing it with a request to call them with my brainstorm. "Hey there, Alex," I say when they've agreed to a call.

"Hi, Emelynn."

My heart flutters when they say my name.

"It's good to hear your voice again," they say.

"Yours, too." I know a conversation is necessary if we're going to keep hearing each other's voices, but for now, I'm too busy smiling.

"So you have some ideas?" Alex prompts.

"I am full of ideas. I wanted to start with what you've done so far. What's already crossed off your list?"

"Um. Nothing?"

"You've been in California a year. You can't have done nothing since you got here. Are you an inside museum or theater kind of person, or an outside beach or hike kind of person?"

"Starting with the hard questions!" They laugh.

"C'mon. Don't overthink. Where would you take me if I visited your hometown?"

"You wouldn't visit Paducah, Kentucky."

"If you were there, I would," I flirt. Because I want to be flirting with Alex. I want to spend time with Alex and not have to be careful.

I hear the smile in their voice and imagine their eye roll when they draw out their reply. "Okaaay. We could go to the Kentucky Dam. Or the Paducah Antique Mall."

I want to ask if this is a date, but I don't want to break character. That gives me pause. Alex started with a pretend opener that made us sound like strangers, but we're not strangers. We've kissed before. We know we're interested in each other. We're not at the very beginning where it's uncertain whether we like each other. I already know I like Alex, and I want this to be a date. "Alex?" I ask.

"Emelynn?"

Again with my name. I bite my lip. "This is us right now, right? For realsies?"

"Yes. For realsies."

"And you want to spend time with me, like on a real date?"

"I want to spend time with you. When I sort out everything in my head, I'm pretty sure I like you, Emelynn, and I was hoping maybe we could test that out."

"That's a theory I would love to test out. It sounds like you'd be into walking around Olvera Street and maybe getting lunch or dinner more than catching a show at the Pantages."

"I don't know anything about either one of those places. I trust you."

I know they are talking about trusting me to choose a good destination, but hearing those words offer me immense relief. "Thanks."

"Yeah. Just one thing. If those places are more than a ten-minute drive, we should take your car. My ride is not exactly comfortable these days."

"Cesar told you to bring him the car!" I chastise.

"No. It's cool. Tom lent me his barn truck, so I'm okay for a while. It's reliable. But it doesn't smell too good."

That makes me chuckle despite the small sting of the boundary line their choice establishes. They are still cautious. I'm still earning their trust. "Fair enough. Maybe we could start smaller. You said you would take me to an antique mall or a historic dam. Are those things you miss about Kentucky?"

"Not really. I miss how green it is. I miss hearing crickets instead of traffic."

"I'm sure California green is way different than Kentucky green. Bonelli Park is pretty nice, and it's close. We could hike around there. Maybe plan a picnic?"

"That sounds nice, Emelynn."

I lean my chin on my hand. Do they know how warm I feel every time they say my name? "When are you free?" I ask.

"I happen to be free tomorrow morning," they say.

"Well look at that," I say. "So am I."

CHAPTER FORTY-FIVE

Alex

"Wow! This is way more green than I expected," I say at the rise of a hill along the hike Emelynn selected. It's more open than back home, less wooded, but the exact green I need.

"For three months, this is about the prettiest place I can imagine," Emelynn says. "Once we're into the warm part of spring, forget it. It'll be hot and dry up here. That's when it's nice to play in the lake. My brothers love their Jet Skis. Have you tried them before?"

"Never," I say, happy to pause with this distant view of the lake she's talking about. I'm equally drawn to the view of Emelynn in her stretchy hiking pants and cropped T-shirt. And glasses! I never noticed that she had contacts in, but she must have, and for her to wear glasses today makes me feel like she wants me to see the real her—the Clark Kent, not the made-up Superman.

I'm wary, though, which she has clearly registered. When she arrived at my house, I could tell that she was disappointed that I was already waiting on the porch. I'm self-conscious about renting where I do. I can't show my meager living arrangements to a woman who owns a house, even if she purchased it with the help of her family in order to flip it.

I enjoy hearing Emelynn talk about the other houses her brothers have flipped, partly because the details interest me, but more so because it matches the story she told me the weekend we hung out during the trial, further confirming her insistence that I know her.

After returning our water to the backpack she happily let me shoulder when we reached the park, we continue on the trail as it dips and rises through hills covered with lush green plants and yellow mustard. It blows my mind that there is this much undeveloped land in Southern California. The sky is vast and deep blue, crisp white clouds zipping across, sporadically blocking the sunlight. It's like being in a real-life time-lapse video, especially because according to this made-up story of mine, this is my first date with Emelynn, yet we have fallen into such a familiar rhythm as we walk.

"So your brothers Jet Ski. Are you into that, too?"

"I'll go for a spin around the lake if one of them is driving, but honestly, I like the lake better this time of year when it's so quiet, especially during the week when we practically have the place to ourselves."

"Do you come for the day to Jet Ski?"

"Oh, no. If they haul out the Jet Skis, it's for a trip. When we were little, our family got a campsite for a week every summer. My dad tried to teach us to fish in the lake. Cooked on a camp stove. Slept on the ground. The works."

"That sounds amazing. My family did a few car trips that I remember, but we never camped."

"Have you camped on your own?" Emelynn asks.

"Nope. It's so overwhelming, all the stuff it involves. Tom's invited me along on a wagon ride. All I'd need is my sleeping bag. He has a crew that does all the cooking, but…I don't know. It's nice for him to invite me, but that's his world. You know?"

She pauses and turns to look at me. She's thinking of me in her world, how I've dipped a toe in already by meeting Cesar and Mateo. "You could camp with us. We haven't gone for years, but I bet I could get my brothers on board. They like you, and not only because you're a good painter." She begins walking again. "Are you hungry for lunch soon? There's a nice spot at the next rise, or if a picnic table would be better, we can hold off. I brought snacks, too."

"I don't need a picnic table," I say, though I'm not really thinking about food. I want to talk more about her family. The hill is steep enough that it steals my breath, so it's not until we're settled on the thin blanket Emelynn spread a few paces off the trail that I circle back around. "What did your brothers say about me?"

"Nothing. That's how I know they like you. They're not making a list of all the reasons you're no good for me." She pulls out sandwiches. "I got my favorites. A turkey and their 'Green Monster,' which is vegetarian. I wasn't sure what you'd be in the mood for since you did tofu when we had Thai."

"That's nice of you to remember."

"I remember lots of things," she says, glancing at my mouth.

I could kiss Emelynn. The trial is over, and if I trust what the studio has told me, I'm finished with all the interview filming I was required to do. Now, all that's left is to wait and keep my mouth shut about the whole project until it releases.

She pauses a moment before she unwraps the sandwiches as if she's thinking about the possibilities of the day as well. When it's clear neither one of us is crossing that line, the moment passes. The sandwiches are cut in half, so we agree to do half of each. Emelynn takes a bite of the turkey and checks with her thumb to make sure she hasn't gotten any mustard on her face. The small gesture makes me smile. As if I need any more reason to stare at her mouth. "What?" she asks.

"Nothing. This is nice, being here without Vicki."

She laughs, a glorious sound that comes from deep in her belly. She has the back of her wrist pressed to her mouth, and her eyes twinkle. I appreciate that she let me start this day with my farce, but it's better to acknowledge the rockiness that the trial caused. "Yeah, she sure complicated things." Her gaze jumps from my eyes to my mouth. She quirks an eyebrow and leans over to kiss my cheek before taking another bite of her sandwich.

The chaste kiss relaxes me. There is no need to rush anything. I can settle into this day together, sit under our wide expanse of blue sky that makes it seem like anything is possible. We don't rush back to the trail once we've finished lunch. Instead, we lie on our backs and watch the clouds slow-dance across the sky as we talk about TV shows we enjoy. It's no surprise to learn that she loves reality TV. There is nothing she can say to interest me in high-drama shows like *Alone* or *The Bachelor*, but considering the company I'd be in, catching an episode of programs I've never heard of that showcase uncommon interests like glassblowing in *Blown Away* or bladesmithing in *Forged in Fire* wouldn't be so bad. "My cousin's husband actually competed in that one," she tells me. "I'd love to show you."

"That sounds great," I say, savoring the ease of making plans together.

"Come on. There's one more thing I want to show you," she says.

The sun is sinking in the sky as we descend the hillside to what she tells me is Puddingstone Lake. She takes my hand and pulls me to a fishing pier jutting out into the water. It's calm and reflecting the soft pink and orange clouds. We are alone, save for several ducks paddling near the shore.

On the hills to the east are houses that must have an unbelievable view. Across the lake are snow-capped mountains, the San Gabriels, Emelynn tells me. "The tallest peak is Mount Baldy. Even when the snow melts, it looks bald because there are no trees at the top. It's another good hike if you enjoyed today."

She barely looks at me as she says this. "How can you have any doubt that I enjoyed this day with you?" I ask, incredulous.

"I guess I just don't want to get my hopes up."

I reach up to caress her cheek. "You know what the best part of today has been?"

"What?" she whispers, her gaze on my mouth.

"Making a list of other things we'll do together."

She hmms and turns toward me, her own fingers lightly resting on my neck, teasing my hair. "I wonder if I could top that."

The way her gaze falls to my mouth, I can tell she wants to kiss me, and I flash back to her kitchen when she'd said she'd wanted to. *What's stopping you?* I'd asked. And now I know. I imagine the battle she waged with herself with Vicki screaming to take a step back and Emelynn insisting that a kiss was all right. She'd tried to put on the brakes to protect us, and I'm the one who hit the gas. I was part of that, too. "What's stopping you?" I ask.

I can tell by her smile that she remembers, too. "Absolutely nothing," she says as she leans forward, her lips finally meeting mine.

This is not our first kiss. I already know if I ask for more, she will meet me. I take my time, though, pulling at her soft lips with my own before I dare to taste her again. She gasps and leans further into me when I run my fingers through her hair. I wrap her in my arms and she pulls my face closer, both of her arms around my neck now, pulling me into her. Heat builds inside me as her hands roam my back, and I cannot hold back a moan. Emelynn smiles against my mouth.

Eyes still closed, I sigh. "You set my world on fire."

"Open your eyes."

I do as she says, and the clouds are red as fire all around us.

CHAPTER FORTY-SIX

Emelynn

"Okay, gold faucets it is." Cesar's voice infiltrates my thoughts.

"What? God, no! Gold faucets are trendy, and I hate trendy."

"Like I don't know that," Cesar grumps.

"Then why would you ask that?" I snap back.

"Because you're in your own little world. You're not helping at all here."

"I'll help. I'm helping," I say, vowing to keep my head in the Home Depot with him. It's difficult to manage when all I want to think about is Alex. Since our hike at Bonelli Park, we've seen each other every day. At first, Alex would text at the end of their workday and ask questions about my day, how it had been, what I was thinking about doing for dinner. They would offer to bring burgers, as if I needed any incentive for their company.

After I cooked a few dinners, they insisted on bringing groceries and helping with the meal. It has never been easier for me to fall into a routine with someone than it has been with Alex. I love hearing about their day as we wash and chop vegetables. I love lounging on the couch pretending to watch reality TV shows while I discover more things I love about their mouth and hands.

"Riiiiiight," Cesar says.

I snap back to the store aisle. "I'm sorry. I was trying to remember what the fixtures were in a bathroom I just saw. Hold on. I have a picture saved." I open my phone and quickly swipe past the lock-screen picture of me and Alex. "Brushed nickel. That's what it was." I book it down the aisle to the brushed nickel section.

"So that's why you're so happy?" Cesar chins in the direction of my phone.

"I'm not happy!" Cesar gut laughs at this, but I ignore him, taking in the selection of fixtures. "This'll work," I say, grabbing the smallest faucet.

"No, it won't. Dudes can't get their hands under tiny faucets like that." He holds his hands out. "I hate cramming my hands under those tiny spouts."

"Thank goodness I don't have to worry about accommodating monster hands like yours," I say, my thoughts quickly shifting to Alex's perfect hands.

"So, you and Alex...When did you two hook up?"

"Excuse me? We have not hooked up!" I say.

He holds up his hands. "Okay, okay. My mistake." He hands me the same faucet style I liked but with a longer neck on the spout.

"Sure."

He grabs another for the second sink and places it in the cart. "Why haven't you hooked up yet?"

"How about this for the shower?" I ask, choosing a set with a nice wide spout.

"Yeah, good pick. There's room for two under that."

I slug him, and he shuffles away, laughing.

"We have not gotten naked."

"Not because you don't want to," he observes.

I don't have any comeback for that and try again to steer the conversation away from me and Alex by asking Cesar about a curtain rod that bends away from the tub to allow for more room. He laughs harder, and I realize I'm still painting a picture of a shower that could accommodate two.

"There's something going on, though? With Alex? Is their name Alex, or was that an acting thing?"

"Alex is their real name, and our show is wrapped, so we're free to..."

"Bang each other," Cesar says on top of me saying "Explore."

"Stop." I scowl.

"What? You always spill."

I push the cart toward the selection of mirrors. "This is different. I haven't ever dated a nonbinary person before. I don't know how comfortable they are with their body. I don't want to make any assumptions."

"But you want to sleep with them."

I glance up and down the aisle, thankful we're alone. Could he pick a worse place to ask me these questions? Our parents' house flashes in my mind, and I'm immediately grateful for where we are. "Well, duh."

"So you say, 'Want to come back to my place?' And then they either say yes or slap you."

"You're really helpful. They've been to my place, remember? We're already at my place."

"So what's the problem? What are you waiting for?"

"It's their call. I almost messed this up already, so I have to be careful. I can't rush them."

I push ahead of him, ignoring him to read the signage at each aisle so I don't have to explain. "Oh, this is cool," I say, an endcap with paint supplies stopping me in my tracks. There's an extension pole that holds both paint rollers and brushes. "Do you think Alex needs this?"

"I think what Alex needs is a good lay. Whether that would help...I don't know. You know more about lesbians than I do."

"I'm being literal here. This is about how many houses there are in California with insanely high ceilings, not about what would get Alex into bed. I don't even know if Alex identifies as lesbian."

"Wouldn't that be a good thing to know about your girl… wait. What do you call someone you're dating when they use they/them pronouns? Your themfriend?"

I throw up my hands. "I don't know! I thought you wanted to get all the things we need for the bathroom, not grill me about my personal life."

"But this is way more fun," he says, putting the pole extension tool in the basket. He winks at me. "Can't hurt."

He thankfully drops the topic to focus on our shopping. By the time we've unloaded everything, he's ready to call it a day. While I wait for Alex, I squeeze the lemons Cesar brought me from his place and make a pitcher of lemonade. I drag a stool to the front porch and prop my feet on the railing to wait for Alex. My mind circles back to what my brother asked about what I call Alex if we're dating. I'm pretty sure we're dating. I'm waiting for them at the end of my day, knowing that they'll be on their way over after they wrap up their job for the day. Isn't that what people do when they are dating?

As I've been doing a lot more frequently these days, I pull out my phone to search the web. Some of the suggestions that come up for what phrase to use completely baffle me. "Enbyfriend?" It cracks me up that Cesar was fairly close suggesting *themfriend* when in the list is *theyfriend*. I try it out, whispering, "Theyfriend. This is my theyfriend." Nope. Does not feel right on my tongue.

Whatever the word is, the sight of Alex slowing to pass my house and back their borrowed truck up the driveway brings a smile to my face. Impatient for their lips to be on mine, I set down my drink and lean over the rail to get my first kiss of the day. I catch the back of their neck so I can run my fingers in their downy hair while I reacquaint myself with their beautiful mouth.

"Is that lemonade?" they ask, smacking their lips.

"It sure is. I'll get you a glass."

They stow their tools out of the way and join me in the kitchen, sipping the lemonade. "Oh, that's good," they say.

"I feel like quite the homemaker, welcoming home her…" They quirk their head to the side, and I put my hand on my hip.

"Okay. Help me out here, because Cesar asked me today what to call you, and I tried searching it up, and what does enbyfriend even mean?"

"Nonbinary."

"Ohhhhh. The two letters." I smack my head. "Gotcha. Do I call you my enbyfriend?"

They set their lemonade down on the counter to wrap their arms around me. It brings our hips together, which brings to mind the other question I want to ask Alex. I want more of them. They thread their fingers through the two closest belt loops. "Cesar asked what to call me?"

"He did." I search their eyes. In this light, they are not solid brown. There are two shades, subtle, like the difference between two river rocks, but it's like a sunburst. They blink away from me, taking away the warmth. "Tell me what you're thinking."

"The last time I tried this, I was someone's girlfriend. When that label didn't work for me, we ended up not working at all."

"I like *you*, Alex." I cup my hand along their jaw, stroking their face with my thumb. "If you want me to say 'This is Alex, the person I'm dating,' I'm cool with that."

"I want to be your person, but..."

"Can we stop there? I like that. I think you could be my person."

"Other people don't get it, and there's always going to be someone new questioning it."

Their eyes betray how heavily being questioned weighs on them. "So let's stay right here. I get you. Can't that be enough?" My lips find Alex's, and the zing of lemon sets off my hair-trigger tingles. I wrap my arms behind their neck, pulling them closer, kissing past the bitter until there is only the sweet. I move to their neck, kissing and nipping my way up to their ear. I want all of them. The way my arms are wrapped around them, the energy between us is my whole world. I take their earlobe in my teeth and pull ever so slowly, releasing it when I hear their breath hitch. "I want you to be my person, Alex. I want you."

I wish I could see their eyes when I speak that truth. They rest their forehead on my shoulder and move their hands to my back. I wrap my arms around them, wanting to erase the hurt they brought from Kentucky. An idea hits me. "I'll tell you what we need. Primer."

CHAPTER FORTY-SEVEN

Alex

"Primer?" I'm completely baffled by Emelynn's shift in conversation. If she's trying to distract me from how insecure talking about labels makes me, she's succeeded.

"Yes! We need mental primer. I don't know what your ex said, but it must be like the neon green that a previous homeowner chose for a bathroom in the last house we flipped. Even the ceiling was green. It felt like stepping into an alien ship's portal beam. It took two coats of primer to keep that awful color from bleeding through."

"Okay," I say, playing with this metaphor she's offering. "Sure. For that one bathroom, you can cover up the bad decision and replace it with something better."

"Like me," she supplies, pulling me into another kiss.

It's difficult to maintain my focus when she kisses me like this. It feels so good when I can keep my mind connected to what my body is experiencing in that moment. Since kissing Emelynn on our hike, it has gotten easier to believe that what I am feeling is safe. Emelynn has never asked me to be anyone but myself. She is better than anything I ever imagined, and the way she kisses me makes me think about more. It's clear that Emelynn's ready for more right now, and that's all I need to be thrown out of the moment.

"I heard a 'but' coming and wanted to chase it away," Emelynn says.

She's running her fingers through my cropped hair. The way she closes her fingers and softly tugs is almost enough to bring me back into the moment. But...I don't want to finish the idea. I want to be settled in my skin and ready to take Emelynn's hand and follow her wherever she wants to lead me.

"But?" Emelynn prompts me again.

I'm reluctant to finish the sentence because I don't want to reveal to Emelynn that I am a work in progress.

"Have you seen the bathroom?" Again, she takes an abrupt turn in the conversation.

"No?" She can't be letting me off the hook this easily, I think, following her as she takes off through the house at California speed. Everyone here walks as if the hills are on fire.

The room is gutted. New pipes for the two-sink cabinet she chose for the space stick out from the wall. The floor is checkered with new sub-flooring. Emelynn points to bright new two-by-fours set into the wall. "Wait until you see the cute tile I picked out once I finally convinced Cesar that a recessed shampoo shelf was the way to go. He'll thank me later."

"Is your point that you have a vision?"

She wraps her arm around my waist. "My point is that I live in constant flux and mess. I don't like the small bathroom in the primary bedroom, but I moved all my stuff in there so Cesar and Mateo can remodel this bathroom, and once they're done, I'll move all my stuff back in here while they demolish another part of the house. That's why I live here. I'm not scared of a mess. Once this house is turnkey, they'll sell it and we'll buy another place that needs a ton of work, and I'll move in and live there while they fix it up. It's how we work! I'm betting your 'but' is about how one bathroom is one bathroom, but there are more rooms in the house and more rooms in other houses. Am I right?"

"Spot on," I say, impressed at her ability to read me. "But it's not as simple as relocating and starting over with people who get me better than my ex or my family did. I appreciate that you say you can cope with messy. It's exhausting, though. Eventually, you're going to want a place that's in order."

She considers this. "Okay. That's fair. When my acting career takes off, I'll for sure want to keep a house we fix up. Let's say I stayed in the house I was describing, and the bathroom looked great after two coats of primer and two coats of paint. Which it did."

"Who did the painting?"

"Someone not nearly as talented as you, but it was still way better. You're not letting me get to the point, though. Eventually, the bathroom would need repainting. If we put on the same paint we picked, 'Barely Lemon,' and a white ceiling—Who paints the ceiling the same color as the room?"

"Agreed," I insert without derailing her.

"I wouldn't need to prime. I could, well *you* could put on a fresh coat, and it would look great."

"You are very optimistic."

"You say that like it's a bad thing." She has her hand on her hip. She's wearing a loose white V-neck tee and low-rise jeans. She's barefoot, her hair in a messy whale spout, and wearing her cute glasses. She is utterly at home and herself in a way I never have been, and I worry about how flighty I am in my body. How can she like me when I'm not absolutely certain that I like myself? "What I want to know," she says, her voice so seductive, "is whether I'm persuasive."

I don't doubt Emelynn's patience with a project, but it intimidates me to be with someone who has a clear picture of how things are going to be. I'm afraid that she sees me as a finished product when I am still in the process of figuring out who I am outside of the box. How did we even get to talking about being together long enough to need a second coat? I trace back in the conversation. Cesar. "Your brother really asked what to call me?"

She lights up. "He did. *And* he told me to get you this." She rifles through a bag and pulls out a tool I can attach to a pole extension that would hold a paintbrush.

"Sweet!" I say. "He told you to get it?"

"Well, I asked if I should get it, and...Yeah..." It looks like a slew of information she doesn't seem to want to share passes through her mind.

"You two are twin close, even as adults, aren't you?" I ask.

"That is such a good way to put it." She relaxes a bit and points to the tool. "Will that be helpful, or is it an endcap gimmick? If it's not helpful, I can return it."

"No. I want to try it out." It touches me that the two of them were thinking about me and talking about me, so much so that my emotion embarrasses me. I place it with my pile of gear. "Thank you for picking it up. Thank Cesar for me, too?"

"Or you could text him. He wants to get back to the Orange Beast. Is it at your place or out at Tom's?"

"At Tom's," I say. "What did you want to do for dinner tonight?"

"I see you maneuvering out of these sticky things, and I'll allow it because I am hungry."

I know she is responding to my question about dinner, but the way her voice resonates on *hungry* reminds me that she narrates sex scenes. The cadence and timbre of her voice pull things tight inside me. If I suggest feeding the hunger I recognize in her eyes first, she will have me in her bedroom in an instant. It's so easy to imagine how I would like to satisfy Emelynn. The hitch is in what she expects from me. Her perception of me is based on how I present myself. Taking off that armor scares me. What if it turns out I'm not what she wants? She has paused on that, providing a space I could step into. I want to be ready to step into that space, but I'm not, so I say, "But?"

Her eyebrows dance, and her mouth is pursed to the side in an indulgent smile. "But promise me you'll think about trusting Cesar with your car? He isn't offering because he wants money. He wants to work on it because he enjoys the puzzle of an old engine, and he likes you, and if you bring him the car, he'll be able to tease me about how much I like you, and he loves to tease me."

"I'll think about it," I promise.

"Good. I'll tell him my person is thinking about it." She leans forward slightly as she tests out the phrase on me.

"Okay," I say without my typical rumination. Everything else we have talked about has gotten tangled in my mind, but that last statement goes straight to my heart, and my heart accepts it without question.

Now a true smile lights up her face. "Okay!" She wraps me in a hug and whispers, "I'm not interested in changing you, Alex. Please don't take any of this paint talk to mean that you need a remodel. I like you for you and whatever part of yourself you'll share with me."

"Thanks," I say, because she's given me so much to think about that I don't quite know how to respond.

"And if anyone needs a remodel, it's me." She steps away from me and smacks her utterly perfect butt. "I need to work out."

"You have to be kidding. You're turnkey."

"Well, a workout never hurt anyone." Her eyebrows dance, so I don't miss her meaning of the workout she's picturing.

CHAPTER FORTY-EIGHT

Emelynn

"Let's bring this home," Alex says as we tap paddles and switch sides of the court. Their eyes and smile compete for sparkle, and it's as hard to resist them as it is for Sarah and Jass to return their serve. "Ten, nine, two." Alex calls the score and smacks the ball crosscourt.

This one Sarah returns smack down the middle of the court. We've already worked out that middle of the court is for whichever of us is hitting forehand, so Alex handily returns it. Jass and I literally stand there doing nothing but watch Alex and Sarah smack the small yellow ball back and forth at such a rapid pace I can hardly keep it in sight. Then Alex switches to a gentle dink to Jass's side, and it bounces twice before Jass can get there.

She's laughing as she joins us at the net to bump paddles and congratulate each other on a close game.

"Yay!" Chloe hollers from the sideline. "Ice cream! Ice cream! Ice cream!"

"It's that time," Jass says. "Want anything?"

I'm about to decline, but her glance between Sarah and Alex clues me in on the right answer. "I'm game. Alex?"

"If you're getting something, an ice cream sandwich," they say.

"You got it."

"You know what I want," Sarah says to Jass with a wink, and I get the impression what she wants is not on an ice cream truck. As we circle the courts to get to the parking lot where the truck is blaring the worst jingle I've ever heard on a fifteen-second loop, Jass thanks me for giving Sarah and Alex a moment to catch up. "Sarah hasn't said much about the project y'all worked on, but she likes to check in and make sure Alex is doing okay. I'm glad you were able to join us this time."

"I am, too. I'm surprised by how much I like pickleball." It stings to hear that Alex has continued to play with them since we started dating and has only now invited me, but I suspect it's for the reason Jass has identified.

"Same. Don't tell Chloe, but it's way more fun to play against a couple. Oh, wait. I'm making a huge presumption there."

"It's okay. Alex is my person." I'm so glad that my brother spurred me to have the conversation with Alex, not just because I have the right language at the tip of my tongue but also because I like knowing that Alex and I are on the same page, at least when it comes to dating.

We all make our choices and exchange a ridiculous amount of money for our treats. I unwrap my Drumstick and take a bite. It's soft enough that I'll have to deliver Alex's ice cream sandwich without dithering, which won't give them much time to chat with Sarah. But they had to have known that when they asked for ice cream, which means they didn't intend to talk in depth about anything, which frustrates me. I told Alex I am good at messy, and I am trying to honor that and give them time to settle in and trust me.

But we are moving glacially slow despite the ways I have tested the water to go further. They don't seem to have any problem when I guide their hands under my shirt. My nipples stiffen at the memory of Alex helping me out of my shirt, lifting it over my head, bathing my breasts with attention. I have felt Alex's weight where I most want to feel their hand or mouth, but only that.

I hand them their ice cream and say, "I sort of feel like I've stepped back to junior high school, like buying you an ice cream will convince you that I like you as more than a friend." I mean it in silliness, but the twinge of hurt on Alex's face makes me immediately regret my words. I try to cover my passive-aggressive comment by saying, "It's probably been that long since I've bought anything from an ice cream truck."

My pitiful attempt falls flat.

The group is now standing in collective awkwardness, and I feel like an enormous shit.

"That's maybe quite apropos given Alex's transition." She turns and rests a hand on Alex's arm. "Please correct me if I'm wrong. I'm merely making an observation based on a memoir of nonbinary stories that I read recently. Several wrote about how they felt like they had to go through puberty again, some more than others. I'm sure that there are many factors."

There's an even more awkward silence.

"I'm sorry if I…I'm sorry I overstepped," Sarah says.

"No! *I'm* sorry. That was inappropriate of me to say." I wish I could disappear.

Alex unwraps their ice cream sandwich, ripping the paper in the middle so their fingers don't stick to the cookie. They redirect the conversation by asking Chloe what they picked.

She holds up her popsicle and says, "Dora!" with a giggle.

Jass rolls her eyes, and Sarah says, "Inside joke."

Alex whispers, "It's not creepy to eat a character's face?"

Humor restores the relaxed atmosphere as we finish our treats before packing up our things and saying goodbye to Sarah's family, but I am still upset with myself. I take Alex's hand as we walk to my car. Once we're inside, I say, "I'm really sorry I said what I did."

"No, don't be. It reminds me of all the stories about teenagers who get kicked out when they come out and inevitably make their way to the West Coast. That is so me. I'm closing in on thirty, but I'm hardly different than a teenager trying to live on their own for the first time."

"You have so much more stability than that," I say.

"But not the maturity."

"God, I am such an asshole."

"Emelynn, stop. I'm not mad," they say. "I know you're frustrated with me because I keep slamming on the brakes."

I can't help interrupting with a string of "I'm sorries," but Alex keeps talking over me. "I've been so worried about disappointing you because we're not teenagers. You know what you want, and I'm terrified about whether or not I can deliver. I relate to the teenager who has no idea what they are doing more than I want to admit."

"Oh." This isn't what I was expecting them to say at all.

"Hollywood is super clear on what cishet women should want, and the lesfic Lilian read explained what I should want if I'm lesbian, but I'm neither of those things, and when I started presenting more masc, Lilian flipped out, assuming that I'd want to top her." They've delivered all of this to the glove compartment and glance toward me to see how it's landing. Their voice is barely above a whisper when they say, "But I never wanted that."

"What do you want, Alex?" They are rubbing their palms on their shorts, and I grasp their left hand. "That's the only question." I want these to be the magic words. The script I am writing has them saying *Let me show you*. And I am down for whatever that is. I don't know whether Alex has had any surgery, but I am sure that whether there are curves or muscular lines under Alex's clothes, they are going to be sexy as hell.

As has been the case for weeks, I'm light-years ahead of them, because instead of telling me to put the car in gear, they rub their thumb along my hand and say, "I don't know."

CHAPTER FORTY-NINE

Alex

I'm absolutely ready for Emelynn to say *Let me know when you figure it out* and drop me off at my truck, but she doesn't. She asks what I feel like for dinner. She says she has leftover chicken we can put into burritos with so many greens that it basically sounds like a salad in a wrap with the chicken thrown in. "Cesar drowns it with dressing, so I have it on hand, but I don't use it. Or I could make beans and we could do bean and cheese?"

I want to ask why we are talking about dinner instead of how I can't express what I want. I lied to her when I said I don't know what I want, and it feels awful.

"Or we could stop for takeout on the way home."

I don't have the brainpower to sort through all the choices. "I don't know. What do you feel like?"

"Bean and cheese, if it's really all the same to you."

When I nod, she starts the car, and we drive the short distance from the park to her house. The car is silent, but my thoughts are loud and unkind. I should not have told her about not wanting to top Lilian. I should have had an answer when she asked what I want. How hard is it to answer one stupid question? I glance over expecting Emelynn to be frustrated, but she's serene and even smiles when she glances my way.

Once we're home, she starts pulling out the ingredients, piling them on the counter. I like being at Emelynn's house. It's not on a major road like my place is, so it's quiet, and I don't have to run to my room to grab my toilet paper if I need to use the restroom. Even though it's not hers, it's clearly a home, not a resting place for misfits. "Why are you doing this?" I ask.

"Making dinner? Because I thought we were hungry?" Emelynn says.

"C'mon. You know I'm not talking about dinner. Why are we having this lighthearted conversation about anything but what we're really thinking?"

She's bent over from studying the contents of her fridge. She hooks her chin over the arm that's holding the door open. "What are we thinking about?"

"About how I don't know what I want." The lie I told in the car tastes even more bitter as I repeat it.

"I'm working on that, actually. It would take me a while to make beans. Is it okay if we switch to chicken?"

"Sure. Whatever."

"But I want you to be happy. Will you be happy with chicken?"

"If that's what you want, yes." We have never had such a lengthy discussion about dinner.

"I like lettuce, celery, and snap peas in there." She slides these things onto the counter. "Any suggestions?"

"Guacamole?"

"Yes. An essential. I make it with lime, onion, cilantro, tomato."

I don't follow why she's outlining all the ingredients. "Are you trying to distract me from what we were talking about?"

"Nope. Trying to make a point. Have you had guacamole with fresh cilantro? It's not for everyone. Some people say it tastes like soap."

"Oh. I don't think I've had it."

"How do you make guacamole?" She's got her hand on her hip now like this is important.

"I add a spoonful of sour cream and a spoonful of salsa. Salt and pepper. That's what I learned."

"Okay. I want to make you happy. Let's do that tonight."

"Are you sure? I mean, I could try your way."

"Let's do yours tonight. If we don't like it, we'll try my way next time."

"This feels really weird."

"Kind of awkward?"

"Exactly."

"We could stop." She pauses.

I'm obviously missing something here. My chest starts to feel tight when it occurs to me that she might be making everything super awkward to point out how we don't match. "Mind if I get a glass of water?"

"Not at all. I'll drink water tonight, too."

After I fill our waters, I am about to start work on my guacamole when I see her chopping. "Wow, the only time I've ever seen anyone chop that fast was on TV."

She laughs. "I worked in a kitchen for a while. Not quite the waiter dreaming about her big break trope, but close."

"Have you done anything before *Civic Duty*? Or is it the break you've been waiting for?"

It's a safe topic. I get to hear about the miseries of being cast as an extra, the stint trying to do stand-up comedy because she'd heard that was a good route to late-night TV. "Turns out I'm not funny. My timing's all fucked up. Cesar says I've been strung too tight since before my first breath. I was stretched out transverse in my mom's belly." She shows me with her arm wrist to elbow between her hips. "He was head down, ready to rock and roll, and my mom says he's the one who popped the amniotic sac. So there she was, going into labor because her water broke, and the midwife is doing everything to slow it down because they've got to wait for the doctor to do the cesarean because she was sure I wasn't coming out."

All the ingredients chopped, she expertly lines the middle of each tortilla and folds them. She hands me one of the plates, which I carry to the table. She sets down her plate and rummages around in a drawer, returning with a pad of paper and a pen. These she sets aside to pick up her burrito.

After a few bites, she says, "This guacamole works. It needs a little kick, though." She puts down her burrito, popping the veggies that spilled out into her mouth. She returns with a slice of lime. "Some?"

"Mine's perfect," I say. Every bite has a nice mixture of texture and flavor. We go back and forth about what types of food we like and what level of heat we can tolerate. She tells me about watching Chef Ramsey on *Hot Ones*. When we're finished, she stops me as I reach to clear her plate. Her hand caressing my wrist, she says in a sultry voice, "That was so nice."

"Um. Yeah. I said it was delicious."

"So it was good for you, too?"

"Wait," I sputter, dropping back into my chair. "Why does it sound like you're talking about sex?"

"Because we made something together. We used words and talked about what we liked and what we didn't, and it was nice, right? Isn't it practically the same as sex?" She pulls the paper toward her and draws a figure that comes out looking like a gingerbread person on it.

"What if instead of talking preferences, we talked about erogenous zones? Shall we start with the top or the bottom?" She taps the head and the feet.

"Feet?" I screw up my face. "Why would you start with feet?"

"I had a partner once who was utterly turned on by a foot rub. Don't get me wrong. I love a foot rub at the end of the day, but it's more likely to put me to sleep than get me in the mood. But." She smiles playfully. "Kiss the backs of my knees? That sends signals." She puts an E next to where the figure's knee would be and then puts another one in the chest area. "I figure you already gathered that I love for my partner to play with my breasts."

She places the pen on the paper and pushes it toward me and collects my plate, taking both to the sink. I'm staring at the gingerbread person. Emelynn has given me permission to start anywhere, big or small. My heart is racing, but it's only us, and the gingerbread figure is detached enough to make the topic less threatening. I decide to follow her pattern. I put an A on the figure's hand. "My hands are super sensitive, like my wrists? If I'm, you know, messing around myself? I kind of…bite them?"

Emelynn returns to the table but sits next to me instead of across from me. She takes my hand in hers, and for a moment, I'm scared she's going to try out what I described, but instead she strokes from wrist to the end of each finger, bottom and then top. "You have such beautiful hands." She kisses each fingertip before setting our intertwined hands on her lap.

"I think yours are beautiful," I whisper. There are so many things I would like to say about how I find fingers erogenous, but I don't feel ready for that. It would be easy to describe how sensitive the area below my hip is or how much I liked it when she pulled on my earlobe with her teeth, but I want to meet Emelynn where she is. "I'm sure you've noticed I didn't do top surgery. I am happy in the body I was born with, and I don't mind my partner touching or kissing my chest. It just doesn't send any signals anywhere. At least it didn't with Lilian, and she wanted to be with someone who was responsive to that kind of touch."

Emelynn squeezes my hand. "Thank you for sharing that."

"It wasn't as hard as I thought it would be. Maybe because you have this ridiculous figure?" I put an A with a question mark parallel with Emelynn's initial at its chest. I put an A where the figure's wrist would be.

She takes the pen from me and places an E and A on either side of the figure's head where ears would be.

"You noticed?"

"I did. But it might be good to double-check." With her hand on my thigh, she leans over and traces my ear from tip to lobe with her tongue. She slowly lets out her breath, awakening the whole area. I shiver and tip my head, wanting her to use her teeth again. She nuzzles behind my ear and starts to use her teeth on my neck. It feels so damn good. I grab her hand and whimper as she does her best to reduce me to a puddle.

I hear her sit back in the chair, but I keep my eyes closed for a few more beats, letting the tingles travel through my body. When I open my eyes, she's grinning wickedly. She's waited to mark another A under the ear area. "Confirmed ears and established your neck area."

Though I have spent a good amount of time kissing Emelynn's neck, I seize the opportunity to test further. I test out the tracing and nipping strategies Emelynn used on me. Her gasps and fingers tightening on my thigh indicate that she is just as much a fan of using teeth as I am. I slide the fingers of my hand into her hair and gently pull to stretch the skin of her neck tight under my lips and tongue.

The way she draws out the word *fuck* fills me with heat. I'm standing now, turning her chair so I can straddle her and get both of my hands in her hair as I kiss her. Her silken lips slide along my own, and her nails scrape along my scalp. Her fingers direct the energy our kiss produces, moving from my head down the sides of my arms and then back up the tender inside. She surprises me with both of her hands pressed soundly under my armpits and running solidly, possessively along my body to rest on my hips.

Her slow hands light up my chest with sensation that gathers in my belly before pooling between my hips.

I have to echo her *fuck*, breaking away from the kiss, arching my body so my muscles pull tight and reverberate with feeling.

That, of course, is when I hear a gasp coming from the wrong direction.

CHAPTER FIFTY

Emelynn

"Cesar! What. The. Actual. Fuck?" I shout as my stupid-ass brother tries to tiptoe across the kitchen in his heavy work boots.

"Don't mind me," he says, running once he hits the hallway. "Carry on!"

If Alex could crawl into my armpit, they would. They jerked when Cesar so subtly entered the kitchen, but I wrapped my arms tighter around them before they could get anywhere. They still have their face buried in my chest.

"Do you think he saw me?"

I laugh so hard, they're forced to sit up.

"Oh! And Mateo is meeting me here. Should be here any—"

"Hey, Alex!" Mateo says, entering the house as if on cue.

"I will obviously be changing the locks and locking the door whenever we are here," I announce to everyone.

"I picked up the cabinet, and this is when Teo could help me carry it in," Cesar says. "Bathroom's clear."

Alex wriggles off my lap and carries our glasses of water to the sink. I quickly grab our erogenous zone map and shove it into a drawer. "Would've been nice for you to warn me about the delivery."

Mateo waggles his phone at me, and the two disappear out to the truck.

I pull out my cell, and sure enough, there are texts from both stating they'll be by. I tip my phone to show Alex. "Guess I was distracted. I'm so sorry."

They're rubbing the back of their very flushed neck. "I should go."

I take their hand. "You really shouldn't. Our conversation was going so well. I, for one, was enjoying it. You?"

They smile sheepishly. "Maybe I can slip out the back and they'll forget I was here."

I scrape my fingernails through the short hair above their ear. "Not a chance. If you leave, you're abandoning me to their ruthless teasing."

They stop my hand with theirs and give it a squeeze. They're looking out the window. "Crap. I'm parked in."

"They don't have to install it tonight. I'll tell them to leave." Even as I say the words, I know there is no hope recovering the mood. My best bet is getting Alex into a space where they feel safe. "Grab your stuff. I'm sure the keys are in their truck."

Relief brings their shoulders down a full inch. "Thank you."

I take what they can't fit in their hands, and we do slip out the back as my brothers grunt and swear the cabinet through the front door. Alex is in their borrowed truck, engine turned over and ready to flee, but I make them roll down the window for one more quick kiss. "I will never forgive them for interrupting us."

"Yeah, you will," they say.

I pat their hand. Because they're right. I will. I jog to Mateo's work truck and pull out of the drive to release Alex, who waves as they leave.

"Crap," I mutter under my breath, parking the truck in the drive. Time to face the music.

They are working the cabinet over the pipes, and it's perfect, but I don't say that. "You two are such assholes!"

"You're welcome!" Mateo says. "You want us to clear out of here, so you can get back to your busy evening?"

"Alex left," I say.

"No!" Cesar says.

"Too late. You scared them away," I grump.

"Where'd that truck came from? They didn't get rid of the Orange Beast, did they?"

"No. I'm working on them."

"Oh, we could see that," Mateo says with a wink.

"Can we not?"

"Oh, we are," Cesar says. "I so knew you were into them."

"You gotta give him all the details since he can't hold on to his own woman," Mateo says. He's the only one of the three siblings who has been able to sustain long relationships. He thinks that Cesar and I ruined each other for relationships by sharing a womb, as if we had any choice in the matter.

"I could if I wanted," Cesar says. "We're just more discriminating than you are."

"I don't need to go out with a hundred girls to know that Esme's the one," Mateo says.

I roll my eyes, not wanting to get him started on his high school sweetheart. "Well, since the two of you have already screwed up my evening, are you installing the faucets?"

"Do we get dinner out of it?" Cesar says.

"Are you kidding me? I'm not feeding you to work on your own house."

He and I butt shoulders and push each other around as we both try to sift through the purchases we made at Home Depot. Once we have everything sorted, the three of us sit in a row in front of the cabinet, my brothers each installing a faucet and me changing out fixtures. I stand, hovering the camera high to get a picture of them.

"Real assholes!" Cesar says when I tell them both to look up.

"Yeah. Doesn't get any worse than us," Mateo agrees.

I decide the best way to get them to stop talking is to stop feeding the conversation. I'm finished way before they are and push my back against the new tub and send the picture I took to Alex. *Not how I wanted to be spending my evening*, I text. Relief floods through me when I immediately see dots come up on my screen.

But awesome progress! they reply.

True. But not as fun as the progress we were making.

"Is that Alex?" Cesar asks. "Tell them we really didn't mean to scare them away."

Cesar says they didn't mean to scare you away, I type.

Probably for the best.

I recoil like I've been slapped. *What? Why?* I type. To my brothers, I say, "I'm making a call. Is the faucet the only thing you two are doing tonight?"

Cesar and Mateo look at each other and start laughing. "We can stop here if you've got plans." Mateo draws out the word *plans* over several beats.

"Doesn't matter," I say breezily, kicking myself for giving them something so easy to throw back at me. "I'm going to clean up the kitchen."

"If you've got leftovers…" Cesar starts again.

"You know what? Go! This can wait until tomorrow."

"I've nearly got it, though," Mateo whines.

I'm still prickly aware of my brothers, but the longer Alex is quiet, the more I worry that they are regretting what we did, so I go to the kitchen and start loading the dishwasher. "Why would you say your leaving is for the best?" I ask as quietly as possible once Alex has answered.

I hear them blow out a breath. "There are things…I like it when…but if I talk about that, it goes below the belt, and…" They growl in frustration. "It should not be so hard to talk about this, but that's why it's better I left."

"Alex, I would never pressure you to talk about or do anything that makes you uncomfortable. Were you comfortable with the stuff we did today?"

It takes a few beats before they whisper, "Yes. I really, really like your hands on me."

"Good. Because I really like touching you." I drop my voice for more privacy. "I would have loved to push your shirt off and feel your skin. You have the best shoulders, and I get the impression it would be okay if I used my nails on your back." I'm worried I've pushed too far, but then they answer.

"Yes. I would love to feel your nails on my back. A lot."

Now it's my turn to growl. This is when Cesar and Mateo decide to mock tiptoe their way through my kitchen, Cesar making kissy faces.

"Emelynn?" Alex asks, their voice tentative.

"Sorry. My moronic brothers were leaving. Thank god." I stand in my kitchen, my hand resting on my chair. My body tingles remembering the weight of Alex on my lap. "You straddling me on the kitchen chair…That was fucking hot, by the way. I can't stop thinking about how I would have rather had that scene play out."

"I've been thinking about it, too," they say.

"Now that I'm alone, I'm picturing what I would have liked to come next. That okay?"

"Yes. That's okay."

"Then I'm going to toss your shirt aside and run my nails down your back while you kiss my neck."

"Um, in my mind, your shirt was off before mine."

"My arms are up to make that easier. Who's taking off my bra? You or me?"

"Let me," Alex says.

I sink into the chair, imagining myself shirtless and Alex tracing the edge of my bra as they undo the clasp. "Okay. It's off. Now yours." I close my eyes to better imagine Alex's shirt hit the floor. "Your skin feels so good."

"Can you do that thing you did when you ran your hands down my sides?"

"With pleasure." I remember how firm their muscles felt beneath my hands and how I barely grazed the sides of their chest with my thumbs. "I love your legs around me. I want to cup your ass and pull you close to me. I want to run my nails along the backs of your thighs."

"Would you…"

"Would I what, Alex?" I open my eyes to my bright, Alexless kitchen. "Tell me what you'd like."

CHAPTER FIFTY-ONE

Alex

What I want is exactly why it's good that Emelynn's brothers walked in when they did, because Emelynn's game was fun above the belt, but I sure didn't feel comfortable talking about what I want below the belt in her kitchen. Now I'm safe in my cave of a room, and I still am unsure about how to vocalize what I want. I tell myself that if Emelynn were here, I'd be able to take her hand, kiss her wrist and her fingertips like she did to mine earlier, and then take her pointer finger in my mouth. Visualizing this turns me on to the point that I am wet between my legs. I close my eyes and slip my hand into my pants. I'm so wet and so sensitive that I moan.

"Alex," Emelynn growls out my name. "Tell me what you're imagining."

My heart hammers in my chest. Emelynn is sitting in her kitchen, waiting on me. It scares me how much I like her and want to be with her. "Emelynn. I want to take your hand."

"Okay," she says.

"Can I put your finger in my mouth?"

"Fuck yes." She groans in my ear, spiking my already piqued desire.

"I want you to feel my lips and my tongue. And when your finger is wet, I want...god..." I can't believe I'm saying this out loud.

"Tell me, Alex," Emelynn says again. "Tell me what you want. You are so sexy, and I will touch you anywhere. My finger is wet."

"I want you inside," I whisper.

I hear her suck in a breath, and then her voice is low and sensual in my ear. "Alex..."

"Yes?"

"You are so wet." I press my fingers against my wetness and follow her voice, slipping my finger inside as she says, "So soft... so warm...so open."

I am. I'm so open. I want more and ask.

"Oh, you like two. You can feel me better now?"

"Emelynn?" What I'm doing feels so good, but it also feels wrong because I have worked hard to erase what puts me in the female box in the eyes of the world, the submissive woman, and this lands me firmly in a passive role, and I don't know if that's right. I don't know what it means to want this.

"Too much?"

"No!" Shit. I'm messing this up, making Emelynn doubt what she's doing, and there is nothing—nothing—worse than being touched tentatively. I need her to be sure. I need her to want to touch me.

"I've got my other hand on your ass. Does that feel okay?"

Imagining her hand cupping me, pulling me, letting me know that she wants me starts to return me to the sensations, my body tightening around my fingers. I am coiling tight, getting so close to the edge of release. I am panting with want.

"Put your hands on my shoulders," Emelynn whispers. "I want to taste your skin. I want your finger in my mouth."

I gasp. "I can't..." I am right on the brink, but I need both my hands. "I have to put down the phone," I whimper.

"Do whatever you need to do. You feel so amazing inside. You feel so good."

I drop the phone onto the pillow next to me and flip to my knees, which is all I need for release to crash over me. I groan and gasp into my pillow as I continue to rock against my hand, my orgasm continuing to ripple.

"Emelynn?" I'm panting as I flip back to my back, my hand tucked in my underwear, resting on my pulsing mound. "Are you still there."

"Oh, yeah. That worked?"

"So good. I really want to touch you now."

"Good. Because I really want you to touch me."

"But not in the chair. I need to lay you out on your bed. Can we relocate?" I close my eyes and imagine her leading me through the house. "I want to feel all of you, no pants. Can we lose those?"

"If you lose yours."

I shimmy out of my pants and undies. My sheets feel wonderful on my skin. "Naked now?"

"Naked," she whispers.

I groan. "I wish I could see all of you. I want to run my hands over your beautiful skin, your hips, your belly. You are so sexy. I want to kiss your breasts, but I already know you like that. I want to explore a little first. Didn't you say behind your knees is sensitive? I'm going to start there and draw slow circles with my tongue."

"But I want your mouth on my breasts. Can I pull you up here?"

This woman makes me swoon from miles away. I shake my head even though she can't see me. "Not so fast. I'm still exploring, kissing your thighs. Your hips. The inside of your elbow."

"You're killing me here. Mouth on breasts. I want your thigh between my legs, so I can feel you."

"Because you're wet?" I ask, imagining being there to test this instead of having to ask.

"Fuck yes."

"Okay. What next?"

She guides my movements, her breath coming in gasps and whimpers that stir my body to life again. "There…yes…don't…

stop…yes…yes…yesssssss." As she is tipping to climax, I press on my clit, wondering if this is what aftershocks might feel like if she is the epicenter six miles away.

"I wish I could take you in my arms. Do you want to be the tree or the koala?"

Her breath continues to come in pants and hitches. "Tree? Koala?"

"If I'm the tree, I put my arm out and you put your head on my chest and hold onto me like I'm the trunk. Or do you want to be the tree and have me snuggle into you?"

"I'm on my back, and I absolutely can't move. That makes me the tree?"

"Definitely tree. Wrap your arms around me."

"If only you were really here in my bed…I'd run my nails on your back again."

"That might get us into trouble." I chuckle.

"Oh, I think I'd like to get into trouble with you all night long." Her voice is smooth as syrup in this postclimax snuggle.

Even though we are not physically next to each other, my breath syncs to hers. "Emelynn?"

She hmms in my ear, but I can tell she does it with a smile. She likes it when I say her real name.

"You don't think it's weird…" Why can't I let us stay in an uncomplicated cuddle? Why does my brain have to start whirling again?

"Think what's weird?" she prompts.

"What I wanted? That I like…that I want you, you know… inside?"

"I do not think it's weird to want what you want. In fact, I think it's super hot to know and ask for what you want. Was it easier to ask for what you wanted without being in person?"

I sigh deeply, sleep pulling at me. "I think so. But now I wish my head was actually on your chest. I wish it was your mound my hand was resting on."

"Oh, a little bit possessive," she says, her voice a sweet tease in my ear.

"I…" When I realize I almost said *I love you* out loud, I startle as if I assumed I was walking on a level surface and missed a step.

"Alex?"

"I'm here. Sorry. I'm falling asleep on you."

"No. Me too. It's all good."

It's more than that as we say our good nights and sweet dreams. I hold the phone to my chest as if I'm the tree holding Emelynn and fall into a deep sleep.

CHAPTER FIFTY-TWO

Emelynn

"Soooooooo?" Cesar is letting himself in as I shuffle to the coffee maker the next morning. "Is Alex here?"

"No." Alex's name sends a wave of heat through my body. The way they made me feel with their voice alone... If they'd stayed the night, I would have had to text Cesar to stay far away until noon, so we could do more research on what turns them on below the belt. I duck my head into the fridge, hoping to cool myself down, and grab bread and jam for breakfast.

"Then why do you look like that?" Cesar asks.

I make a show of scanning my sleep-rumpled self, still in pajamas and a light robe with my glasses instead of contacts. "Like what?"

"Like you had sex on the kitchen counter until midnight."

"In your dreams. Not until I change the locks..." I place my hand on the cold composite surface. "Even then...nope. Cold counters are a definite turnoff."

"But Alex turns you on," he tries again.

I don't know what mistake I made with my face, but he's jumping around the kitchen clapping his hands like his Lakers just won another NBA championship.

"So?" He interrupts my coffee maker to pour himself a cup. I glare at him and turn my attention to the toaster like that will make it speed up, so I can disappear back in my room. He pours in milk from my fridge and leans against the counter, slurping like he knows I hate. "What happened after Teo and I left?"

"We talked on the phone for a while." As hard as I try to mask my elation, he's my twin, and he knows something happened.

"You had phone sex? Oh my god. You had phone sex with Alex!" He pulls himself up to sit on the counter.

"Get your ass off where I make my food," I say, moving his coffee to the island where he can sit on a stool like a civilized person while I put butter and jam on my toast.

"Do not try to change the conversation!"

"Oh, the conversation has changed, my friend. I am not discussing my sex life with you."

"C'mon! You're never shy. Was it hot as hell? Like, hotter than when you gave Jordan a hand job on Ghost Rider at Knott's?"

"That is so far from the hottest sex I've had. You just think a hand job on a roller coaster is hot because you're a guy."

He grumbles like a child as he sips his coffee. Even though we're technically the same age, he has yet to mature. I can't say I disagree with the overall tone of his musings, though. Last night was a first for me. I'd call myself sexually adventurous, but until now, that has been something I express in a physical... place. I have to be careful to keep a neutral face when I recall the location of my riskier hookups. My college roommate finger fucking me during the movie night in our dorm living room with all of our suitemates there... The hood of Rick's Triumph TR7 in the Hollywood Hills before he figured out he was gay... With Ruby on the play structure when we were stuck at her family's barbeque at the park...

The coffee is finally finished, so I pour and fix myself my own cup, glad that I have another reason to have my back to my brother. The element of risk is typically a turn-on for me, and yet I don't remember any previous experience moving me the way being with Alex last night did. My eyes drift to the drawer with our map of erogenous zones. I started it for Alex, but now I can see how that conversation and being forced to use our words on the phone last night made for an intimacy that touched deeper than the physical.

"Okay, no talking about sex, but this means you fixed everything with them."

"Fixed everything?"

"You said you messed things up before and you had to be careful."

"Oh, that." In the bubble of me and Alex, I am confident that we are good. "Mostly? I think?" Last night is a hurdle cleared, and I eagerly anticipate enjoying their company in my bed, hopefully tonight. I'm not sure I can think of much else until I get my actual hands on them. When I expand the question to include the show, I'm not as certain. I have not been considering how the show's release will impact us. Do I owe the producers an update on our relationship status?

My coffee and toast both prepared, I head to my bedroom. "You working with Mateo today?"

"Nah. All that's left on the bathroom is the finishing stuff. The mirror, light fixture, all little things I can do myself. Then you'll be ready to paint." His face lights up. "Maybe you can get Alex to do the paint."

"They don't owe me."

"They will when I get my hands back on the Orange Beast."

"When do you think you'll be finished with the finishing touches?"

"Two hours, tops."

"I'm not sure why you're still sitting on your ass."

I text Alex. *Hey, what's work look like for you today?*

Nothing on the books. Why?

Cesar says the bathroom is ready for paint this afternoon. He says if you paint it, he'll order up the stuff for your car.

Cesar takes his mug to the bathroom to begin his work, which gives me the counter space back. I grab my laptop and open my email, hoping to find a reply on a demo I sent in for an audiobook narration.

The subject line *Press Junket* catches my eye, and I open that first, my heart rate spiking as I see the release date is three weeks away and our promotion begins in a week. Relief pours through me, knowing that having to keep silent about the show and how I know Alex is finally coming to an end. And I'm excited, too. I'm so proud of the work that we did. My part is inconsequential in comparison, but it's Alex who is meant to shine, and I am positive that the message is going to come through. My phone rings, and Alex's name lights up the screen.

"Hey! I'm so glad you called. I was just thinking about you," I say.

"Have you seen your email?" Their breath is coming fast.

"Hang on. Are you okay? Do you need to sit down? It sounds like you're hyperventilating."

"Did you see the email about the show?" they ask again.

"I did. Tell me what's going on."

"I can't do this."

"The press junket?"

"The whole thing!" Alex's voice is high and tight.

"Hold on. The press junket isn't a big deal. It's basically speed dating with a bunch of people who have questions about what it was like filming *Civic Duty*. You can even talk to the producers about the kinds of things you're willing to talk to reporters about."

"You're an actor, Emelynn. You were aware that we were being filmed with secret cameras. You went into that job wanting to be on some stranger's television set. This means that there are strangers watching this, laughing at me. Once this comes out, my whole family is going to see it. They're going to watch me defending a lesbian, and they'll think I'm even more screwed up than when I came out here. I can already picture my mother pulling her hair and asking what child would do this to their parents."

"Try to slow down your breathing," I say. Hearing their breath come so fast in my ear sends my body back to our call last night. I fleetingly consider saying so but quickly reject the idea. That would not help Alex at all. I press my palm to the cold tabletop. "Breathe in, Alex. Fill up your lungs until you can feel your tummy pooch out and then blow it out like you're trying to fill up a balloon in one go." I model the breaths I'm suggesting they take, quietly sitting and breathing with them. When it seems like they are calming a bit, I say, "You knew you were filming a documentary, right? This isn't so different."

"A documentary is *real*, Emelynn. This is completely fake. Think about it. How many people are going to watch a documentary about jury duty? How much would they market a documentary about jury duty to the general public? But a show where only one bozo thinks it's all real? That is *very* different. You have to see that."

Cesar walks through the kitchen on his way to his truck. He pauses and mouths *Everything okay?*

I wave him off and keep the steady breathing going until Alex's breath comes at a more normal pace. "I hear what you're saying. We've got a week to prepare. That's why they sent the email. Let's take one step at a time. I can help you."

"Okay. Great. Super. How would you answer when reporters ask how stupid a person has to be to not notice the whole thing was fake?"

I open my mouth, hoping that in doing so, my mind will get the message that it's supposed to supply me with words. "You do not look stupid in the show, Alex. The whole point was to trick you." Ugh. That sounds awful. I try again. "Listen. I don't think that people are going to focus on the fact that you were duped. They're going to be left thinking about how important it is to take jury duty seriously. You model how people on a jury have to think beyond themselves. That lesson is so much bigger than how they achieved it. You come across as a good and honest juror and an incredible person. That's something to embrace and be proud of!"

Alex says nothing, and I sit helpless in my kitchen, not sure there are any words I can say to fix this.

CHAPTER FIFTY-THREE

Alex

"Come over. Or let me come to you," Emelynn pleads. "You don't have to do this hard thing by yourself."

"Thank you for offering. I can't right now. I just need to disappear, okay?"

Emelynn is reluctant to end the call. She is trying her hardest to talk me off the ledge I'm teetering on, and I appreciate her efforts. Honestly, I do. But I decline her offer and hole up in my room instead, thankful I didn't have a job to get to. I leave my room only to use the bathroom and make myself a quick PB&J. A few of the other renters are home, so I keep my head down. I don't want to be seen today. I'm used to keeping to the margins. Being invisible takes less energy than facing people's questions about whether I'm a man or a woman or, worse, being misgendered. Now all I can think about is whether this show is going to permanently push me into a spotlight I can't escape.

I'm sitting with my legs crossed on my bed, scrolling through my phone searching for a distraction, when my phone rings. I recognize the prefix as local but not the number. I have to answer since it could be someone who needs a painter.

"Hi, Alex. It's Sarah. I wanted to call to see how you were doing."

"Emelynn called you?"

Her hesitation confirms what I thought. I'm not sure whether I'm touched or mad that Emelynn reached out to Sarah. I appreciate that Sarah doesn't try to bullshit me. "I did think about you when I checked my email this morning, but I was planning to wait for you to reach out. But Emelynn called. She was worried about you."

"Worried about me?"

"You said you wanted to disappear."

"Oh! Wait. Shit! Emelynn was worried I was going to hurt myself? That's not what I meant at all. It was just too much this morning. I was overwhelmed and didn't know what to say and didn't feel like I could be around people. All I wanted was to hide in my room."

"I can understand how the email would make you feel vulnerable. Do you want to talk about that? Or would you rather have me let Emelynn know you're fine and to give you some space?"

"What about the show? Do you have to tell them that Emelynn thought I might hurt myself?"

"Can you tell me more about what you meant by needing to disappear?" she asks.

I let out a long breath, sounding like a leaking balloon. "Emelynn wanted me to come practice what the interviews might be like with her."

"That's a good solution for managing anxiety."

"I know. Logically, I know that practicing will make it less overwhelming, but it also makes it more real. If I do this press junket, I'm one step closer to this reality I'm not ready for."

"What's your biggest fear? The show airs, and…What is it you visualize?"

I explain how the show will make it impossible to hide and what a toll being visible brings. I tell her how Emelynn was trying to get me excited, sharing how positive and impactful the show's message is. "It all sounded great, but she has to say that."

"All of what you are saying is true. Having seen the arc of the story and how your integrity inspired people to look beyond the surface, I am excited for that to be amplified. But I can also see how being put at the center, you have an additional weight becoming the spokesperson for challenging social norms. I'm trying to remember…I know you use they/them pronouns, but I don't remember you ever explicitly talking about being nonbinary during the filming."

"No. I only talked to Emelynn privately about being nonbinary, and she made sure people used they/them pronouns even when I wasn't in the room."

"Some of the folks I've talked to on my podcast say that it's pretty amazing to have friends advocate for them. Imagine the opportunity you have to use this show to raise awareness. That's one of the things that makes you so special as a person. You naturally challenged people on the jury to view the defendant differently. And in promoting the show, you have the chance to challenge the assumption that people make when they identify someone's gender simply by looking at them. When I meet with reporters, I can introduce myself using my pronouns, but they are already going to use she/her pronouns in their story, if they even talk about me at all. I don't think I'll be able to convince them to say that they talked to Sarah Cooper who, by the way, uses she/her pronouns. You, on the other hand…"

"That makes a lot of sense," I say slowly.

"Let me be clear. I am in no way saying you *should* use the platform. I'm merely pointing out that it is an opportunity. What would it have meant to a teenaged you to stumble upon someone talking about how gender is more than a binary while promoting their show?"

My chest aches to imagine this. I have lived the difference between stories my parents and teachers read that mirrored their world versus the ones I have painstakingly searched out on my own. It would have meant the world to me to hear someone talking about my lived experience. I recall how Sarah talked about public criticism at the park and how she holds on to the fact that her show has a positive impact on vulnerable people, which is why she's calling me in the first place. "It would have been huge."

"Yes," she says softly. "Naturally, the most important thing for you to do is what's best for your mental health. I hear how draining it is to maintain your sanity in such a gendered world. Please excuse me for trying to drag you onto my soapbox."

"No, that might have been exactly what I needed to hear."

"Oh, thank goodness." I can hear Sarah's long exhale. "For a minute there, I was kicking myself. I would *never* advise a therapist to speak like that to a client struggling with anxiety. But I couldn't help myself. This is all so exciting! You are such a remarkable soul. You have a special sparkle that is a true gift. I am a better person for knowing you, and you elevated this show to a level that nobody expected. It is such an honor to have been a part of it all. I want the whole world to witness how good we can be to each other if we choose kindness and empathy like you naturally do. You have a unique opportunity here."

"You really think that?"

"Alex, I would never say anything that I didn't believe with all my heart. Oh, speaking of which, you said something earlier about Emelynn seeing a potential impact. You didn't believe her. What did you say? That she had to say positive things about the show? What did you mean by that?"

"She and I…well. How do I put this? If Jass tells you that your podcast is the best…Doesn't she kind of have to because of being your partner and all?"

"Ah. I see what you're saying. People we love do often try to protect us by saying nice things. But the best people are those closest to us who know that we need to hear the truth, even if it's hard, because that's what makes us better. Jass would never tell me an episode was good if it didn't work. She loves me and wants me to succeed, and once in a while that includes critical feedback, and luckily, a good part of the time it includes praise."

This is part of being someone's person, I realize. I know that Emelynn did not want to hear that she had hurt me, but I told her because I wanted her to be better, and she has been better. Can I trust that she is doing the same for me and honestly thinks the show is that good? As usual, Sarah has given me a lot to think about. "Thank you for calling me," I say.

"You are more than welcome. Maybe you'll share with Emelynn that you're feeling more settled about the press opportunity?"

I don't miss how she has renamed the event happening in a week. "I will. Hey, Sarah?"

"Yes?"

I search for annoyance at my pulling her back but don't hear any. "Do you think…Say there was something happening with me and Emelynn. Would we need to tell the producer people?"

"If you're asking about contractually, no. The filming is over, and *Civic Duty* was centered on a court case and how people arrive at a verdict. Who we date should not and did not influence our case, right?"

I weigh this for a moment, checking my biases and asking myself if they influenced the case. Sarah chuckles. "What?" I ask.

"Do you know how quickly most people will say 'right' without even thinking about it? Most people don't question themselves. This is what I'm talking about when I say that you have something important to share with people."

"So, I don't have to tell anyone that Emelynn and I are a couple?"

"First, thank you for trusting me with that."

"Oh. Yeah. Um. You're welcome." I chuckle. "I guess I figured you knew after pickleball?"

"Jass did share what Emelynn said about you being her person, but I thank you all the same for telling me. When Jass and I started dating, I wrestled with how to tell people we were together, and I did so on a public scale. Without stepping onto the soapbox again, that was a decision I made with intention, and it has had the desired impact."

"I think I get what you're saying," I say.

"Soapbox. Sorry. The takeaway is do what is best for you. Always."

"Okay. I appreciate your time."

She says again how it's her pleasure but in more words than that. I'm not exactly listening anymore because of what she said about Emelynn claiming me as her person. I'm her person. Hearing how she shared our being together with Jass started a shimmer in my chest that now extends out to my fingers and toes like fairy dust that might actually make me fly. If I believe.

CHAPTER FIFTY-FOUR

Emelynn

I throw my arms around Alex the second they walk through the door.

"Whoa, whoa, whoa. Let me put this stuff down." They laugh, setting down a tray loaded with paint gear. They take me in their arms and kiss my neck. "I'm sorry I made you worry."

"No, no. Don't be sorry." I'm burying my face in their neck, in their smell and solidness. My arms around them, I lean back so I can look at them. "Are you suddenly taller?"

Alex squeezes me closer and kisses me, really kisses me, down to my toes, to the point where I'm starting to think it might not be so bad to be pressed to the cold countertop because this kiss sets me on fire. "Thank you," they say, which is ridiculous, them thanking me when they've kissed me off my toes.

"For what?" I'm grinning from ear to ear.

"For making me feel like this," they say.

"Like what?" I place my hand on the flat of their chest, my fingers tracing the fine bone of their clavicle.

They shut their eyes, and their breath catches, and I'm certain that last night's phone call is flashing through their mind. They place a hand on top of mine and lean forward until their forehead presses against mine. "Important."

"C'mon. It's not like that's hard," I say.

They squeeze my hand. "But it is for so many people, and it gets so heavy. And being around you...I can take off all the armor. When I saw the email about the press junket, I thought I needed more armor, and then Sarah and I talked, and I have such a different vision of what next week can be like. You'll help me get ready?"

"Of course! This is what I do."

"Yes! So I was thinking. We don't have to sit to practice, do we? I was thinking...You said the bathroom is ready to paint? Do you have the paint, or do we need to pick it up?"

I bite my lip to keep myself from kissing them. It's terribly difficult, but there is a transformation happening before me, and I do not want to get in the way. "I have the paint already."

"Great. Because I was thinking. If I sit and think about all of it, I start to feel overwhelmed, but if my hands are busy, I'll be able to keep myself focused on what I want the interviews to be like."

"It sounds like you have a plan."

"It's crazy." They light up again as they gather their tools and walk to the bathroom. "When I read the email, it felt like a wave was about to crash over me again, like I had no control over anything. My mind stuck on how stunned I felt when the judge said the show was all about me. But talking to Sarah..." They set down the tools in the bathroom. Hands on their narrow hips, they survey the space—the mirror that Cesar put in that covers nearly the entire wall above the cabinet and the fixture I found with three flared sconces. They meet my eye in the mirror. "This looks so good!"

"Right?"

"And everything brushed nickel? I love that finish."

Keep talking, I think, *because I will never get tired of listening to your voice.* I come up behind them and wrap my arms around their waist, going on tiptoe to hook my chin over their shoulder. "But, talking to Sarah...?" I prompt.

"Oh, yeah! She opened my eyes to how much control I actually have. She reminded me that the filming is over. They can't trick me again. And now people are asking me to talk about it, and it's an opportunity to be visible, you know, for other people like me." They hold out their arms to match the expanse of the mirror. "It's like this."

They look at me to see if I follow. I don't yet. "Like the mirror?"

"Like going from a tiny medicine cabinet mirror where you can barely see yourself and then…" They make the sound of an explosion. "You can see so much more. There's room for so much more." They raise their arm and pull me close. "I can see so much more."

I wrap both arms around their waist and take us in. They aren't pointing out another truth—that the bathroom is unfinished—but it doesn't matter. I like existing in a space where it's easy to imagine it looking even better.

They fall into the work of painting, peppering me with questions about the press junket. We work through what I anticipate the main questions will be. They'll be focused on how Alex signed up for the filming of a jury service they thought was real. They'll want to know how Alex has coped since the reveal. They'll ask what the most difficult part was and whether anything positive came out of the experience.

When I lob that question at them, they set the brush they're using to edge around the wall on the open pint of paint and turn to face me. "Am I allowed to say you?"

I'm sitting on an overturned bucket, typing a list of the questions and making notes about what they've said as we talk. I'm so focused on typing the question I pitched that it takes me a moment to process what they said. "Me?"

"Meeting you. Being with you. Can I say that?"

"You mean how we're a couple?"

"Yeah. I mean. It's another *kaboom!*" Their arms fly up, mimicking the explosion of a firework. "I haven't said a word to my family. Or Tom. Not that he'd read about it before I have a chance to tell him, and if you want to tell your family before any of this comes out, I guess that would be fine? It's not like it impacts the show, right..." They trail off, a bit of the newfound spunk fading.

I stand and set the computer on the bucket so I can wrap my arms around Alex. "I would love for you to say we're a couple. I..." I am staring at the sunburst pattern in their eyes again, and I feel this explosion of emotion inside. I love their energy. I love their careful consideration of things followed by headlong commitment. I love...them. "I love you. Am I allowed to say that?"

"I'm pretty sure you just did," Alex says. "I almost said it the other night, after..." They lift their shoulders in the most adorable, unapologetic shrug. "After we touched each other. Can I say that?"

"If I can say that the next time we're naked, we had better be in the same room." I know my voice is suffused with the heat inside me by the way Alex's gaze falls to my lips before bouncing to the wall they started.

I understand the rules of painting. I don't like to paint, but I've learned that it's best to roll a wall that is freshly cut in order to blend the two sections. I am fully prepared for Alex to return to their work.

Instead, they turn and move the brush to balance on the roller and replace the lid on the can of paint. They wet a small towel in the sink and drape it over the rolling tray. "We're going to regret that later," they say, and then their mouth is on mine, and I can't get them to my bedroom fast enough.

CHAPTER FIFTY-FIVE

Alex

I swear I did not head over to Emelynn's house as a way to get into her bed, but now that my mouth is on hers, it is the only logical destination. We bump along the short hallway from bathroom to primary bedroom, pulling at each other's clothes. I know from last night to expect a bra underneath Emelynn's soft green tee, but now I don't have to imagine how beautiful she is. I can see with my own eyes how perfect her breasts are and hold their beautiful weight. I am desperate to take her dark nipples in my mouth and suck them into hard peaks, but she keeps my mouth where it is, one hand cupping my jaw and the other wrapped around my crown as she leads me to her bed.

She stops a few feet away to peel off her pants. I don't take my eyes off her strong thighs or her neatly trimmed mound as I shuck off my white work pants. She pushes her covers back, exposing deep purple, sexy sheets that match Emelynn perfectly. She sits and grabs me by the ass, pulling me to her as she rakes her nails up to my shoulders and pulls me on top of her.

This is exactly where I want to be. I press into her, my body flushed with heat coming into contact with her cool, smooth skin. Her mouth is on my neck, sucking and pulling and nipping, and when she pulls at my hips to mash my mound against hers, I can't help but cry out. Her body fits perfectly with mine, and I move by instinct into a rhythm she matches with urgency. We are pumping furiously, and heat is building inside so quickly I think I could come without her even touching me.

"Wait!"

Did she say wait? I can barely process, but I try to respond, try to slow my body. She grips my butt again, but not to keep me in rhythm, to stop me.

"Wait. Hold on."

Inexplicably, she rolls out from under me and pads to the door, which she shuts and locks. "Just in case," she says, her chest heaving. I am aching for her to return, but she stands there across the room, staring so long I feel increasingly more naked. She licks her lips, and my hand moves to my wetness. "Yes," she says, finally returning to the bed. "About that."

As much as I loved being on top of her, she is able to push me onto my back with a single finger. She straddles me, her center too high for me to get any friction. I run my hands up her stomach, loving the way her muscles tighten under my touch. "Why are you so far away?"

"Because if we don't slow down, I won't be able to stop."

"Who said anything about stopping?"

"Last time, we got interrupted," she says, "so we never got to clarify boundaries." Then she's leaning forward enough that by propping myself up on one elbow, I can wrap my other arm around her to pull her close and take a nipple into my mouth. My pull brings her to all fours. Now, I can use both my hands and my mouth to caress first one and then the other breast. "Alex," she moans, her hips moving in time to the languid strokes of my tongue.

I hum my appreciation of hearing my name on her lips, which brings forth the most erotic gasps I have ever heard in my life. But then she is moving away from me again, bending lower to bring her mouth to mine as her hand traces a path down my sternum to my belly button, pausing with her fingers at my mound. I arch my hips, trying to get her hand to continue to my center, but she drags it back up between us. "I want to feel you inside," I growl.

"You think I don't remember what you like?" A cheeky little grin on her lips, she quirks an eyebrow and places her finger on my lower lip. I hold eye contact with her, slipping my tongue to the tip of her finger. I lift my head enough to wrap my lips around her finger and suck hard. Her eyes shut, and her eyebrows knit as I demonstrate what I would like her to do to me with her mouth. "I have a whole box of things I thought might interest you." She opens her eyes again, asking the question without speaking.

"Is that what you want?"

"Right now, all that matters to me is that you get what you want. I want you to know you can ask for what you want, always."

I am so tempted by her offer but also unsure. That Emelynn has a box of things that I have fantasized about but have never been able to ask for is thrilling but also magnifies how inexperienced I am. With just the two of us, I finally feel confident to want what I want, and right now, all I want is for Emelynn to touch me. I take her hand and guide it between our bodies once more, making sure that this time she feels how aroused I am. "Next time," I say. "Right now, I only need you. But I need you right now. I'm already so close."

Finally, she drags her fingers through my wetness and finds her mark. "I knew you would feel just like this," she whispers. "Tell me what you like. Can I put my mouth on you?"

"Yes," I breathe, watching her as she rearranges herself, her gentle strokes as steady as her gaze.

"You have such a wonderful body. I love touching you so much."

I am utterly present in my body as she adds the heat of her mouth to my center. She splays the hand not buried inside me across my belly but stops short of my breasts. I want Emelynn to know all of me, and it feels right to guide her hand to my left breast.

"This?" she asks, massaging in slow circles. "Or this?" She pinches my hard nipple. My hips jerk, and she pinches again.

I tip my head to the side, lost in sensation. Hands still holding hers, I guide it up to my lips and take her finger in my mouth again. As my lips wrap around her finger, it's as if I've closed a circuit, and the current sweeps through me, pulsing and pulsing.

Emelynn rests her face on my hip, staying buried inside me until my body ceases to spasm. I release her finger and open my eyes to find her staring at me. I have to throw my arm over my eyes to settle back into myself. Emelynn is back next to me, lying on her side, stroking from my hip to my leg.

I take a shuddering breath. "I want you to feel like this. Do you want to get out your box? You didn't say anything about it yesterday. Did you want to?"

"We hadn't fully talked about what you liked below the belt, but if you're up for that now…" Emelynn waggles her eyebrows. "Is this what you meant by next time?"

"We didn't get to what you want, either. Maybe it's easier for you to show me?"

She pauses for a moment, like she wants to give me time to change my mind, but nothing in that box is going to make that happen. Nothing she shares is going to scare me. The only thing that scares me is having another person shame me for what I want. And Emelynn is not going to do that, not if she, herself, can share so openly. I nod to encourage her, and she shimmies to the edge of the bed, lifting a box out from underneath. She flicks open the lid and studies my face.

My heart flutters. "You have so many!" I have multiple questions, but sitting naked on her bed with the box between us does not seem like the time to ask. I don't want to reveal to Emelynn how inexperienced I am. For years, I shut down any thought of using toys because Lilian said the whole point of being a lesbian was having sex without a penis or something shaped like one. But Emelynn isn't Lilian, so maybe it is the perfect time. I don't know.

Pointing to items in the box, Emelynn breezily explains how sometimes she likes vibration, but not all the time. She has some that are more realistic than others, and the one that she calls a rabbit looks comically silly to me. "I tried these brief-style ones, but honestly, I like the harness better." She drops her voice to an extra-sultry low and says, "More control."

"You like to strap?" I must not be as good at hiding my surprise as I think because she throws her head back and laughs from her belly.

"What? You think a femme can't rock a cock?"

I fold myself over and bury my head in the sheets as if I can hide from Emelynn. "I think you can do anything. How are you this relaxed talking about…" I sit up and gesture to the box.

"I'm a very curious person," she says. "And I like to experiment. You haven't? Not even by yourself?"

"I would never have dared to keep anything like this in my room at home. My parents would die," I say. "And it wasn't the first thing that came to mind after I broadened my horizons by moving out here. Trying out sex toys wasn't one of the things Tom and I talked about when we discussed goals, you know?"

She's studying me, then leans over to kiss me. "What about today? Should I push this back under the bed, or do you want me to pick something?"

"I want…" I'm too overwhelmed to find words. All I know is that I want Emelynn. She's beaming at me as if I've given the right answer when I've given her none. "What?"

"Progress! You didn't say I don't know. You're thinking, and I love that. I don't want to pressure you, but there is one that I'm confident you'd like."

I bite my lip. "But I want to use what you like."

"Oh, I like this one a lot."

She sets a few things on her bedside table and plops the box back on the floor before turning to me. Lying back on the sheets, she come-hithers me with a crooked finger. "Come warm me up again. You remember?"

I nod as I graze my hips and belly against her, and now I have the freedom to kiss her breasts without reaching. I can kiss and nip and suckle as my hands roam and pinch and tease. It is so easy to relax with Emelynn, who is so at home in her body. I kiss my way down to her center, ask if I can put my mouth on her, think this is what home tastes like. I am mesmerized by the rhythm of her hips and the sounds I can elicit with my tongue.

I could stay here forever, but she pulls me up and reaches for a toy that I'd been curious about. I'm reluctant to bring up my inexperience, but it occurs to me that Emelynn would not have known at first, either. But now she does, and this is what she wants, so I will learn.

"I'm not really sure how that works," I admit.

"As we confirmed, you like something inside. So do I. The way this one works, you insert the bulb, and then you can use this part…" The way she slides her hand along the phallus makes my insides tighten. "…to fuck me."

She hands over the toy and the lube, leaving the choice to me. I wait for it to feel wrong, but it doesn't. I'm curious, and Emelynn has given me this avenue to pleasure her, and I really want to pleasure her.

I'm grateful for lube and laughter as Emelynn and I fit ourselves to the toy and then, I realize, to each other.

And it's magical. It's not perfect. The toy is not my body, and I worry about whether I'm going to hurt Emelynn, but she doesn't make me guess, and she's right—her telling me what she wants, hearing her say that what I'm doing makes her feel "So. Fucking. Good" is so hot I could almost come again.

She shifts me again to where I can feel her heat against mine, and she pulls on my hips to guide my movement and speed, and in this moment, I transcend my body and find the deepest connection I have ever experienced. Because it's not just about how good it feels. And it feels really good. It's about how I'm not hiding a single thing right now, and she wants me. Not only wants me but also encourages me to explore how I might be more myself. It surpasses the current I found before because once Emelynn tenses and shudders beneath me, electricity flows from her to me and back again until I am reduced to a puddle next to her, sweaty and spent.

"Next time…" She is panting and smiling at me. "Next time, we can switch."

"I'd like that. A lot," I say.

She wraps me in her arms, and I am getting dozy thinking *next time…* Next time after we doze? Next time tonight after dinner? "Fuck," I say, remembering I have to finish painting the bathroom.

"Yes, please."

"No, not that. I mean, yes that. Lots more of that. But first I have painting to finish. That puts a crimp in next time."

"Not if you plan on staying tonight. Can I say that?"

"I would love to. I'd like to stay many nights. Can I say that?" I look up to find her smiling at me. My head rises and falls with her deep sigh.

"As many as you want."

"I'm going to want a lot. I hope you don't get sick of me."

"Never. I'm never getting sick of you."

Her voice is fading as she drifts. I trace a pattern on her belly until I can slip out from her arms. I have work to finish, after all, and the promise of a return to Emelynn's bed later.

CHAPTER FIFTY-SIX

Emelynn

A week later, we're all gathered back at the courthouse. Since it's not in use, which is how we got it for filming *Civic Duty*, they've been able to secure it for our press junket. Reporters have been given the opportunity to scope out the hidden camera locations as well as where the control room and monitors were set up.

I'm glad for the week that Alex and I spent running through possible interview questions to work through Alex's jitters. I have a few interviews with journalists before the video interview with full cast and crew is recorded in the courtroom, but luckily mine are scheduled for slightly after Alex's, so I can stand by for emotional support as they get started. They're wearing an outfit I helped pick, a navy suit with a great cut with a crisp white button-down. They have the jacket draped on the back of the chair and the shirt sleeves rolled up, and they look both hot and relaxed, and that's the most important thing.

The reporter points out that most people try to avoid jury duty and asks Alex why they would not only answer what they thought was a legitimate jury summons but also volunteer to be on a documentary.

Alex and I have practiced this question, and they glance in my direction before they launch into a variation of the answer we practiced. Alex is well prepared to shake up their responses to keep their answers fresh for each reporter. The look they send me sets off a flurry of butterflies so strong, I place my hand on my stomach.

"They look like a natural, don't they?" Sarah says, pausing next to me.

"Absolutely," I agree. "You have a busy schedule today?"

"Just a handful." Sarah nods in Alex's direction. "It's all about Alex."

"Yeah." I sigh.

She pushes me and laughs. "You are so far gone."

"It's that obvious?"

"On the both of you. It's adorable. And it's good? I mean, I'm assuming things are good with the two of you and that has something to do with how well they're doing in this environment."

"We've been practicing all week," I offer.

"I bet you have," she says with a smirk. I do my best not to acknowledge her and give her any ammunition. She bumps my hip anyway and says, "I'm happy for you both. What a wonderful thing to come out of all of this."

Before she ducks out, she assures me we'll see each other in the courtroom. I hate to leave Alex, but it's time for me to find my own interview. It's clear that Alex doesn't need me, so I offer a thumbs-up, which they breezily reciprocate. I'm mentally running through the talking points I anticipate about the concept of the show, the audition, and the character I play, when my phone buzzes.

I've got all the parts. Can Alex bring the Beast this weekend?
Sure, I type. *We're free.*
Who said anything about you?
Punk.
We can grill afterward.
Sounds good.

I'm unprepared when Alex rests their arm across my shoulder but relax immediately when I feel their familiar warmth and breathe in their soothing mixture of cologne and hair product.

"What's wrong?" Alex asks.

"Nothing's wrong."

"That's not what your face says."

"You know me so well."

"Not nearly well enough yet," they whisper in my ear. They point to my phone. "But seriously, everything okay?"

"Cesar has the parts to get the Orange Beast all tuned up. He invited us to grill this weekend. Some of these articles are going to be out by then, the teasers. I'm worried what my family is going to think about my part in all this. It doesn't feel great talking about how we worked to fool you."

"I appreciate that," Alex says. They squeeze my hand. "I'll tell him it's cool, and it'll all be fine."

"Who's the optimistic one now?" I ask.

"Must be rubbing off." Their eyes twinkle and their gaze drops to my lips for a second. In this setting, it's as good as a kiss, and I can see they're thinking the same thing. "Tell him thanks and we'll be there. And stop worrying. It all worked out."

I hold Alex's goodwill through my solo interviews, happy when the last journalist I'm scheduled to talk to wants to talk about the diversity represented on the show, noting the prominent lesbian on the jury and the subplot spurred by Alex's suggestion that Marlene had been in a relationship with her college roommate.

"And you're lesbian, is that right?"

"Queer suits me better. It doesn't work for me to use a label that is predicated on a gender binary."

"Did you find that this environment was supportive of that kind of nuance?"

"Oh, absolutely. Alex uses they/them pronouns, and the whole crew worked to make sure not to misgender them, even more so than some of our actors, actually."

"That's interesting. Thank you for that angle," he says.

The rest of the interview follows the questions I anticipated, and I run through the talking points on autopilot, eager to wrap up my final interview and get to the group interview on camera. He must sense my distraction because he mercifully wraps it up.

I hustle over to the courtroom, meeting Jean on the way. As we approach the jury box to take our seats, I ask how the courtroom feels.

She holds out her hands, tips back her head, and takes a deep breath. Then she snaps back and cackles, "How the hell should I know?"

Everyone laughs.

It feels good to be gathered as a group again, this time without the obvious hurt radiating from Alex. The interview starts with the producer talking about the show's conception, her love of *The Truman Show* that merged with her concern about what she sees as an erosion of morals and values. This guides the interview into a surprisingly deep conversation about the value of jury duty.

Brittany says, "The most amazing thing about the show, really, was how watchable it was. I mean, we had to schedule long hours of boring material to build up a sort of believability bank that we could make withdrawals on to get the fun content in. So there were many long court days."

The whole room groans in confirmation.

"But people got sucked in. I remember one day I was stuck at home watching material from the stationary camera in the courtroom, and my teenagers stopped dead in the middle of the kitchen and couldn't walk away. It was the day Alex was convincing the judge not to move the energy crystal, and they were transfixed. That's when I knew we had something special."

"And it wouldn't have been what it became without Alex," a scriptwriter says. "Brittany brought the concept, but Alex brought it to life. We had an outline of what challenges we wanted to put in front of them, but we did not anticipate the level of compassion they brought not just in considering the evidence but also in mediating the jury."

I'm so proud of who Alex is but also impressed that nobody on the team needs any reminders about Alex's pronouns. That alone captures Alex's ability to impact those around them.

The interviewer smiles. "I have to say that you all seem unusually close."

"I'm hoping to stay in touch with Alex. We haven't talked specifically about their career options after this, but I'm hoping that this won't be Alex's sole performance for the camera," Brittany says.

"What do you say to that, Alex?" the interviewer asks.

"I've dipped my toe in far enough," they say, glancing at me. We've already talked about how I thought I wanted this show to launch my career. I'm thankful that Alex supports me whether that happens or not, and I haven't pressured them at all to audition for other roles.

"I can see where your perspective about the success of the show is quite different. What would you say the best thing has been for you?"

This is the question Alex has been waiting for. Their whole face lights up as they look first behind them to Sarah and then to me. "I found my tribe here. I've made friends who have helped me put down my roots." They subtly raise the thumb on their left hand, and I nod. They take my hand. "And I found my person."

It takes a moment for the room to put our joined hands and Alex's words together. The cast and crew erupt in questions and proclamations of "I knew it!"

I hear Nick's frantic voice asking if there is time to add this revelation to the show before it goes public.

Alex rolls their eyes and leans in to kiss me.

Flashes go off, capturing our first public display as a couple. Questions fly not only from the interviewer trying to regain control of the interview but also from journalists pouring in from the hallway.

"Look what you've done," I whisper. "Now it's going to take forever to get out of here."

"Like you don't love the attention," they whisper.

I press my forehead against theirs, gently rest my hand along their jaw. I want to block it all out for a moment to share this moment with them, my person. "Not as much as I love yours."

EPILOGUE

Six Months Later

"Hey! How'd the reading go?" I ask, leaning in to kiss Emelynn. She texted me to meet her at "our" In-N-Out to celebrate the anniversary of our first dinner together.

"Good! So good!"

Seeing the receipt with our order number, I sit down. Emelynn spins her phone around to show me Cesar's text. I read her message to him, telling him where she is and thanking him again for how supportive he's been.

Ask Alex how's the Orange Beast and if they got pulled over again. It's followed by a laughing emoji and a heart.

My ears flush red remembering both the first experience of seeing flashing lights behind me on the freeway and for being let off when the police officer recognized me from *Civic Duty*. That's a perk of celebrity I never expected and still feel guilty about. *It was only once!* I type out before pushing the phone back.

A message pings, and Emelynn reads, "Hey Alex!"

"How does he know?"

"You didn't call him a punk. You could."

"I know." She says this because her whole family has made it clear that they are my family now, too. My folks watched the show before they came out to visit, and while it managed to convey to them that I do know my own mind in a way my words never could, it did not magically draw us together. Their visit to Los Angeles went better than I had anticipated. Still, there is a formality and stiltedness with them that is absent with Emelynn's family, maybe because of the letters I received from my extended family that the studio forwarded after *Civic Duty* aired. Among the letters from strangers, I discovered newspaper clippings with *How could you do this to your family?* scrawled on a Post-it and cards telling me that god still loves their niece from a few of my aunts and uncles. Emelynn encouraged me to throw them away and refuse to engage. Sarah agreed that trying to talk to them would only add fuel to their salvation campaign. I'm not here to ruminate on the past, though. I want to hear about the present, which includes the table read that Emelynn had today for the sitcom she landed after the excellent reviews *Civic Duty* received when it aired. "Tell me about today."

"I love what the writers are doing, and I can tell that we're really starting to jell as a group. David's comedic timing is... ugh...inspiring and frustrating. I'm definitely the weak link there."

She launches into an example, and I bask in her radiance. Shoulders back, hands flying, she explains the backstory necessary to understand the scene. It's hard for me to believe that this is my life, the setting sun illuminating the palm trees crossed behind her and sliding down the San Gabriel mountains.

I'm not the only one who notices Emelynn. Heads turn as customers walk into and out of the restaurant. Eyes flick to see who she is sitting next to, but it's clear which one of us is meant to be in the spotlight. The mom sitting next to us with her teenager has spent their entire meal glancing in our direction. Emelynn is completely unaware of her audience and continues to talk animatedly until our order is called.

I've had my eye on the receipt next to her, and when the numbers match, I take the paper. "I'll get it."

"You sure?" She rests her hand on my arm as I rise.

"Happy to."

I'm turning to enter the restaurant and find the woman who was staring at Emelynn right next to me.

"I'm sorry to interrupt," she says. She glances toward her teen, who hides under a hoodie, probably mortified. "You were on *Civic Duty*. You're Alex."

I'm so used to Emelynn being the focus of attention that I'm not sure what to say. Emelynn stands and takes our receipt from me. "Yes, they're Alex."

"I'm so sorry to interrupt the two of you!" The woman covers her mouth when she recognizes Emelynn. "I'll be so fast. I promise. I just..."

Emelynn excuses herself to get our dinner, and the woman glances back to the teen, and when she looks at me again, I see tears are welling in her eyes. "My son..." Her voice wobbles. She closes her eyes and takes a deep breath. "My child told me that they are nonbinary. If I hadn't watched *Civic Duty*, I wouldn't have even known what they were talking about. They were obsessed with the show and told me I should watch it. I binged it in one day, and then after I watched them all, I watched every interview I could. I'm sorry. I'm babbling and your dinner is ready. But I had to say something when I recognized you. This isn't easy for me to understand, and you...well, I think you helped my kid work up the courage to talk to me. You can't tell from this..." She motions to the teen studiously ignoring us. "But we're closer than we have been in a long time, and I have you to thank for that. Bless you." She squeezes my hands.

Emelynn returns and sets our tray on the table. She stands next to me. I return the slight pressure she applies to my side, letting her know I'm fine.

The woman smiles at us and places her hands against her cheeks. "Thank you, both of you, for sharing who you are so publicly. It makes me worry less about Jax knowing that the two of you found each other. I hope the world is nothing but good to you." She takes a deep breath and nods before scurrying back to the table where her child chances a look in our direction as they unfold from the table.

My heart is so full in the split second the youth and I make eye contact before they turn away to clear the trash. Their mom follows, wrapping an arm around their shoulder as they walk to their car.

Emelynn wraps her arm around my shoulder and says, "I love you."

"I love you." Throat tight, I look from the mom and her child to Emelynn and say, "Right now I don't know which is better, you loving me or that mom thanking me. Can I say that?"

"Luckily, you don't have to choose."

I never considered myself lucky, but in this moment, I could not ask for anything more than this life I've been gifted.

If you enjoyed meeting Sarah, I hope you will check out *Falling All In*, the story of how she met and fell in love with Jass.

More Titles from Bella Books

Hunter's Revenge – Gerri Hill
978-1-64247-447-3 | 276 pgs | paperback: $18.95 | eBook: $9.99
Tori Hunter is back! Don't miss this final chapter in the acclaimed Tori Hunter series.

Integrity – E. J. Noyes
978-1-64247-465-7 | 228 pgs | paperback: $19.95 | eBook: $9.99
It was supposed to be an ordinary workday...

The Order – TJ O'Shea
978-1-64247-378-0 | 396 pgs | paperback: $19.95 | eBook: $9.99
For two women the battle between new love and old loyalty may prove more dangerous than the war they're trying to survive.

Under the Stars with You – Jaime Clevenger
978-1-64247-439-8 | 302 pgs | paperback: $19.95 | eBook: $9.99
Sometimes believing in love is the first step. And sometimes it's all about trusting the stars.

The Missing Piece – Kat Jackson
978-1-64247-445-9 | 250 pgs | paperback: $18.95 | eBook: $9.99
Renee's world collides with possibility and the past, setting off a tidal wave of changes she could have never predicted.

An Acquired Taste – Cheri Ritz
978-1-64247-462-6 | 206 pgs | paperback: $17.95 | eBook: $9.99
Can Elle and Ashley stand the heat in the *Celebrity Cook Off* kitchen?